The King's Sword

LEAGUE OF RULERS, BOOK TWO

JENNIFER ANNE DAVIS

Published by Reign Publishing

Cover Design by Phoenix Design Covers
Proofreading by Allyssa Painter and Leah Alvord
Map by Annika Jost

ISBN (paperback): 979-8-9864009-5-2
ISBN (ebook): 979-8-9864009-4-5

Library of Congress Control Number: 1-13707565801

CASTLE
PALACE
CUSP
LYNK
AVONI
PORT RITE
GATE
GATE
LEAGUE HOUSE
PALACE
CARLON
SKYFALL RIVER
NISK
LARK
LY FOREST
BAKLEY
CASTLE
N
W
E
S

Chapter One

Sabine gulped down another cup of water, wanting to clear the giplig from her system. She couldn't believe she'd been kidnapped in the middle of the masquerade ball. She handed the cup back to her captor who was sitting on a chair beside the bed. So far, she'd gathered she was on a ship but had no idea what time of day it was or how much time had passed since she'd been taken.

"You and King Rainer are married?" the man asked, his pale green eyes narrowing, as if he didn't quite believe what she'd said.

She nodded, recognizing him. He was part of the Avoni delegation, which meant he was most likely an assassin.

He ran his hands through his hair and cursed. "Maybe I should take you back to Lynk," he muttered.

"I think that a wise idea," Sabine replied with false bravado. Her mother's words came back to her: *I'd rather die than be at the mercy of my enemy. I pray you never find yourself in that situation. It is a fate worse than death.* She shivered. To make it through this ordeal, she'd have to be strong.

"When did the two of you marry?" he asked, resting his elbows on his thighs.

"Why does it matter to you?" she countered, shifting on the bed.

"I suppose it doesn't." He mumbled something unintelligible under his breath. "And you've probably been crowned as well."

"I have. You can release me at the next port. I'll return unharmed to the palace. Hopefully, my husband won't wage a war against your kingdom for stealing me."

"You don't understand." The assassin sighed.

As far as kidnappings went, she hadn't expected him to be so passive. Not that she was complaining. "I understand perfectly. You kidnapped me to prevent the marriage from taking place." She held up her hand revealing her wedding ring with the Lynk crest etched on it. "Just because we don't have the League's approval or you don't want Lynk uniting with Bakley doesn't give you the right to kidnap someone." She tried to remember what he'd said on the balcony that day he'd warned her about things not being what they seem.

The man withdrew a letter and handed it to her. "Maybe this will help explain."

Sabine took the letter, examining it. The Bakley seal was on it and intact. "Where'd you get this?" Cold fear slithered through her like a snake crossing a garden path.

"Just read it." He stood and started pacing in the small cabin.

With shaking hands, she broke the seal and saw the familiar handwriting of her father.

> Sabine—
> We haven't received any correspondence from you and are becoming quite concerned. Your

mother is worried. Our spies are reporting conflicting stories. I fear Lynk may have had something to do with the missing Bakley children. Please be careful. We're sending Otto north to try and get in contact with you. Be safe.

 All my love,

 Your Father

She turned it over, but nothing more had been written. She'd sent several letters to her family, and they should have received them by now. Since they hadn't, she wondered if someone had intercepted them or if they'd never been sent. "Why do you have this?" She was no longer part of Bakley now. The fact that her father had written to her about this was very concerning. It reinforced that not all was as it seemed.

"Your brother, Otto, gave it to me to deliver to you."

"Why are you only giving it to me now?" He'd had plenty of chances at the palace to do so. She examined the letter again. This was definitely her father's handwriting and seal.

"Otto asked me to check on you while I was in Lynk. He said to get you out if you were in danger." The assassin stopped pacing and turned to face her. "I'm sorry I had to go to such extreme measures to get you out of there, but you'd be dead by now if I hadn't taken you."

The ship rocked up and down, making odd creaking noises as it did so. Sabine closed her eyes, not feeling quite right. When she opened them again, she found the assassin watching her. "I was in danger," she admitted. "That is one of the reasons King Rainer and I married—to try and keep me safe from the *Avoni* assassin trying to kill me."

The man resumed pacing. He rubbed the back of his neck,

not looking her way. He appeared to be about her age, eighteen or so, with dark red hair and penetrating light green eyes. "I thought I spotted someone…" His voice trailed off and he eyed her sidelong.

She lifted her brows, curious what he had to say about one of his fellow countrymen trying to kill her. When he looked away, she shifted her weight, trying to sit up more on the hard bed. The butterfly wings of her dress dug into her back. The layer upon layer of fabric for the skirt made it hard to tell where the edge of the bed even was.

The assassin's head turned her way as he tracked her movements. "Are you strong enough to stand yet?"

She had no idea. A sheen of sweat broke out over her forehead and she shivered, suddenly cold. It had to be residual effects from the giplig.

He came over to her, taking hold of her elbow and helping her to her feet. "If you're going to be ill, you need to do it over the side of the ship and not in its only cabin." He led her out of the room and up a dark, narrow stairwell.

Her foot kept getting caught on the hem of her dress, making it difficult to climb the steps with the ship's constant movement.

When she stepped onto the deck, crisp air greeted her along with another wave of nausea. She ran to the rail and vomited over the side. When she finished, she slid down and wrapped her arms around her legs. Thankfully, it was night and she didn't have to deal with the bright light of the sun. If only the ship would stop moving so much.

"Do you get seasick often?" the man asked, squatting beside her.

Sabine didn't know why he acted like he cared. "I have no idea." She'd never been on a ship before. But if this was what it felt like to sail, she'd never step foot on one again. She rubbed her tired face and looked about. The boat was smaller than she expected. And then she remembered him saying the cabin below was the only one. "Where is the rest of the Avoni delegation?" And what about the crew? Not only did she not see another person, but there was no way a dozen people could even fit on this ship.

"I presume back at the Lynk palace." His brows pulled together. "The Avoni delegation has nothing to do with you being here. I acted on my own, independently of them."

When she had snuck into the suite the delegation was staying in, she recalled seeing their bags packed as if they were ready to leave directly after the masquerade. "Wait," she said, "I'm alone on this ship with you?"

"Yes."

Another bout of nausea hit her and she groaned, leaning her cheek against her knees, trying to soothe her shaking body to no avail. As the large sail whipped in the wind, a metal piece attached to a rope kept clinking against the mast. She had no idea how one person could sail this ship without having someone else help. Maybe this man was more pirate than assassin. But she remembered him jumping from the roof above her bedchamber onto her balcony. Then when he'd left, he'd scaled the side of the palace. It seemed this assassin-pirate had many talents.

The ship hit a larger swell. Perhaps it would be better to look at her surroundings rather than be curled up on the deck. Reaching above her, she gripped the railing and pulled herself up. She couldn't afford to be vulnerable or ill right now. Not when water surrounded the ship in every direction for as far as she could see in the moonlight. "Where are you taking me?"

"To meet your brother, Otto."

She eyed this strange man, trying to determine if he was lying to her or not. "Why?"

"Because he wants to make sure you're okay."

"But why *you*?"

"He asked me to."

"You're from Avoni." And her brother lived in Bakley. She had no idea how this man knew her brother. Maybe he was going to demand her brother pay for her safe return. Or maybe her brother had hired him, especially since there was an Avoni assassin after her.

He shrugged. "Your brother asked. I agreed. It's as simple as that."

Sabine assumed there had to be more to it.

"It's late. Do you want to sleep below deck in the bed?" he asked.

She shook her head. "I feel better up here, out in the open."

He stood and turned toward the stairwell.

"What's your name?" Sabine asked.

"Evander." He descended the steps without another word.

***

Sabine barely slept from not only the rocking of the ship, but trying to figure out what, exactly, was going on. Her family had been trying to get letters to her, but it seemed they were being intercepted. And now she was on a boat on her way to see her brother. She'd never been kidnapped before, and so far, the ordeal wasn't what she had expected.

When morning came and the assassin-pirate finally decided to make an appearance, Sabine watched him carefully.

"How are you feeling?" he asked as he adjusted the sail.

"Better," she said.

He opened a box off to the side, pulling out two loaves of bread and handing one of them to her.

Her stomach growled. She had no idea when she'd eaten

last. Lifting the bread, she tore off a bite. "I'm not sure what you find so amusing," she grumbled, irritated that he was watching her eat. She wasn't a barn animal.

"It's not often I have a butterfly on my ship," he said with a wink.

She rolled her eyes, wondering what he'd done with her mask. Her dress had been so beautiful the night of the masquerade. That dreadful night when she discovered Lottie was responsible for hiring the assassin to kill Alina and Sabine.

They hit a particularly rough swell, and she knocked her head against the side of the boat.

"Hold on," Evander called out as he ran to adjust the sails.

Glancing at the sky again, Sabine took note of the dark clouds rolling in. It was going to rain. And when it did, being on this ship would be even more awful.

"Don't worry," he said. "We'll be disembarking shortly."

"We've arrived in Avoni?" she asked. She must have been given a strong dose of giplig which caused her to sleep for a few days if they were there already.

"Not quite," he said as he walked past her and started tying a loose rope around the mast. The sail swung to the other side, and the boat turned.

Sabine stood and gazed out at the water, spotting the shoreline not too far off. Relief filled her. Was this strange man, this assassin-pirate, really taking her to her brother? She remained there for several quiet minutes, contemplating her options.

Hearing a noise, she glanced over her shoulder and noticed Evander coming up from below deck. He'd changed his clothes from solid black to dark brown, his shirt a lighter shade than his pants. The change in colors made him look less intimidating than before, especially with the top button undone. He handed her a bundle of clothes. "I need you to change into these."

Sabine took them from him. "Why?"

"We're going into port. Wearing that dress will garner the wrong sort of attention."

Thunder boomed through the sky.

She hesitated.

"The choice is yours. Change and come with me, or tell them who you are and return to King Rainer." He turned and went below deck, giving her some privacy to change.

Sabine quickly considered her options. If this man was lying to get her to comply, they'd disembark and he'd take her to a dungeon, toss her in, and torture her. She'd be used as a bargaining chip. However, if he was telling her the truth, he'd take her to see Otto where she'd possibly learn something of importance.

The urge to scream in frustration inundated her. As much as she wanted to return to the palace and avenge her sister's death—which would be much easier now that she knew Lottie was the culprit—she also wanted to find out if what this man said was true. If her family had been trying to get information to her, and someone in the palace had been preventing it, she needed to know.

Sabine started pacing. The last thing she wanted to do was return to Lynk if there was another danger she didn't know about. The best course of action would be to disembark with Evander and if things didn't look or feel right, she'd leave him and go to the palace.

She quickly removed her outfit and pulled on the brown pants and matching tunic. Dressed in the scratchy, generic clothes, she picked up the beautiful butterfly dress, trying to decide what to do with it. Since she'd never wear it again, she tossed it over the side of the ship. It landed on the water, floating for a few seconds before it began to slowly sink, disappearing from sight.

"Now that you're dressed appropriately," Evander said, joining her on the deck, "I need your help getting this ship into port."

Folding her arms, she looked at him. "I've never sailed before." And if he'd managed to make it to Lynk on his own, he could figure out how to get into port on his own.

"I just need you to steer the ship." He pointed at the wheel. "Keep us heading toward that red building due south."

The idea of steering this vessel excited her. Smiling, she went over and took hold of the wheel, feeling the smooth wood beneath her hands. Once she spotted the building Evander had pointed out, she made sure to keep the ship headed that direction. The wind blew against her face, tossing her hair back.

As they got closer to the shoreline, there were dozens and dozens of boats she had to navigate around. While she steered, Evander pulled in all the sails except for one of the smaller ones. The ship slowed and cut through the water at a much smoother pace.

When Evander came over and took control of the wheel, Sabine moved to the front of the ship, watching the other boats and the people aboard them. Some had cages of fish, others crates of goods. Evander steered the ship to one of the docks that jutted out from the shoreline. Once in a slip, he dropped anchor.

After he tied the ship to the dock, he went below deck, leaving Sabine alone. She stood there realizing she could easily run away from her kidnapper if she wanted to. It almost made her believe that Evander was telling her the truth about meeting up with her brother.

He returned a few minutes later carrying two bags and

handing one of them to her. "We're in another kingdom," he said. "Make sure you stick close to me. Try not to use my name. And don't look anyone in the eyes or stare."

"Why would I stare?" she asked as she followed Evander off the ship.

"Given your upbringing, this seaside town is going to be a bit shocking to you. I just don't want you to stare all wide-eyed at some commoner and offend him or her." They made their way from the dock to the shoreline.

"My upbringing?" This assassin-pirate better not be implying what she thought he was implying.

"You know, being a pampered royal." He looked sidelong at her. "You were born a princess, raised in a royal household, never had to lift a finger, and now you're the queen of another kingdom. You're totally spoiled."

"I am not." She folded her arms as they headed along the road that paralleled the shoreline. He knew nothing about her or the sacrifices she'd had to make. Being born a princess didn't mean she had an easy life. Unlike him. He could go anywhere he wanted, do anything he wanted, and marry anyone he wanted. He was the spoiled one, not her.

Most of the people they passed had darker skin and hair. What little conversation she managed to overhear sounded like they were speaking the same language she did, only with a thick accent.

"Let me ask you this," Evander said as he slid his arm casually around her shoulders. "Have you ever wandered around a seaside town such as this one before?"

"Of course not."

"And is my arm making you uncomfortable?"

It was but she didn't have to tell him that. Instead she asked, "Why is your arm on me?"

"I don't want you to get bumped and lose your way." He steered them down the street on the right.

Sabine gaped at the crowded market area straight ahead where dozens and dozens of carts were lined up with people selling all sorts of goods.

"Keep moving," Evander said, pulling her along. "Remember, foreign kingdom. Don't want to attract attention." He looked pointedly at her.

She forced herself to keep walking, taking it all in. There were carts with beaded jewelry, food, candles, and swaths of fabric. The pungent smells of exotic food and the noise of people haggling prices were different from what she was used to.

Evander led the way down another street, taking them away from the market.

"Do we have to go already?" She wanted to spend time looking at everything.

"Yes." He glanced around. "It's not safe here."

Several of the nearby wooden buildings had missing windows. A few of the people they passed wore clothing that had holes or tears. Some faces were smeared with dirt.

If it wasn't safe, then he should have chosen a better place to meet her brother. "Where are we?"

"We're in Nisk."

Nisk? That meant he'd sailed the boat from the ocean into Skyfall River.

The road they were on led them straight out of town. The surrounding land was mostly low rolling hills with brown brush covering them. It was actually quite ugly.

"How far do we have to go?" she asked.

"Not too far." Evander removed his arm from her shoulders, and the two of them walked in silence.

A bout of nausea hit her. She stopped and bent over.

Evander turned and faced her. "Are you pregnant?"

She almost laughed and told him she hadn't shared her husband's bed. However, she thought better of it. "No." She stood and pushed the loose strands of her hair from her face. "I feel like we are moving up and down even though I'm on solid ground."

"I forgot you don't like sailing." He turned and resumed walking.

"It's not that I don't like it," she said, hurrying after him. "I just don't like feeling this way."

"You'll get over it." He reached into his bag and pulled out a small root. "Chew on this. It'll help."

It had an odd smell but she took it anyway, breaking off a piece and putting it in her mouth.

She didn't see anything around for miles other than the town they'd just left. "Are we going the right way?"

"Yes," he replied.

"Are you certain?"

"Yes."

"We couldn't have sailed closer to our destination?"

He mumbled something under his breath.

"What did you say?"

"I said *women*. You're all the same. Always questioning everything us men do, and you're never able to be quiet for more than two minutes." He picked up the pace.

Sabine had to practically jog to keep up with him. "You must not have any sisters, and clearly you're not married."

He chuckled. "I have three."

"You have three wives?" she asked, horrified by the prospect.

"No. Sisters." He shook his head.

"Are they older or younger?" Not that she cared, but questioning him helped pass the time.

"Older."

"I have five older siblings." And then she remembered she didn't. She stopped walking and closed her eyes. She missed Alina terribly. "I mean four," she said, her voice softer as she opened her eyes. "I have four older brothers." And no sister.

"Are you okay?"

"I'm fine."

"We need to keep moving." He glanced up at the darkening sky.

They resumed walking.

Thunder boomed, and big fat raindrops started to fall.

"We need to run," he said.

"How far?" Sabine still didn't see any homes or structures nearby. Just the dirt road they traveled on and ugly dry brush covering the hills all around them.

"It's about a mile from here."

While the boots he'd given her were rather large, she'd managed fine up to this point. "Okay." A mile wasn't that far, and she should be able to make it without any problems.

He nodded and took off sprinting.

Sabine jogged after him, the bag hitting her back as she ran. After about five minutes, the rain started to come down even harder, soaking through her clothes and making it difficult to see. The road turned to slick mud. She tried keeping her head down in order to see better.

After a few more minutes, Evander turned onto a narrow road. Sabine ran after him. It felt as if they'd already gone a mile and she was just about to ask him when she glanced up, spotting a nondescript wooden house not too far away, barely visible through the rain.

Sabine's foot caught in a divot in the road and she flew forward, landing sprawled on her stomach in the mud. She'd managed to keep her head up just enough so it remained mud free.

If Evander was lying and her brother wasn't in that house, Sabine was fairly certain she'd strangle him.

Without saying a word, Evander approached and reached

down, grabbed her arms, and hoisted her to her feet. Her shirt and pants were covered with thick mud.

Sabine glared at Evander, as if falling in the mud were his fault. Somehow it had to be.

He looked at her and pinched his lips together, quickly glancing away, trying not to laugh.

As she stood there in the pouring rain, some of the mud began to wash off.

For some reason, even though Evander's clothes were soaking wet and his hair had fallen across his forehead, he managed to look more rugged and manly while Sabine appeared to be a pathetic pig who couldn't stay on her feet.

Huffing dramatically, she stormed past him, walking the rest of the way to the house. She climbed the steps of the porch and was about to knock when the door flew open, revealing her brother, Otto.

"What happened to you?" Otto said, looking her up and down.

She wanted to throw her arms around him, hugging him, but refrained from doing so. There was no reason for the both of them to be covered in mud.

Before she could answer, Evander joined her. "Turn," he said, pointing behind her, cutting her reunion with Otto short.

Sabine did as he said, trying to figure out why he wanted her to look that way on the porch when she heard him stripping out of his clothes behind her. Being sure to keep her back to him, she started to shake from being drenched.

"Okay," Otto said.

She turned back around and Evander was nowhere to be seen, but his boots and clothes were strewn on the porch. Not wanting to get water in the house, she bent over and removed her muddy boots as well. There wasn't anything she could do about her clothes though—she wasn't going to run through the house naked.

"Come inside," Otto said. "We have a lot to discuss."

Sabine stepped into a sitting room. "Who's house is this?" she asked, closing the door behind her. A fire roared in the hearth, warming the room.

"It belongs to the League."

Several things clicked into place. "Are you Bakley's representative?"

He nodded. "Go and get cleaned up, then we'll talk."

"Is there a room I can use?"

"Upstairs, last door on the left."

Sabine looked at Otto. It had been weeks since she'd seen him. His hair was a little longer and his cheeks were sunken in a bit more. She reached out and grabbed his hand, squeezing it. "It's good to see you." She turned and headed upstairs, her wet socks leaving marks as she went.

She entered the room Otto had indicated and closed the door. A slew of emotions overwhelmed her. She wasn't in a dungeon, she was safe, and she was with her brother.

Chapter Two

After washing up, Sabine found a pair of pants and a shirt in the armoire. Both items were large but clean. She quickly dressed then went downstairs, eager to spend some time with her brother. She found him alone in the sitting room, resting on the sofa, Evander nowhere in sight.

"I put a few more logs in the fire for you," Otto said by way of greeting. "Sit on the chair closest to the hearth so your hair can dry and you can warm up."

"First, I need a proper hug." Now that she wasn't covered in mud.

Otto smiled and stood, wrapping his arms around his sister and squeezing. "It's good to see you. We weren't sure you were even alive." He held her at arm's length, looking into her eyes. "Are you okay?"

"I'm fine. You know, other than Evander kidnapping and scaring me half to death." She sat on the chair, curling her legs up under her.

"Kidnapping you?" Otto said, his voice slightly higher-pitched than normal.

She shrugged. "He gave me giplig, put me on a ship, brought me here."

Otto's face reddened. "Excuse me." He turned and sprinted up the stairs.

Sabine sat there, wondering what he was doing when she heard a door bang open, followed by angry shouting, then another bang. Otto ran down the steps now looking flushed.

"What was that?" she asked. She'd seen her brothers argue and fight enough to know Otto was furious. "I thought you asked Evander to bring me here?"

"I did." He flopped on the sofa. "But not like that." He pinched the bridge of his nose. "He was supposed to tell you what was going on, not steal you away."

"I wouldn't have gone with him," she admitted while rolling her sleeves up. She would have remained in Lynk with her husband.

"Why is that?" Otto asked, running a hand through his shaggy dark hair. The skin under his eyes appeared slightly gray, as if he hadn't slept in days.

"Because I wouldn't have believed him." If her parents had been concerned, they could have sent a letter to Markis. While she understood they'd be worried about her after Alina was assassinated, there wasn't much her parents could do to protect her, especially from so far away. So asking her to leave with a man she didn't know wasn't something she would have even considered doing.

"We became concerned after you didn't respond to Father's last letter."

She groaned, thinking about how her dog had destroyed that letter. "That's because I never read it." She quickly explained how Harta had eaten the paper.

"So the letter arrived, but you never read it?" Otto asked, leaning forward on the couch.

A chill slid through Sabine as she thought over the

incident. At first, she'd assumed Harta had been misbehaving and trying to get her attention by destroying the letter. However, knowing how well-trained the dog was, Sabine was now inclined to believe someone had told the animal to eat it. "No," she whispered. "I did not. What did it say?" Fear and apprehension filled her. She couldn't even trust her own dog.

"Father wrote in code stating that he believed King Rainer was manipulating the situation in order to marry you so he could get soldiers on the ground in Bakley to surround Carlon and Nisk." His words hung heavy in the air, the information buzzing around like bees ready to attack.

Sabine rubbed her forehead. "I don't understand." When and how had her father come upon this information? The fire crackled in the hearth, startling her. She shivered even though the room was warm.

"It all started when the League reviewed the new contract with your name. I noticed an increase in the number of soldiers father requested, which I thought was strange since he never mentioned it to me."

Sabine had heard Rainer talk about the increase in soldiers.

"Father said he didn't make any changes other than putting your name in place of Alina's." Otto scooted over on the sofa so he was in front of Sabine. "I informed the other League members, and we decided not to approve the marriage until we could investigate further."

"And did you?" she asked.

Otto nodded. "We managed to arrange for the Avoni delegation to travel to Lynk under the guise of wanting to witness the wedding ceremony knowing the marriage hadn't been approved yet. We hoped they'd discover nothing was amiss, and your marriage could proceed as planned."

"I'm guessing that since I'm sitting here, things didn't go as planned." She rubbed her eyes, suddenly exhausted.

"No, they did not. Avoni discovered soldiers preparing for battle. Weapons are being amassed in caves near the border, armor is being made, and there are tent cities with soldiers ready to enter Carlon and Nisk at a moment's notice."

Sabine stared into the fire, thinking over everything her brother had revealed. "How did Avoni come across this information?" It wasn't like the delegation was running around Lynk. They were at the palace. And she'd traveled through the kingdom and hadn't seen anything to support this.

"The delegation took spies with them."

"And we trust their spies?"

"I don't know."

She leaned forward, taking her brother's hands. "An Avoni assassin killed Alina. An Avoni assassin is after me. We can't blindly trust them."

"I understand." Otto squeezed her hands. "And I do need to discuss the matter with Evander."

"Are the two of you friends?" she asked, skeptical that Otto had friends she didn't know about. Granted, he'd been a League member and she hadn't known that.

"We are. I've known him for some time." He leaned back in his chair. "Now tell me, did Rainer confide in you? What have you learned? Did you discover who hired the assassin to kill Alina?"

So many questions that she didn't even know where to begin, so she started with the first. She explained how Rainer never confided in her. Then she went on to tell him how she'd discovered Lottie was trying to take her brother's throne and had hired the assassin to kill Alina.

Otto nodded. "And did you overhear anything about the kidnapped Bakley children?"

"No."

"Rolf sent out spies to watch the border and report back on who was conducting the raids and stealing our children." He looked at her, the lines around his eyes deepening, as if not wanting to continue.

A sick feeling wormed its way into Sabine's stomach. "What did he discover?" she asked, knowing she wouldn't like the answer. Before going to Lynk, she'd been so sure Carlon was responsible for everything.

"There is conflicting evidence, but there is viable proof that Lynk soldiers are raiding the borders and doing the kidnappings."

Sabine rubbed her temples. The man she'd married couldn't be responsible for these awful things. "What's the conflicting evidence?"

"A few of the men had something tying them to Avoni."

"So we know it's either Lynk or Avoni who is causing Bakley all these problems."

"Correct," he replied. "Did you see anything to support any of this at the palace?" Otto asked. "Did Rainer mention anything to you at all?"

She shook her head. She'd been so wrapped up in finding Alina's killer that she hadn't been paying attention to anything else. Sometimes she felt her young age and lack of political knowledge keenly—this was one of those times. If she'd paid more attention to her studies, if she'd attended more meetings with the dignitaries from other kingdoms... there were a lot of ifs. She needed to rectify these things. She needed to protect Bakley.

"You're not looking well," Otto said.

"I need something warm to drink. Can someone bring me a cup of tea?" Hopefully, the beverage would soothe her stomach.

"You want tea?" Otto asked around a chuckle as he stood from the sofa. "You're turning into Mother."

She rolled her eyes. "I'm cold and hungry is all."

"There aren't any servants, so we'll have to make it ourselves." He led her to the kitchen.

Sabine had never made her own tea before and wasn't sure how one went about doing it. "Why aren't there any servants?" And who would cook their supper? The kitchen had an alcove with a small hearth containing a fire. Next to it, several pots and pans hung. There were also two long counters for cutting vegetables or kneading bread. Below the counters were stacks of plates and pewter mugs. In the middle of the kitchen, a long table with a bench on either side took up a majority of the space.

"We don't have servants because we don't want anyone to overhear our conversations. It's safer this way." Otto went over and grabbed a pot.

"Are all of the League members here?" Sabine asked, taking a seat on one of the benches.

"All but one."

She pinched her eyes shut, realization dawning on her. "Is Evander Avoni's representative?" She looked at her brother, fearing the answer she already knew.

"Yes." Otto filled the pot with water.

"Which means Evander is a member of the Avoni royal family?"

"He is." He hung the pot in the hearth, above the low burning fire.

Sabine drummed her fingers on the table, contemplating this new information. Originally, she'd thought Evander was simply a member of the delegation. Then when he'd appeared on her balcony at the palace, she figured he was an assassin since he seemed to possess stealthy skills. Then he went and kidnapped her. And now she found out he was a prince. An assassin-kidnapper-pirate-prince. A man of many talents. She snorted.

Otto poured some steaming water into a mug, handing it to Sabine. Then he got a jar of tea leaves and added some into a strainer, giving it to her.

"Why is the League meeting here today?" she asked, taking the strainer and setting it in her mug to steep.

Otto sat across from her. "We're here for two reasons. One, to discuss your marriage to King Rainer. And two, to do a little spying." The corners of his lips rose in a half smile.

"Spying?" Sabine wrapped her hands around the mug, warming her fingers.

"Yes. We're going on a trip tomorrow to investigate. Our spies have discovered that certain caves and tunnels are being used to transport weapons from one kingdom to another. We're going to go and take a look to see for ourselves. The League can't act on this information unless we're one hundred percent sure it's true and accurate."

After taking her tea strainer out and setting it aside, she took a sip of the hot tea, letting its warmth fill her. "About my marriage to King Rainer," she said as she set her mug back on the table, "we secretly married." She quickly told Otto what had transpired before the Avoni delegation arrived in Lynk. When she finished, she leaned across the table and whispered, "The marriage hasn't been consummated." She sat back down, waiting for his response.

He sat there motionless, staring at her, his face revealing nothing.

"Don't you have anything to say?" she asked, unease filling her as she shifted her weight on the bench.

His face remained unreadable. "Let me think this through. Tell no one."

She nodded, knowing this was a tricky situation. One in which she had no idea how to navigate through. She was married, but the marriage was not consummated. She was crowned queen of Lynk but no one knew except for a handful of people. A thought suddenly occurred to her. "Is Anton here?" Since he was Lynk's representative, he should be present.

"He is due to arrive the day after tomorrow. We wanted to talk with you and then do our spying mission before Anton got here."

Evander came strolling into the kitchen dressed in clean clothes, his hair wet. "Tea?" he said, shaking his head as he eyed the table. "You Bakley people and your plain tea."

Sabine glared at him but didn't respond. Instead, she took another sip, reveling in the warmth of it, even if it was rather bland.

Evander glanced at Otto. "Are we good?" he asked, his eyebrows raised.

"Do you plan on kidnapping my sister again?" Otto asked, folding his arms.

"I don't think so."

"Then we're good, so long as you don't lay a hand on her. Are we clear?"

Evander raised his hands in surrender. "I won't touch her." He went over to the hearth and poured himself a cup of hot water. "It must have been tiring growing up with four older brothers," Evander said to Sabine as he approached the table.

For once, Sabine happened to agree with him, though she'd never admit it.

Evander sat on the bench beside Otto, pulling out a small black satchel from his pocket. He opened it, revealing leaves. Sabine watched him take the tea strainer she'd used, fill it with said leaves, and put it in his cup to steep.

"You're making tea?" she asked. "After just making fun of me for drinking the same thing?"

He nodded, his lips curling into a conciliatory smile. "I was making fun of you for drinking *plain* tea."

"As opposed to exciting tea?"

He lifted a single eyebrow, his lips still curled in a smile as he removed the strainer, stirred his freshly-made tea, then pushed it toward her. "Try it." The way he said it made it seem like a challenge.

"The last time you gave me something," she said, pointing at him, "I found myself waking up on a ship."

He smirked and made the sound of a chicken.

"You did not just do that," she said, looking at him in disbelief.

Otto chuckled and shook his head. "I'd watch it if I were you," he said, elbowing Evander. "She isn't like most women."

Evander shrugged. "Fine." He reached out to grab the mug, his eyes never leaving hers, amusement dancing in them.

Irritated that it felt like defeat for not tasting the tea, she swiped the mug before Evander got it, lifted it to her lips, and took a tiny sip. Her intention had been to prove she wasn't some pampered princess who backed down from a challenge. She wanted to show him he didn't scare or intimidate her. However, the second the warm liquid hit her tongue, a sense of peace filled her. The tea tasted like a luxurious sweet treat she'd have after supper.

"Did you just moan?" Otto asked Sabine. "What did you give her?" He turned to Evander.

Evander chuckled. "Hand it back." He reached for the mug.

Sabine pushed it over to him. "That's the most delicious thing I've ever had." It didn't even taste like herbal tea.

"Like I said, you Bakley people drink *plain* tea."

Evander really was quite irritating. Especially when he was right.

"If the two of you are done bickering," Otto said, "I'd like to know what Evander saw in Lynk."

Evander rubbed his eyes then looked at Sabine. "I know you told me Rainer wasn't holding you at the palace against your will, but I think he was." He spoke gently, as if afraid to hurt her feelings.

She hadn't been a prisoner in the palace. "I was free to leave my room." She took a sip of her drab tea. "I mean, so long as I had guards with me, but that was for my own protection. I was only confined to my room those first few days." As she said it out loud, it sounded worse than it was.

Evander looked at Otto. "See. She was being held there without her even realizing it." He took a sip of his tea and smiled at her.

Prick.

Otto scratched the side of his face. "Did you visit any nearby towns?"

"I went through one on my way in," she explained. "You have to understand, there was an assassin after me. I had to be careful. Rainer didn't want me wandering around and getting myself killed. I wasn't locked up, and I wasn't in a dungeon." Rainer wanted to ensure her safety. He'd been so upset over Alina's death that he'd been overly cautious with Sabine.

Otto sat there staring at her, his face unreadable.

"I wasn't forced to do anything I didn't want to do," she said, hoping her brother understood.

"It's such a shame you married the guy," Evander mused. "Now your fate is tied to his. I kidnapped you hoping to save you from being involved in a nasty war."

"There's not going to be a war. Not if I can help it." She rubbed her temples.

"You know she's married?" Otto asked Evander.

"She mentioned it on the ship. If I'd known beforehand, I never would have taken her."

"Rainer has been nothing but kind to me," Sabine insisted. He always seemed concerned with her wellbeing and safety. Granted, he needed her to produce an heir. But he'd never been mean to her. Not really. Her face reddened thinking about how he made her feel on occasion, the clothes he insisted she wear, or even the way he expected her to behave. She remembered him training her. The way his muscles felt beneath her hands. He really was one of the most handsome men she'd ever seen.

However, now she was forced to examine things from a different perspective. Had Rainer been manipulating her into doing what he wanted? She didn't know what to believe anymore. "I'm exhausted from my journey and wish to retire to bed." That way she could think through her time in Lynk without having these two men sitting before her, scrutinizing her every move.

Otto stood. "Come, sister. I'll escort you to your room." He led the way up the stairs. Stopping outside her room, he whispered, "You know Evander is not someone you can push too hard or challenge."

She stepped inside the room, hearing the rain pounding on the roof above her. She went over to the bedside table and lit the candle. While the room was small, containing only a single bed and armoire, it was clean and warm. It would be much better than sleeping on the deck of a ship.

"Why is that?" she asked, curiosity getting the better of her. Evander looked to be about her age. While he was tall, he didn't have the same wide shoulders and muscles that Rainer did. "Is it because he's from Avoni and has been trained to be an assassin?" Now that she knew he was a prince, she wasn't so sure if he was either an assassin or pirate anymore. She didn't see the need for members of the royal family to learn the art of assassination or pirating. Not when they had people who could perform those tasks for them.

Otto peered over his shoulder at the staircase before stepping into her room and closing the door behind him. "You need to be careful around Evander," he whispered.

"Why?" she asked, wanting to know more about the man who'd managed to kidnap her from the palace and get her out of Lynk undetected. She shivered, wondering how he'd managed such a feat on his own. She couldn't envision him carrying her since there wasn't much to him.

Otto whispered, "Evander is the only son of King Kai and Queen Sherilda Botoko, he is a trained assassin, he's Avoni's League member, *and* he is one of the most wealthy and powerful men in Avoni." He looked pointedly at her, as if making sure she understood each and every one of his points. "Most importantly, he is the leader of the Crimson Cloaks."

"The what?"

"One of the five assassin leagues." He folded his arms. "I'd say it's the most exclusive, most elusive, and most difficult to join."

She blinked. "Evander?" The red-haired man who'd kidnapped her? He seemed so...young for all those things. If anything, she'd say he was slightly awkward, a bit of a goof, and he seemed more of a joker than an assassin. She couldn't imagine him being wealthy or powerful either. However, he'd managed to take her from right under Rainer's roof. All on his own. And she'd seen Rainer fight and had heard stories of his army. He wasn't someone to trifle with. Yet Evander had.

Otto put his hand on Sabine's shoulder. "Evander is not only intelligent but an excellent fighter."

She hadn't seen Evander fight and had trouble imagining him being able to hold his own against someone like Rainer.

"Never underestimate him," he added.

"How do you know this?" she asked her brother.

"I've known him since I was five. But that is a story for another time. Get some sleep—we have a big day ahead of us tomorrow."

She nodded and pulled back the blankets on her bed. "Now that I'm here with you, I don't have to worry about Evander." They'd go their separate ways, and she wouldn't have to deal with the assassin any more.

Otto left the room.

Sabine crawled under the covers. The rain had lessened to a soft patter, hitting the window in a soothing sort of way. She fell fast asleep, thoughts of Evander the assassin-pirate-prince inundating her dreams.

Someone shook Sabine awake. She peeled her eyelids open and found Otto standing next to the bed, already dressed. The room was only just starting to lighten, so it had to be too early to wake. "What's going on?" she mumbled.

"We're leaving to go spy. Do you want to come with us or stay here?"

Shocked he was giving her the option, she immediately agreed to go and shoved the covers back.

"Wear pants and dark colors," Otto said before closing the door so she could change.

Sabine quickly put on black pants and a tunic. She pulled her hair back, braiding it. After rolling up the pants so she wouldn't trip, she headed downstairs where she found four men. Two she recognized as Otto and Evander, and the other two had to be the League representatives from Carlon and Nisk.

"Sabine," Otto said when she neared. "This is Thad." He

pointed to the shorter man with black hair. "And this is Seth." He indicated the older man with dirty-blond hair. "We don't use titles here."

"Good morning." She noticed each had a jacket and hat in hand.

"Let's get going," Otto said, opening the front door.

She went out on the porch where she found her muddy boots. After putting them on, she straightened. Otto stood there holding a jacket out for her. She slid her arms in. The thing was large on her, but it was warm.

"There's a hat in the pocket," Otto said. "Let's go." His breath came out in a white cloud.

The two of them followed Evander, Thad, and Seth. The group made their way toward the back of the house before cutting across the field, no one talking as they walked. The sky continued to lighten though the sun had not yet risen.

Sabine shoved her hands into her pockets, trying to stay warm.

When they reached the forest, they walked single file between the trees. After a solid hour, they exited the forest and found themselves at the edge of a steep cliff. The four men all got on the ground, lying on their stomachs as they inched closer to the edge. Reluctantly, Sabine did the same, positioning herself on the end next to Otto. Below, the forest stretched out as far as she could see. A narrow path cut between the trees, just wide enough for two horses to ride side by side.

The five of them remained there, lying on their stomachs, no one talking, for hours. If this is what spying entailed, Sabine found it rather boring. The sun shone above them, basking her in warmth. Her eyelids became heavy, and she managed to doze off.

Otto shook her shoulder, waking her, then he pointed to the forest below them.

Sabine lifted her head and looked. At first she didn't see anything. After a few minutes, she spotted a group traveling on the path. She squinted, trying to see better. At the front were a handful of men dressed in nondescript clothing. Behind them, walking in two lines, were dozens of children.

Fury and panic filled her. Where were these men taking these kids? She had to intervene.

Otto placed his hand on her back, keeping her low to the ground. He shook his head and motioned for her to stay quiet.

The end of the line approached, and Sabine spotted another half dozen men at the back. Once they were out of sight, no one in her group moved for several minutes. Sabine considered everything she'd seen. Nothing had indicated where those people were from or where they were going. She hadn't heard them speaking, so she didn't catch any particular language.

Evander suddenly stood and climbed over the side of the cliff. Sabine watched him scale down it, as if it were something he did every day. When he reached the bottom, he took off running the direction the children had gone.

"What's he doing?" she whispered to her brother.

Otto tilted his head behind them. Sabine scooted back then stood. The others did the same. They began to make their way back through the forest. Every time Sabine tried speaking, Otto glared at her, making it clear no one was to talk.

When they reached the house, Sabine stormed inside and rounded on Otto. "Why didn't we stop them?"

Thad and Seth removed their jackets before heading to the kitchen.

"We were outnumbered," Otto said. "There was nothing we could do. Besides, what, exactly, did you see? Could you tell where those men were from? Or what was going on?"

"Bakley children are being kidnapped. I think it's safe to assume those were our children." She folded her arms, glaring at her brother.

"And the men?"

"I don't know," she admitted.

"They could be Lynk's soldiers," Otto said, putting his hands in his pockets.

"Or Carlon's or Nisk's." They were in Nisk after all.

Otto nodded. "Exactly. Until we have more information, we will not act."

"Then what's Evander doing?" she asked, hoping he'd gone to free the children.

"Evander went after them to see what's going on." Otto removed his hat and ran his hand through his hair.

"It doesn't make any sense for it to be Lynk," she said. "I'm married to Rainer. He has no reason to force Bakley into an alliance with him since we already have one."

"That's why we went today," Otto said. "To gather information. So far we know that once a week, about two dozen kids are taken north into Lynk."

This entire ordeal made her sick to her stomach. "Those children are innocent."

"I know."

"I want every single one returned home."

"That's the plan."

She went into the kitchen to look for something to eat. Thad and Seth were sitting at the table with a warm loaf of bread.

"Want some?" Thad asked.

She nodded.

He cut off a chunk and handed it to her.

She took it and went outside, wanting to be alone. Sitting on the top step of the porch, her jacket and hat still on, she nibbled on the bread, thinking about those children and what she could do to help them. Hours went by, and she still hadn't managed to come up with a single idea other than confronting Rainer and demanding to know what was going on—which wouldn't accomplish anything.

Feeling utterly useless, Sabine rubbed her forehead.

"Are you okay?"

Startled, she peered up and saw Evander approaching. She nodded.

"How long have you been out here?" he asked.

"Not long." She shrugged.

"Your nose and ears are bright red." He sat on the top step next to her.

She looked at him. His green eyes held a dark sadness to them. "What did you discover?" she asked.

"I'm sorry," he said. "Those were Lynk soldiers taking Bakley children north to your kingdom."

Her kingdom. She felt sick to her stomach. "What are they doing with the children?" she asked. Since Lynk was her kingdom, she had a responsibility to do something.

"They're using the children for manual labor." He gazed out at the land before them. "They're making weapons."

"The children are?" she asked, wondering why they couldn't use adults for that.

"Their hands are smaller, and it's easier for them to make arrows." Evander rubbed his face.

"And this is happening in Lynk?" She wanted to be absolutely certain. Maybe Rainer didn't know about it.

"There are tunnels in Lynk," he said. "And caverns. They're in one of the larger caverns on the other side of the wall. I'm sorry."

She wondered how Evander had gotten past the wall to discover all of this. Maybe he'd grabbed one of the soldiers and interrogated him.

The door behind them opened. "I thought I heard talking

out here," Otto said. "Why don't the two of you come in since it's starting to get dark."

Evander stood, reaching his hand out to Sabine. She took it, letting him pull her to her feet.

Inside, they went to the kitchen where Thad and Seth were sitting at the table. Otto and Sabine sat on the empty bench across from them while Evander sat next to Thad and Seth.

"Any luck?" Thad asked.

Evander sighed. "I was able to confirm that we saw Lynk soldiers traveling with children from Bakley."

"I think it's safe to conclude that King Rainer is planning to go to war," Thad said. "We have seen his boats filled with soldiers off the coast of Carlon. We now have proof he is stealing Bakley children, using that as a reason for Bakley to align with Lynk. He intends to take over all the land."

This was the first Sabine had heard about the boats.

Evander stood and went to the hearth, returning a moment later with two steaming mugs filled to the brim with tea. He set one in front of Sabine.

"The point of the League is to prevent wars," Seth pointed out. "I'm not sure how we can stop this one."

Sabine had seen nothing in Lynk to support any of this. Although, now that she was looking at things differently, she had witnessed Rainer training with his soldiers. However, she'd assumed that was something he did all the time.

"I don't know what this means for Bakley," Otto said. "We already have Lynk soldiers in my kingdom. Rainer could easily take control."

Sabine took hold of Otto's hand, squeezing it. "I won't let him hurt any of you." Although she didn't know how much power she held over Rainer, if any. Another thought occurred to her. "Where does Avoni fit into this?"

"When I was in Lynk, Rainer asked me to marry Lottie," Evander revealed.

Then Rainer knew who Evander was.

"My guess is Rainer wants Avoni under his thumb in the same way he wants Bakley controlled," Evander said.

"What did you tell him?" Sabine asked.

"I haven't given him an answer yet. He simply proposed the match. I must discuss it with my father first."

She nodded, clutching her hands together, unable to look at anyone.

"What's the matter?" Evander asked.

She shook her head.

"You can tell him," Otto said. "We hold no secrets here. Each of us is required to speak the truth when we meet in this house."

Sabine took a deep breath, letting it out slowly. Then she said, "Lottie arranged for Alina's death. She's the person responsible for killing my sister." Lottie had to be brought to justice, not sold off in marriage to another kingdom.

"Are you certain?" Evander asked.

Someone banged on the front door. "Are we expecting anyone else?" Sabine inquired.

"The only person it could be is Anton," Seth muttered as he got up and left the table.

Sabine looked Evander directly in the eyes. "Yes, I'm certain. I heard Lottie speaking with the Avoni assassin she hired. They were discussing his disastrous attempt to kill me and how the next time he couldn't fail. They planted evidence in the Avoni delegation's quarters to make it look like Avoni was responsible for Alina's death."

Evander's eyes narrowed. "How do you know this?"

"I, uh...was in the Avoni rooms when they came in to plant the evidence. I overheard them." She ducked her head.

"You did what?" Otto asked, his voice high-pitched.

"Why were you in there?" Evander asked, his voice as cool as water on a crisp fall day.

"I was searching for my sister's killer."

"In the Avoni delegation's rooms?" He placed his palms flat on the table.

She chose not to answer that. "When they left, I grabbed the evidence and returned to the masquerade in search of Rainer. I wanted to tell him his sister was trying to kill me in order to take the throne. You kidnapped me before I had a chance to do anything with my newfound information."

"What happened to the evidence?" Evander asked.

Voices came from the adjacent room.

"I don't know. I hid it in my dress." Either Evander had found it, or it had sunk with her dress to the bottom of the ocean.

"Did you at least have a chance to look at it?" he asked.

"I did. It was in another language, and I couldn't read it."

Evander cursed.

"Greetings," Anton said as he came into the kitchen with Seth, his focus going straight to Sabine. "You have managed to create quite a stir back in Lynk," he said as he took a seat next to her.

She figured her kidnapping would have infuriated Rainer into taking up his sword and declaring war. "I knew he'd be upset when he noticed me missing. What's he telling people?"

"No one knows you're gone," Anton said. "Everyone is talking about you because Rainer announced to Lynk, and all the other kingdoms, that the two of you are married and he crowned you queen."

Chapter Three

"Why did Rainer do that?" Sabine asked. They didn't have the League's permission to marry yet.

"He did it to ensure your safety," Anton replied, looking at Evander as he spoke. "No one would dare harm a king or queen. If someone did, there'd be major ramifications for such an act."

"Does Rainer know what really happened to me?" She wondered if someone from the Avoni delegation had told him Evander took her.

"No, he doesn't," Anton said, his focus going to Sabine. "He declared to everyone at court that you're in bed. Most assume you're with child and that's the reason for your confinement."

She couldn't figure out how any of this made sense.

Anton reached out, placing his hand on her arm. "My brother thinks you've run away, and he's worried about you."

Evander snorted.

"I thought he'd find me missing and be ready to raise his sword against the other kingdoms," she said. "Not because he cares, but because it's a good excuse to go to war."

Anton sat there observing her. "I guess your interpretation of events depends on what you've seen and been told." He turned his attention to Evander. "I'm assuming you're the one who convinced Sabine to leave her husband and come here?"

"I have not left my husband," Sabine said. "I am here to see my brother."

"That's right," Otto said. "I was concerned because my sister hasn't responded to my family's numerous letters. Something seemed amiss."

"My brother has given you a fortnight to return," Anton said. "I've been tasked with coming here to speak with the League to see if by chance you came here for clarity, safety, or some other misguided notion." He squeezed Sabine's arm before letting it go. "I really hope that what you said is true. If he discovers otherwise, if he even thinks you've been taken, there will be no stopping him."

Sabine didn't think this had anything to do with Rainer caring for her. But rather, this was him making sure he didn't lose his crown. Since they were married, he had a very limited timeframe to produce an heir, or Lottie would inherit the throne.

"Now that we know Rainer and Sabine are married," Evander said, gaining everyone's attention, "any hope of keeping Bakley and Lynk from uniting is gone. If the League doesn't approve, it'll be like we're declaring war against Lynk. We have no choice but to consent to the marriage." He rested his elbows on the table.

"I agree," Thad said. "Let's give our official approval and move on. We need to decide how to stop Lynk from invading the other kingdoms." He looked to Sabine, as if he didn't know if he could say more in front of her.

Sabine rubbed her temples, a nasty headache starting to form. "I will do everything in my power to prevent my husband from going to war against another kingdom." She tried to speak as strongly as possible so these men would know she was serious. She looked at Anton. "I need to speak with you privately." She stood and left the kitchen, heading straight for the door and going outside without looking to see if he followed.

The sun had set, and the air was turning cold. She strode down the steps of the porch and went a few feet from the house, not wanting anyone inside to overhear her conversation. Anton joined her a moment later. She folded her arms, trying to stay warm.

"I know you married my brother and were crowned, but—"

"No," Sabine interrupted him. "You don't get to speak right now. I am your queen." She glared at him, trying to make him cower. He didn't. No matter, she would still act strong, even if she didn't feel it. "I don't know whose side you're on, but I'm going to do what's best for Lynk."

"I'm loyal to Lynk as well," he insisted.

She tilted her head to the side, considering him. Since he wasn't the previous king's blood, she wasn't certain if his loyalties were to the royal family or not. Rainer's father had Anton's mother, the queen, and his father, the queen's guard, killed. "Your sister hired the assassin who murdered Alina." She waited for him to speak, wanting to know if he was aware of Lottie's treachery. She had no idea how close the twins were to their sister.

"Lottie wants the throne?" he asked, his breath coming out in a puff of white in the cold air.

"I overheard her with the assassin. She sent him after me. I am the assassin's next target." Out here in the dark night, her words came out crisp and clear, cutting through the air.

Anton cursed. "I need to get home. With you missing, who knows what she'll do."

His response seemed reasonable. And if he cared for Rainer, going home to warn him would be the right thing to do. But she had a few more issues she wanted to discuss with him. "Rainer knows."

Anton stilled. "That's why he married you," he said, realization dawning on him.

She nodded, kicking the tip of her shoe against the ground, the only sound in the still night.

Anton let his head fall back as he chewed on his bottom lip. "I knew it was someone close to him, but I didn't know it was Lottie." An owl hooted in the distance. "You running away and wanting to see your brother makes more sense now." He sighed.

"I need you to be honest with me," she said. "Do you know who's responsible for the raids at Bakley's border and kidnapping the children?"

His eyes narrowed. "Why don't you tell me what you know, and I'll say if you're right or not."

"Just answer the question." She knew Anton helped run Lynk's network of spies. He had to know.

"I can't tell you anything," he said. "I swore an oath to Rainer."

"It's Lynk, isn't it?" she demanded. "This was all an elaborate plot to get Bakley's food and land." Tears filled her eyes.

"That's what you think?" he asked, stepping closer to her.

"It's what I know."

He stared at her a full minute before saying, "The situation is more complicated than that."

She noticed he hadn't denied anything.

"You know, as well as I do, that both kingdoms gained

something from this marriage," Anton said. "And why do you care anyway? It's not like it's a love match."

She wiped the traitorous tears that slid down her cheek. "I care because my kingdom is affected. People I'm sworn to protect."

"And which people would that be?" he asked, his voice low. "Lynk? Or Bakley?"

"Both."

He nodded slowly. "I think it best if I let Rainer explain everything."

"How could you let this happen?" Had he no heart? No morals or values?

"No one *lets* Rainer do anything," Anton said, a sharp edge to his voice. "Rainer does what Rainer wants. He always has."

"And you blindly follow him."

Anton lifted his hands, palms facing her, before turning and walking a few feet away.

"We're not done," Sabine said, her voice cracking. This entire time, she thought Carlon was the enemy, not the man she was going to spend the rest of her life with. "I'm going to be ill." The land around her seemed to spin.

Anton chuckled, the sound humorless. He approached Sabine, taking hold of her arms to steady her. "Are you okay?" he mumbled.

As if he really cared. "I'm fine."

He leaned in and whispered, "I'd ask if you're swooning because you're pregnant, but I'm guessing you're not." He looked pointedly at her, as if he knew her marriage hadn't been consummated.

She looked into his eyes but didn't say anything.

"Let's get you inside. You need to go to sleep. We have a long journey ahead of us tomorrow."

The gravity of his words sunk into her mind like boulders

being hurled into a lake, plummeting to the bottom. She started pacing, needing to move so she didn't vomit. She couldn't return to the palace knowing all these things about Rainer. "I want some more time. I'm not ready to go back yet." She needed a few days to gather her thoughts and come up with a plan.

"When you disappeared, I assumed you'd left with Evander. No one else could have gotten you not only out of the palace, but out of the kingdom. I told Rainer you confided in me. You said you were homesick. I recommended you discuss the matter with him and said perhaps one of the women from the Avoni delegation could escort you to see your brother who was visiting nearby in Nisk."

A bold lie. "And what did Rainer say?" she asked, chewing on her thumbnail—a terrible habit she tended to do when nervous.

"He assumed you'd gone through with your plan without discussing it with him. However, he was furious you managed to leave the palace without your guards—a feat he can't figure out how you accomplished. And...he was hurt you didn't talk to him about it. Axel laughed and said you had no reason to confide in him. That only upset Rainer all the more."

"How long have I been gone?"

"Five days."

Longer than she'd expected.

"When Rainer finally calmed down, he bid me to go after you. I'm bringing you home. I told him it would take me roughly a fortnight."

Which was why Rainer had given a fortnight as the deadline for her return. She eyed Anton, wondering if he was being truthful with her. If he could so easily lie to his brother, what was to prevent him from lying to her?

Grabbing her braid, she pulled it over her shoulder,

removed the tie, and started undoing it. "I can't go back to the palace with Lottie there." Rainer knew his sister was responsible for killing Alina. However, instead of telling Sabine, he'd kept it a secret. He'd chosen to hasten their marriage, assuming that would protect her. She glanced at the ring on her finger. It felt like flimsy protection to her.

"You don't need to worry about Lottie," Anton assured her. "If she's after the crown, Rainer will stop her."

Evander opened the door and came outside, jogging down the steps and joining them. "I hate to break up this family reunion, but I'd like to remind you that Lottie hired an assassin to kill you. I'm guessing if Anton came looking for you, the assassin is probably following Anton to get to you. It's not safe for you to be exposed like this." He nodded his head to the surrounding land.

Sabine scanned the horizon, not seeing much under the dark night sky. She shivered.

"There could be someone hiding in the nearby forest," Evander said. "He could have an arrow trained on you right now."

Sabine shoved past him and ran into the house, moving away from the window. How was she supposed to live knowing someone was hunting her?

Anton and Evander came inside the house, closing and locking the door.

Otto, Seth, and Thad were sitting on the sofa near the fire.

"I must return home tomorrow," Seth said. "Sabine, does the League officially have your word as the queen of Lynk that you will do what you can to prevent our kingdoms from being invaded?"

She nodded. "I don't want to see my family involved in a war."

"And which family is that?" Seth asked. "Your husband?"

She understood what he was saying. Her Bakley family was no longer her family now that she'd married Rainer. "I will do what I have to in order to maintain peace."

"That's all we can hope for at this point," Seth said as he stood. "I'm turning in for the night since I'm leaving at first light. It was nice to meet you, Sabine." He bowed his head then went upstairs.

She sat on the sofa Seth had vacated.

"Thank you for your support and reassurance." Thad stood. "I am going to bed as well. I hope all you say is true." He left the room.

"Are you leaving tomorrow?" Sabine asked her brother.

He nodded. "There's nothing left here for us to discuss. If anything, I need to get home to let Mother and Father know you're well and to warn them of the state of things."

She reached out and took his hand. "Let our parents know all that has transpired—all of it." She looked pointedly at him, knowing he'd understand what she wasn't saying out loud. She didn't want anyone else to know her marriage hadn't been consummated. "Tell them I love them, and I'll find a way to fix this mess."

He stood and kissed her forehead. "I'm not sure you can. Just try and be safe." He left the room.

"We'll leave tomorrow after breakfast," Anton said to Sabine. "I'm going to retire for the night." He turned and headed toward the staircase.

"I'm not going with you." Sabine clasped her hands together, not looking Anton's way.

He stopped at the bottom of the steps and opened his mouth, about to argue with her.

"I will return to the palace." She finally looked at him. "Only, I won't be returning with *you*."

"I don't think it's wise for you to travel alone," Anton said.

"She's not," Evander said, coming farther into the room. "I'm escorting her."

"Rainer won't like that," Anton said, looking between the two of them.

Sabine knew Rainer wouldn't like her traveling alone with another man. He'd been upset when she'd traveled with Markis on her way to Lynk, and she'd seen firsthand his insecurities with her guard. "I'll write a letter to Rainer, and you can give it to him explaining everything."

"I can't allow this," Anton said.

"Then it's a good thing it's not up to you," she said as she stood. "I have an assassin after me. I'll be safest with Evander as my escort." She went into the kitchen, wanting a cup of tea to calm her nerves before she went to bed.

Alone in the kitchen, the events of the day pressed down upon her. Everything was a complete disaster—and she didn't know how to fix any of it. The life she'd originally wanted had been stripped from her the moment Alina had left for Lynk. Then it changed again when that man murdered Alina. And then yet again when Sabine chose to take her sister's place. And now, any hope for a quiet life with a loving husband was out of the question. She'd married a soldier king who commanded a massive, brutal army. She'd have to use everything in her power to try and maintain peace between the kingdoms. Any sort of future that she wished for was irrelevant. All that mattered was protecting her people.

She heard mumbling coming from the living room. Curiosity got the better of her and she moved closer to the kitchen door, pressing her ear against it and listening.

"She can't go with you," Anton said. "It's out of the question."

"I understand you have orders to bring her home safe and sound to your pretty little palace on the mountaintop," Evander said. "However, it's best if I accompany Sabine."

Anton mumbled something Sabine couldn't hear.

"Your sister has set an assassin after Sabine. Do you think yourself so adept with a sword that you can keep the queen of Lynk safe? From a trained Avoni assassin?"

"Then why don't you come with me?" Anton said. "The three of us can travel together."

"If we're traveling together, then you're coming with us," Evander said.

"Why?"

"Because my ship isn't far from here. Once we reach it, it's a quick sail over to Lynk."

"Ship?" Anton said. "I can't sail. I get violently ill." There was a long silence. "It'll take the same time whether it's by land or sea."

"I travel roads I know. That's the only way I can be sure I'm not taken by surprise and I can keep Sabine safe."

"Fine," Anton said. "We'll travel separately. But I want a letter from Sabine explaining why I'm showing up without her. And you better have a good explanation as to why you are."

"We very well may arrive before you," Evander pointed out. "But I'm sure she'll write a letter for you. And I plan on letting your brother know I'm accepting his offer—I'll marry Lottie. I assume he'll want me to take her to Avoni immediately to be wed. This saves me a trip."

"Fine."

There was a shuffling noise. "Out of curiosity," Evander said, "has anyone told Lottie about this proposal?"

"I doubt it. Lottie is a problem Rainer needs a solution to. It seems you're it."

Yes, Sabine thought dryly, what better way to get rid of Lottie than forcing her to marry into a family of assassins. At least Lottie couldn't hurt anyone in a kingdom known for killing. If anything, she'd fit right in.

Sabine found Otto packed and ready to leave when she came downstairs in the morning. Her chest tightened at the thought of saying goodbye to him. But it had to be done.

"Evander is in the kitchen and Anton is still upstairs," he said as he stepped forward, wrapping his arms around her in a hug. "Thad and Seth have already left." He held onto her tightly. "Be safe."

"I wish things could go back to the way they were," she whispered. She didn't want to return to Lynk but knew she had to. Not only was she married to Rainer, but she had to stop a war from breaking out.

"I know," he said as he released her. "I miss Alina—even if she was a pain in my ass sometimes."

For Sabine, it was more than that. While she missed her sister, she felt as if she'd lost her entire family since she no longer lived at home. She wanted to be with them, and she longed for the days when she had no responsibilities. Or people trying to kill her.

"I need to be on my way," Otto said. He kissed her cheek before shouldering his bag and heading out the door.

She went over to the window, watching him walk away.

The stairs creaked as someone descended. "I'll be heading out as well," Anton said from behind her.

"I wrote two letters," she said, still watching her brother's retreating back. "One for Rainer, and one for Markis." The letter she'd written to Rainer had been simple and to the point. She figured saying less would be more effective and not get herself into trouble. With Markis's letter, it took her far longer to write since it was in code. She had to make the letter appear normal, casual, as a royal speaking to her guard and nothing more. All the while she needed to tell him what happened, where she was, and who she was with. Markis was going to be furious. She tried to reassure him as much as possible knowing he'd feel responsible for her kidnapping. Which he wasn't.

"Are you certain you don't want to go with me?" Anton asked.

"Yes." She didn't trust Anton to keep her safe. Granted, she didn't trust Evander all that much either. However, between the two, the assassin-pirate-prince seemed the better, safer option. He could protect her, and she felt no attraction, friendship, or loyalty to him. And right now, that seemed the best bet.

"Are these the letters here on the desk?" Anton asked.

"Yes."

"Please be careful," he said.

"I will."

"Hang on," Evander called from the kitchen. He emerged a moment later, drying his hands on a towel hooked to the waistline of his pants, a young woman following him. His sleeves were rolled to his elbows, as if he'd been cooking. The tips of his fingers were dark green and black. A red tattoo wrapped around his wrist.

Sabine and Anton exchanged glances—he seemed as confused as she did.

"For all intents and purposes, this is Sabine," Evander said, gesturing to the woman now at his side. She had similar brown hair and was about the same height as the real Sabine. "She will accompany you," he said to Anton. "You will call her Sabine and treat her as you would your queen."

"Is this necessary?" Anton asked.

"It is." Evander went over to the closet and withdrew a cape. "Here." He handed it to the fake Sabine. "Put this on."

Sabine watched the young woman. "Do you understand what you're doing and why?" she asked her, hoping Evander hadn't found some innocent person who had no idea what she was getting herself into.

"I do," the woman replied. "I am your decoy. You can trust me to do a good job."

"Don't worry," Evander said. "She's being paid handsomely for her services and time."

The fake Sabine tied the cape around her shoulders. The bottom portion of her dress, along with her boots, still shone. The woman reached up, pulling the hood on before making sure a strand of her hair escaped beneath it.

"Perfect," Evander said. "You have the dagger?"

"I do," she answered.

"Good luck."

Anton rubbed the back of his neck. "Fine," he said with a sigh. "Let's go."

The woman joined him, and they exited the house.

"Stay away from the windows," Evander said. "In case the house is being watched. I don't want anyone to suspect you're still here." He went back into the kitchen.

Sabine went over to the hearth. The fire was just about out. She squatted, trying to warm her hands with what little heat there was. She couldn't help but wonder when Evander had left the house to find a woman to pretend to be her. Granted, it would make her journey back to Lynk much safer. However, it emphasized the fact that Evander was a trained assassin. She would need to keep her guard up around him. She also hoped that woman made it safely to Lynk with Anton. If the assassin killed her, Sabine would never forgive herself.

Banging came from the kitchen. She wondered what Evander was doing in there. She was just about to go in there to find out when he opened the door, heading toward the staircase.

"Do I even want to know what you've been doing?" she asked.

The right side of his lips curled into a half smile. "Probably not."

She stood and folded her arms.

"I have a few things left to pack then I'll be ready," he said. "I have to grab something from my room. If you go into the kitchen, do *not* touch anything." He ran up the stairs.

Curious, Sabine went into the kitchen, wondering what he'd been cooking. She opened the door and froze. It was a disaster. Pots and pans were strewn all over the counters. On the table, there were half a dozen piles of crushed leaves and powders.

Evander returned, stepping around her. He placed several containers on the table and began packing the piles using spoons, being careful not to touch anything with his skin.

"Are those poisons?" she asked, remembering when her mother had taught her to identify the most basic of poisons. She thought she smelled one or two of them right now.

He paused what he was doing and glanced up at her. "Why are you asking me a question you already know the answer to?"

Seeing Evander like this—an assassin—terrified her. She shivered.

"Why don't you go and pack," Evander said. "I'll be ready in fifteen minutes. Take enough clothes with you to last a week. I put a bag in your room to put everything in. Make sure you dress in pants and tie your hair back. I want you to try to look like a man."

She nodded and backed out of the kitchen. Her sister had died from poison. She clasped her shaking hands together and ran upstairs. The more she learned about Evander, the more she realized she didn't want to know him. This assassin-pirate-prince.

Sabine and Evander headed toward the town they'd arrived in. While she didn't mind walking since the weather was pleasant, she would much prefer to be riding a horse. She hadn't ridden in weeks and missed it.

"Everything okay?" Evander asked, walking at her side.

She nodded. "I was just thinking that I hope Rainer isn't furious with me for leaving." When she showed up alone with Evander, he'd at least be suspicious.

"I've been thinking," Evander said. "It might be best if we arrive in Lynk with a handful of royal Avoni guards."

She peered over at him, her eyes narrowing.

"What?" he asked. "You don't like that?"

"No, I think that is a wise idea." It unnerved her that she'd been thinking about that very thing.

"Then we'll need to make a slight detour on our way there," Evander said.

"That's fine." She was in no rush to return to Lynk. She still needed to come up with a plan on how to handle Rainer and what to do with all of the information she'd learned.

"Plus," Evander said, "I have to take Lottie to Avoni with me. Having guards will make the engagement look more official."

While Sabine knew she should keep her mouth shut since it wasn't any of her concern, she couldn't refrain from asking, "Why'd you agree to marry her?" Curiosity really could be difficult to overcome sometimes.

"Honestly?" He glanced sidelong at her.

She nodded.

"Two reasons. One, to save my own ass. I'm hoping Rainer won't question why I left with you in the first place if I not only return you to the palace unharmed, but I also manage to solve a problem for him."

She supposed that made sense. "And the second reason?"

"If Rainer declares war and raises his army against other kingdoms, I'm hoping he'll leave mine alone since his sister will be residing within its border."

Again, another reasonable answer. "Do you really think Rainer will be satisfied being king of all kingdoms except for yours?"

"That is a problem for another day." As he walked, he kept his focus on his feet. After a moment, he looked at Sabine and said, "Who knows, maybe you'll stop a war from happening."

"Maybe." While Sabine would do everything in her power to try to stop a war from breaking out, they both knew it was a long shot. Whatever plan Rainer had, he'd set in motion a long time ago. It would take more than Sabine, a mere woman, the sixth-born child, to stop Rainer.

They walked in silence for a few minutes. The sun warmed her skin, making her smile. As much as she hated to do this, it had to be done. "Thank you."

Evander almost tripped, coming to a halt and facing Sabine. "Did you just *thank* me?" he asked, his eyebrows raised.

"Yes," she replied with a forced smile, trying to remain polite instead of punching him like she wanted to.

"For what?" he asked, seeming genuinely confused.

"For escorting me back to the palace. I didn't want to travel with Anton." She resumed walking, hoping he wouldn't press the issue.

Evander caught up to her. "Why is that? Anton is a decent fighter. He seems like a good guy."

"I can't explain it, but it's a feeling I have." Ever since her sister's death, she'd learned to trust her instincts even when they didn't seem rational.

He tipped his head back and laughed. "So you're saying

that you feel safer with me, the man who kidnapped you, than you do with your own brother-in-law?"

When he put it that way, it didn't sound good. But yes, that was how she felt. She chose not to respond to him. There was no point trying to explain it.

"You know the Lynk border is only about fifty miles from here? Which means Anton could have had you safely behind its walls in two days."

"Maybe I'm tired of being confined," she said, keeping her attention straight ahead and not once looking at the man next to her.

"It's about time," he muttered.

She chose not to respond to that, but she happened to agree with him wholeheartedly.

"Out of curiosity, what did you tell Rainer in the letter you wrote to him?"

"Not much. Just that I didn't feel safe there with his sister trying to kill me, so I left. I told him I'd return once it was safe."

His eyes widened, and he started laughing. He held up a finger to her, so she waited. But he kept laughing. Harder and harder.

"I don't understand what's so funny," she said.

"You stood up to him."

"No, I didn't."

Evander nodded. "You implied he couldn't protect you," he pointed out when he finally calmed down. His face turned serious as he looked at her. "He commands a large, lethal army. And you point blank told him you didn't feel safe in his home. I'm not going to lie, that was a bold move on your part. Rainer won't like being made to feel incompetent. I hope you're prepared for the consequences."

She hadn't intended to make him feel that way. She'd only been trying to have a reasonable explanation for leaving. "He needs an heir," she said, her voice soft. "Until I give him one, I'm safe."

"Why go back?" Evander asked. "Why not run away for good?"

She shrugged. "Because I have to find a way to save those Bakley children. I have to stop Rainer from going to war."

"And if you can't do either of those things?"

"Then I'll die trying."

"You're not at all who I thought you were." Evander placed his hand on her lower back, gently urging her on.

The two of them resumed walking.

She turned his words over in her head, realizing she wasn't the person she thought she was either. She was stronger than she realized. And she would make it through this.

Chapter Four

Gripping the ship's steering wheel, Sabine kept them heading in a northerly direction. Manning the wheel turned out to be rather enjoyable. It gave her the opportunity to watch Evander run around the deck, cursing as he turned the mast to move the sail. When they first boarded the ship, he noticed the hook on the mast had broken. After he spent a couple of hours trying to find a replacement one, he gave up and they set out. The result was him having to manually move the sail. Sabine was thankful she didn't have to do anything beyond steer. She tilted her face to the wind, reveling in the feel of it across her skin.

"We're going to have to stop at the next port," Evander said as he came over and stood before Sabine with his hands on his hips. "I need to repair that part on the mast and from the looks of it, it's going to start raining. Normally, I'd still sail in a storm but since the rope isn't holding, I don't want to get stuck."

"I think that's a wise decision." She'd rather be safe than sink. "Is the port in Nisk?"

"No. We're north of Nisk. We'll pull into an Avoni port."

Which meant Sabine would get to see a new kingdom. Since she'd seen so little of the world, she wanted to experience as much as she could when she had the opportunity.

Evander sighed. "It'll take us longer to get north to Cusp where my guards are, but I don't see a way around it. I'm sorry."

"It's fine," she assured him, unable to hide the smile on her face.

"It won't take long to repair, and then we'll be on our way."

As if on cue, a light rain started to fall.

Evander moved to stand behind Sabine. "We need to head east. Do you know which direction that is?"

With thick clouds concealing the sun, Sabine had a hard time keeping her directions straight. Since she spotted a bit of land to the right, she pointed at it.

"Good."

She turned the wheel, steering the ship that way. "Are you just going to stand behind me?" she asked. "Don't you have a rope to tie or a mast to move?" The idea of having an assassin standing at her back made her uncomfortable. Like a spider crawling on her neck.

He sighed. "I do." He ran over and started bringing in the larger sail, then rolling it up.

The ship quickly made its way closer to land. "I see a red flag ahead," she called out.

"Head toward it."

She did as he said. When she got closer, she realized the flag was at the tip of a point, marking it so ships didn't run into it. "Now what?"

"There should be an inlet right past the flag. Steer the boat that way."

The rain came down harder, making it difficult to see.

Sabine did as Evander said and turned the ship just past the flag, entering the inlet. It opened to a large bay. Her arms shook from a combination of being cold and from fear of crashing. As to why Evander trusted her enough to steer this thing was beyond her.

The choppy water rocked the boat. Through the rain, she could barely make out several docks jutting out from land.

Evander came over and took the wheel from her. "You did a great job," he said. "But I'll take it from here." He turned the ship and steered it directly toward one of the docks where there was an empty slip. When they got close enough, he dropped the anchor then ran to the side, tossing a long rope onto the edge of the dock. Evander expertly jumped over the side, landing with grace on the dock where he proceeded to tie the ship up as if he'd done this hundreds of times.

Sabine noticed Evander's movements were always smooth and graceful. And silent. He barely made noise when walking around the ship or jumping onto a wooden dock.

"Grab the bags," he called out.

She ran below deck where she found it much warmer since there wasn't any wind or rain. After getting their bags, she went back up.

"Toss them over," Evander called out when he saw her.

She threw each bag to him. He expertly caught the bags as if they weighed nothing.

"Your turn," he said.

Too wet and cold to argue, she climbed up and over the side. Evander reached out, grabbing her around her waist and setting her on the dock.

He looked at her, his brows drawn together, as if she somehow surprised him.

"Now what?" she asked, glancing around. A warm fire sounded lovely. And a hot cup of tea. Preferably that stuff Evander made and not her *plain* Bakley tea.

"Let's go to an inn," he said. "Once you're settled, I'll come back and fix the broken part." He lifted their bags, hoisting them over his shoulder.

"I can wait below deck while you fix it," she suggested. She'd never been to an inn before and had no idea what it entailed.

He eyed her. "I have to get the part. I don't want to leave you alone on the ship."

"But you'll leave me at an inn?"

A smile slid over his face. "I'll leave you at the *right* inn."

She had no idea what he meant by that. However, she was too cold to argue with him. Besides, if going to an inn meant seeing Avoni, she would do it. "Fine." She gestured for him to lead the way.

Evander headed along the dock toward the land. Turning to the left, he walked along the road parallel to the water. Sabine followed him, taking in the small town. Most of the buildings were brown and black single story structures with oddly shaped green roofs. There were people out and about as if it weren't raining, heading to the docks or in and out of the businesses.

After three blocks, Evander stopped before a building with an odd sign hanging over the door. It had symbols instead of words, so Sabine had no idea what it said or meant. There was an odd similarity to the papers she'd gathered from the Avoni delegation's rooms. "Do people in Avoni use another language?" she asked. The members of the delegation had all spoken the same language as her, so she never thought to ask about it.

"Some still speak an ancient tongue. However, everyone knows the common language." He went to the door, holding it open for her.

Sabine stepped into a rectangular room with only a counter on the one side, a young woman standing behind it.

There were no pictures, no furnishings, and no decorations. Just dark brown wood walls and a ceiling to match.

Evander went over and spoke to the woman so softly that Sabine couldn't hear what they were saying even though the room was rather small. When their whispers became harsh, Sabine wondered if there was a problem. She was just about to ask when Evander came over and took hold of her elbow, pulling her toward the back wall. He reached out and touched what looked like a knot in the wood, and a door swung open, revealing a long hallway.

"What's going on?" Sabine asked, her heart beating quickly, sensing something amiss.

Evander ushered her into the hallway, closing the door behind them. He led the way down the corridor, stopping at the third door on the right. After unlocking it, he grabbed the handle and slid the door sideways, gesturing for her to enter the room.

Evander came in after her, closing and locking the door before dropping their bags on the floor. He began pacing, his hands on his hips.

Since Sabine had never been to an inn before, she ignored him and observed her surroundings. A large bed took up the middle of the room. But it wasn't like the beds she was used to because this one was on the floor, leaving no space beneath it. No other furniture was in the room. The pale yellow walls held no artwork, and there wasn't even a curtain at the window. She imagined this was what the servants' rooms at her parents' castle looked like—simple, small, and clean.

She removed her wet cape, setting it aside so it could dry. While she wanted to change, she refused to do so with Evander in the room. She sat on the edge of the bed and watched him, waiting for him to finally tell her what was bothering him.

He stopped and looked at her. "We have an issue."

She'd gathered that. When he didn't extrapolate, she asked, "What is it?"

"About an hour ago, a man was here in town asking about someone matching your exact description." He folded his arms.

"It probably doesn't mean anything," she assured him. "Or it wasn't even me he was asking about. We hadn't even planned on coming here, so no one would be here looking for me." She reached down and removed her wet boots.

"He's from the Black Daggers," he said as if speaking to a child.

She had no idea what that was, so she shrugged.

"It's one of the five assassin guilds here in Avoni."

"Are you certain?" she asked as terror gripped her chest.

He tilted his head and looked pointedly at her.

She hadn't realized her question was that stupid to him. "Do you think it was the man Lottie sent after me?"

"That would be my guess."

"I thought he would be following Anton and the decoy."

"He probably was. When he realized it was a decoy, he changed course and set out after us." He rubbed a hand over his face. "We did spend that extra time in port, so it makes sense he would have arrived here before us."

"But why here?"

"Because this is a major trading port in Avoni. It's a place we'd stop for food or supplies. He knows I prefer sailing over walking."

Then she asked the question she feared the answer to. "Is he still here in town?"

"No. He immediately moved on. But..."

"But?"

"I know him. His name is Ex. He won't stop until you're dead."

The room seemed unnaturally quiet. Sabine was afraid to move. "What are we going to do?" she whispered, hoping there was a *we* in this and Evander wouldn't abandon her to save his own skin.

"That's what I'm trying to figure out." He pinched the bridge of his nose. "Ex is hunting you. He wont stop or give up."

Cold fear like ice slid over her. "Let's head back to the ship and go to a different port."

"We can't sail in this rain with the latch on the mast broken."

At first she'd assumed being here would give her a chance to explore the town and experience its culture. Now, being here terrified her. "Is there another ship we can take?"

"Yes, but he'll just track us."

She couldn't hide at this inn for the rest of her life. "What are our options?" Her voice came out softer than she'd intended.

"Given the situation, I'm not comfortable traveling north to Cusp. I'm certain that route is being watched. Our best bet is to do something unexpected. And I'd like to get you someplace where you'll be safe." He went over to the foggy window and peered outside.

Sabine sort of thought she was already doing something unexpected. She stood and started pacing, trying to think of what she could do to keep herself alive.

Evander snapped his fingers. "I've got a plan." He twisted his head and looked at her, a smile on his face.

"Are you going to tell me this plan?" she asked, wary of his grin. Nothing about this situation called for that sort of reaction.

"The safest place in Avoni is at my family's compound."

Sabine blinked, trying to understand what he was saying.

"The royal palace?" she asked, just wanting to be sure she understood him.

He nodded.

Which meant the king and queen of Avoni would be there, Sabine would be at a compound filled with assassins, and it would delay her journey home to Rainer.

"You look like I just suggested I kill you for Ex," Evander mumbled. Then louder, "Look, at my family's home there will be plenty of highly trained guards to keep you safe. And, if Ex does come after you, it's the perfect location to deal with him. Once he's out of the way, we'll take the necessary guards and a much larger, reliable ship, and we'll sail to Lynk." He made it sound simple and easy. As if there weren't any risks involved.

Sabine sat on the edge of the bed again, massaging her temples. She should have just gone with Anton. However, if she had, the assassin would have already found her by now. She hoped her decoy hadn't been killed. "Okay," she said, "if we do go through with this plan of yours, how are we going to *get* to the palace?" In one piece and without being hunted or assassinated along the way.

Evander came over and sat on the bed beside her. "We'll have to travel as quickly and discreetly as possible. We want Ex to catch wind of where we've been, just not until we've left. We're going to have to deal with him, and I'd rather it be here in Avoni, specifically near my palace, rather than someplace with unknown factors I'll have to account for."

She slowly nodded as everything began to make sense. "You want to lure the assassin after us."

"Yes."

"So you can kill him?"

"Yes."

His plan was insane. "Why are you helping me?" she asked, peering into his green eyes, wanting and needing to understand his motives. Because she didn't trust this assassin-pirate-prince.

"I'm doing it for me and my kingdom."

"I don't understand."

He sighed. "If I don't return you safely to Lynk, Rainer will have a reason to turn his army toward Avoni. Even if I get you home, if you're killed shortly thereafter by an Avoni assassin, Rainer will take it out on me and my family. Therefore, helping you is really self-preservation."

She turned his words over, trying to see if she was missing anything.

"So?" Evander said. "What do you think?"

"I think you've got yourself a deal on one condition."

"And that is?"

He was going to laugh at her. Steeling her resolve, she said, "I want you to train me. Not self-defense necessarily, but more along the lines of helping me stay alive. I want to learn how to be stealthy, spot someone following me, lose a tail, and know the best places to hide. Things of that nature." She hoped he didn't think her request was too outrageous.

"Given who your husband is, I think that is a wise idea. I'd be happy to train you."

Sabine relaxed her shoulders. "I think this is a good plan so long as it doesn't take me too long to return to Lynk."

"Anton knows you're with me. Maybe we can send word to him that you'll be away another week or so?"

She was glad she'd written that letter to Rainer so he knew she was safe.

"Since we're not taking the ship, I don't need to repair it. Let me go to the kitchen and get us something to eat. You can change while I'm gone. You look like a fish out of water." He stood and went to the door, the corners of his lips pulling into a wicked smile, lighting up his piercing green eyes. "We can have our first lesson tonight." He winked before leaving the room.

Sabine grabbed her bag and found dry pants and a shirt. After she changed, she felt warm and safe. As if wrapped in a fuzzy blanket. Contentment filled her.

A few minutes later, Evander returned carrying a tray loaded with food and tea.

The two of them sat on the floor, facing one another, the tray between them.

The bread had a wonderful rosemary flavor to it, the salted fish she found a little bland, but the tea was perfect.

"First rule," Evander said around a mouthful of food, "is to never eat food someone gives you."

She nodded, thinking back to what her mother had said about that as well. "I'm eating the food you gave me," she said, suddenly not hungry.

He glared at her. "I didn't poison you."

"I thought maybe you were going to make a point. You know, teach me a lesson."

He shook his head. "Me, you can trust. Everyone else, you don't trust."

"Okay." She wondered if there was anyone Evander trusted. "What else?"

"Assassins love to use methods that physically keep them away from their targets if possible."

"Like poison?" she asked, thinking of Alina.

"Exactly. It allows an assassin to place a lethal dose somewhere and then watch from a distance. It gives them the opportunity to get away quickly once the death occurs."

"Anything else?" she asked.

"Bugs."

"What?" Her eyes widened in horror.

"Did you notice the towel I placed under the door?"

She hadn't seen him put it there. "I take it there isn't a draft from the hallway?"

"No. It's so no one can slip a venomous scorpion, snake, or spider under the door."

"I'm never going to be able to sleep again." She shivered. The thought of a spider crawling onto her arm or face and biting her was horrid enough. But to have it bite and kill her was another level of torture she didn't want to think about, much less consider.

"Speaking of sleep," Evander said, "we need to get some. I want you rested and ready for the journey ahead of us."

Sabine glanced at the bed. It was large enough for the both of them, but highly improper for them to share. "Are you staying in here with me?" They shouldn't share a room, but she didn't want to be by herself knowing a man was out there hunting her.

"Yes. It's not safe for you to be alone." He placed the tray out in the hallway, then closed the door and put the towel back along the bottom of it. "Don't worry that pretty little head of yours. I'll take the floor. I prefer it anyway."

Not having nightclothes to change into, Sabine pulled back the covers and examined the blankets before crawling under them. The thought of a bug hiding in there made it hard for her to relax, even after she'd looked with her own eyes.

Evander snuffed out the single candle illuminating the room then laid on the floor next to the bed. "Goodnight."

"Night." Even though Sabine couldn't imagine sleeping after everything he'd told her, she rolled onto her side and her eyes grew heavy. Somehow this assassin-pirate-prince made her feel safe.

"Sabine," Evander said, shaking her shoulder.

"I'm sleeping," she mumbled, swatting his hand away.

"We need to get moving, little butterfly. Let's go."

She rubbed her eyes and sat up. "It's still dark out." Knowing she was being hunted like an animal, she'd much rather travel during the daylight when she could see.

"It'll be light in an hour. Let's go."

She flopped back on the bed with a dramatic sigh. She was exhausted and could easily sleep for another hour.

Evander yanked the pillow out from beneath her head.

"Oye," she said. "What was that for?"

"I said to get up. Now."

"I was. I don't just jump out of bed like a grasshopper. It takes me a minute." She swung her legs over the side and stood.

"Grasshopper?" he said, one eyebrow raised. "Have you seen a grasshopper before?"

She rolled her eyes and stretched. "It is far too early in the morning for this." She stepped around him and grabbed her cape, putting it on before shouldering one of the bags. "Well?" She gestured for him to lead the way.

He picked up the other bag and opened the door, peering into the hallway, then waving for her to follow. They exited the inn.

Much to Sabine's surprise, dozens of people were out and about already. "Does no one sleep?" Maybe it was some sort of assassin thing. Or a cultural thing. People were on the docks loading up ships while others were hurrying from one place to another. Thick clouds covered the sky though it wasn't raining anymore.

"Keep your head down," Evander murmured. "Walk with purpose, and don't look around."

Since Sabine wasn't fully awake, she had no problem doing that.

Evander never left her side as they made their way through the town. He expertly guided her around people and put his hand to the small of her back when they needed to turn onto a different street.

After traveling half a dozen blocks, they stopped before a store that had an open window with a person standing on the other side of it.

Evander handed the man a few coins. The man glanced between the two of them before turning and leaving. He came back a moment later, handing two cloaks to Evander.

After thanking the man, Evander handed one of them to Sabine.

"I have a cape," she pointed out.

"These are waterproof and have large hoods." He put his cloak on. "They're far better than what you have."

Sabine quickly removed her old one and put the new one on. It was heavier and warmer.

"Let's go." Evander took her elbow, guiding her down a different street that brought them to a narrow canal. There were several short docks with tiny boats tied to them. He stopped before one of the boats. "Get in." He tossed his bag in the back.

Sabine stepped into it. There were only two benches, so she sat on the front one, shoving her bag beneath it. The sky was starting to lighten, and the streets were becoming more crowded.

"Put your hood up," Evander said, pulling his own hood on. He reached down and untied the boat. Before it had a chance to go anywhere, he stepped in, sitting on the back bench. He grabbed a long pole that was attached to the outside of the boat and used it to push them farther out into the water.

There were several other boats of similar size out on the canal, all heading in the same direction.

"Do you not know how to ride a horse?" Sabine asked, trying to figure out why he preferred being on the water as opposed to land.

"We don't have a lot of horses in Avoni."

"Why is that?" she asked. While she hadn't seen much of the kingdom, so far, she hadn't noticed a single horse.

"We have hundreds of waterways that we use for travel and transporting goods. There's no need for horses. Besides, they're expensive to maintain. And they're loud. Not an assassin's ideal choice of transportation." Evander used the pole to steer them to the middle of the canal, then he hooked the pole back to the side of the boat. The strong current carried them along.

"We're moving faster than I thought we would." As they made their way along the canal, Sabine watched the shoreline pass by. Single story structures with oddly slanted roofs lined both sides. She wondered if they were homes or stores. "Does it rain a lot here?"

"All the time. Why do you ask?"

"The roofs." She figured they had to be designed that way to keep water from pooling on them. Plus, a lot of the buildings had a hint of green mold to them, as if they never dried out.

When Evander didn't respond, she asked, "How long will it take us to reach the palace?"

"A couple of days."

"What are we going to do if the assassin finds us before we arrive?"

He groaned. "Do you normally talk this much?"

She narrowed her eyes. "I'm sorry," she replied curtly. "Would you rather I quietly sit here, not speaking the entire time we travel, so I don't bother you? Let's not forget *you're* the one who kidnapped *me* and got me into this situation in the first place." She folded her arms, pouting, though she wasn't actually serious. She was just teasing him because it was so easy and fun to do.

He sighed. "Since we'll be stopping at night, I plan to leave a clue for Ex. He'll eventually figure out where we're headed. I expect he'll be a day or two behind us by the time we reach the palace."

"Aren't you worried about luring this assassin to your family's home?" While she understood this was a kingdom known for producing assassins, and Evander had said the palace was well-guarded, it still seemed dangerous to bring this man there on purpose. It didn't seem right to endanger the royal family.

He chuckled. "Trust me when I say that no one in my family is afraid of a single assassin."

She supposed that when one was trained in the art of killing, a single assassin wouldn't be as much of a threat as he would be to a commoner. "What about two assassins?"

He considered her. "Personally, I'd be concerned if I encountered six or seven. That's where I have difficulty protecting myself."

"Is everyone in your family trained like you are?" She recalled Otto telling her that Evander was the leader of the Crimson Cloaks. At least she thought that was what Otto called the assassin league. She didn't know how that worked with regards to the royal family. She also knew that the Avoni kingdom had originally been ruled by five families until one managed to take over and establish control. To this day, there were still five assassin guilds.

"Yes. And each of us is trained to handle a situation such as this one. You have nothing to worry about."

She found his situation fascinating. While her brothers had been trained to either be the future king, leader of the army, a League member, or simply be a flirt, Evander and his siblings had learned the art of killing. She shivered and pulled her cloak tightly around her. She wanted to ask him how he came to be the leader of his assassin guild. However, she wasn't sure she was ready to hear the answer. She'd have to ask him another time. Maybe once Ex was taken care of and she was safely in Lynk.

"To be honest, I'm not sure my family will be at the main palace," he said, reaching into his bag and pulling out a round loaf of bread. He tore it in half and handed a piece to Sabine. "We have several palaces and we move around constantly. I chose to go to the main one simply because it's the closest to our present location."

She took a bite of bread.

"Are you ready for your next lesson?" he asked.

She nodded, eager to learn more.

He angled his head so she could see directly into his green eyes. "Today's lesson is to learn the art of being quiet."

She huffed as she ate her bread, glaring at him.

"Instead of talking to fill the silence, I want you to learn to listen to your surroundings."

She suspected he just wanted her to stop talking. Maybe he truly enjoyed it being quiet. What a strange man.

"If something sounds off, then there's a problem. For example, if you're outdoors, and the birds are suddenly quiet, you'd better hide. It means that someone is near and has probably already spotted you."

Sabine shivered.

"Also," he continued, "pay attention to what's around you at all times. Like now, what do you see?"

She shrugged. "A few boats in the water, some homes on the shoreline."

"Good. So, if all of a sudden, there's an increase or decrease in the number of boats, you'd want to take note. Right now, I know without looking, that there are three boats behind us and two ahead. I know the number of people in each one, whether they're male or female, and if they're carrying supplies."

She hadn't noticed any of those things.

"Your lesson for today is to start paying attention to everything around you. Not only what you see, but what you hear as well."

"I can do that."

"It's harder than you think," he said. "It means you have to clear your mind from thinking of other things and just be in the present moment."

She nodded.

"Shall we give it a try?" he asked.

"Yes." Sabine sat there, observing her surroundings and listening to the water lapping against the boat, the frogs on the shoreline, and the birds overhead. She didn't know how long they'd been traveling, but the homes and stores on both sides of the canal hadn't stopped yet. She supposed most people would want to live close to the canal since it was used for transportation and exchanging goods. She wondered how many blocks deep the towns were. And if this was one large town or several all lined up next to one another.

A piece of bread hit her on the forehead. She blinked, startled.

"Focus," Evander hissed.

Sabine just ignored him because he was right. Paying attention to her surroundings proved to be rather difficult when her mind kept wandering to other more interesting topics.

They traveled all day without any additional conversation. Every time Sabine went to say something, Evander would pelt her with a piece of bread and tell her to focus on her surroundings. He said it was not only for her benefit, but his as well. He didn't want her distracting him since he knew Ex was tracking them. To catch an assassin, they had to think like one. She honestly couldn't tell if this was the truth or he just didn't want to deal with her. It wasn't like she was all that chatty. But seriously, it was boring sitting in a boat all day floating along a canal. Not talking.

At sunset, Evander used the pole to steer them to one of the docks jutting out from the land. After tying the boat up, they got out.

"Stay right next to me," he said. "And keep your hood up and head down."

They entered the town. All of the structures were made from similar dark wood and had those oddly slanted green roofs. Signs hung above the doors to the buildings. They had strange markings Sabine couldn't read, so she had no idea what they were looking for as they made their way along a narrow wooden pathway, a stream next to it. Evander had mentioned that there were a lot of waterways, and Sabine was beginning to think that Avoni had been built on water.

Evander guided her along with purpose, as if he knew exactly where they were going. He'd said he wanted to travel where he was familiar, so perhaps he knew these towns well. He led her across a narrow bridge and to one of the taller buildings. Inside, lanterns hung from the ceiling, providing just enough light to see. There were about three dozen tables, most full with people. Evander reached out, taking hold of Sabine's hand, and leading her to the back wall where they sat at a table next to one of the open windows.

Sabine peered out, seeing another stream directly below. "Do boats travel through these waterways as well? Or only in the larger canal?" She hoped she was permitted to talk and she didn't have to make it through supper doing another exercise in observing her surroundings.

"Just the larger canals," he said, waving a server over. "I'll order food for the both of us."

Sabine nodded. She'd never eaten in an establishment such as this and had no idea how one went about deciding what to eat. While Evander spoke to the woman, Sabine examined her left hand. The one Evander had held. It meant nothing, of course. But the feeling of his skin against hers had been warm and comforting. Strange that a simple touch could feel that way. By an assassin no less.

Once the server left, Evander leaned back in his chair. "These waterways are too narrow for boats. There are thousands of them crisscrossing the towns."

"Avoni is a fascinating kingdom." It was beautiful and unlike anything she'd seen before. So different from the flat, farming land in Bakley and the mountain towns in Lynk. Sitting there, she scanned the room, looking at the faces of those around her. There was a mixture of skin tones and hair color. While she hadn't seen many people with red hair before, Evander didn't stand out as much as she thought he would since there was such a variety here.

Like the delegation that had visited Lynk, most of the people here wore long-sleeved shirts, pants, and many even had on gloves. Granted, it was colder here so it made sense, but she still found it strange. "Do women not wear dresses in Avoni?"

He leaned forward, closer to her. "They do. But it's not necessarily practical. Women mostly wear dresses for special occasions."

The server returned with two bowls of soup. After she left, Evander examined and smelled both of them. "It's safe," he mumbled, shoving one of them in Sabine's direction.

"I'm surprised you can eat anything you didn't prepare yourself." Lifting her spoon, she took a small bite. It tasted wonderful, though she had no idea what kind of soup it was.

"I'm trained to detect most poisons," he said. "I also carry a handful of antidotes with me. And I know the owner of this establishment. Otherwise, I wouldn't be eating here."

She remembered seeing him in the kitchen at the house in Nisk. She'd assumed he'd been making poisons, not something to neutralize them.

As they ate, along the waterway, people began to light the lanterns hanging outside the buildings. The light reflected on the water like stars, giving the town a magical feel.

When they had finished eating, the server approached them again. She said something to Evander in a language Sabine didn't understand. He thanked her and she left.

"What was that about?" Sabine asked.

"She said, as of now, Ex hasn't been spotted in this town."

"Did you ask her about him?"

"When I ordered the food I did."

"Does she know who you are?"

"Yes, but not in the way you think." He leaned forward on the table, closer to her. "This establishment is loyal to my assassin guild." He tapped his wrist, where his tattoo was, hidden by his long sleeve. "The information I receive, and the loyalty of this place, is from being a part of that guild and not because I am a member of the royal family."

She reached out and took hold of his hand, pushing his sleeve up just enough to catch a glimpse of his tattoo. She traced her finger over the marking. She'd never seen anything like it. It was a deep red line encircling his wrist with thorns on it. So many questions she wanted to ask, but she knew now was not the time or place.

"It's one of the reasons we wear long sleeves. We only reveal our association as needed." He pushed his sleeve down then twisted his hand, taking hold of hers and pulling her up. "Let's be on our way."

The two of them wound their way past the tables and toward the door. Sabine noticed a few people glance at Evander but quickly look away. She wondered if they knew who he was.

Outside, he tilted his head to the left, and they headed to the building next door. "We'll stay here for the night." He opened the door.

Like the previous inn, this one had a plain room for receiving guests. After Evander paid for a room and got a key, he took Sabine down the hallway to the last door on the left.

The tiny room contained a bed on the floor and nothing else. There was barely enough space for the two of them to move around the bed.

Evander shut and locked the door. "I'm sorry, but this is all they have available."

"There's no room for you to sleep on the floor," she pointed out.

"I know. We're going to have to share the bed."

"But..." She couldn't share a bed with another man. It wouldn't be appropriate. The ramifications if someone found out were astronomical.

"You can try to sleep on the floor if you don't trust me to keep my hands to myself," he said. "You're smaller and you might fit between the bed and the wall." He removed his cloak, rolling it up and placing it along the bottom of the door.

"That's not it." If Rainer found out, her reputation would be called into question and he'd never forgive her.

"Ah," Evander said, a smile on his face. "You're afraid you won't be able to keep your hands off me."

Her eyes narrowed, not having expected him to joke with her in such a way. She removed her cloak. "We can't share a bed," she said. "If people find out..." Rainer could have her killed. Just like his father had done to his mother. Her hands began to shake.

"We're sharing a room," he pointed out. "If anyone discovers that, it makes no difference if we're in the same bed or not." He sat on the edge of the bed, removing his boots. "It's not safe for you to be alone." He stretched out on the bed, on top of the blankets. "If you're worried about your husband, I'm sorry. It's unfortunate he doesn't trust you or believe what you say. The fact of the matter is I am here as your protection. If Rainer values your life, and I think he does, he has to understand I am only here to keep you alive. If something happens to you, I'm sure he'll make it his mission in life to kill me for your death."

Everything Evander said made sense. However, she'd been brought up knowing how important perceptions were. Not seeing a way around it, she removed her shoes, she snuffed out the candle, then slid under the blankets, keeping her back to Evander.

"Goodnight," he said, amusement dancing in that one single word.

"Night," Sabine mumbled, trying not to let her frustration seep through. It wasn't his fault they had to share a bed.

Lying there, a strange sensation filled her with the realization that she'd never been in bed with a man before. She'd assumed she would have slept at Rainer's side on their wedding night. However, not only had they not shared a bed, they hadn't even consummated their marriage.

She couldn't help but think of the stark contrasts between Rainer and Evander.

Sabine peeled her eyelids open, finding her left arm draped over Evander's chest, her leg on top of his. "Oh," she murmured, wondering how that had happened with him on top of the covers and her beneath them. She glanced up at his face and saw him staring back at her. "I'm sorry." She extricated herself from him and sat up.

"No need to be sorry," he said, his voice gravelly. "But we should get going." He rubbed his eyes.

Horrified *she'd* been the one cuddling with *him*, Sabine went over and gathered her cloak and bag.

Evander stood and did the same.

She put the cloak on, pulling the hood up. "I'm ready."

He tilted his head to the side, stretching his neck.

"What's the plan for today?" she asked, not really caring but wanting to break the odd tension between them.

"Same as yesterday." He opened the door.

The two of them went down the hallway and exited the inn. The sky was just beginning to lighten. However, dark clouds covered the sky, promising rain. The two of them headed along the wooden walkway.

Sabine lifted her hands to her mouth, blowing hot air on them, trying to warm up. "It's vastly different here than in—" She didn't get to finish her sentence because Evander yanked her to the side and into an alcove.

He shoved her against a door while covering her body with his. His green eyes turned furious, making her cower with the intensity and hatred in them. He released her and turned so his back was now against her front.

She was about to ask him what was going on when he removed his hood, exposing his face.

"The only way to her is through me," he shouted. "Would you dare kill your own prince and commit treason?"

Cold terror slid through Sabine. The assassin had found them.

The door she was leaning against opened, and she fell backward.

Chapter Five

Sabine landed on the floor, the wind knocked out of her. She rolled to the side, trying to catch her breath. Two large black boots came into view. Unable to speak, she said nothing as the man reached down, grabbed hold of her shoulders, and hoisted her to her feet. He pulled her back against his front, covering her mouth with one of his beefy hands while his other pinned her arms down.

Evander cursed. "Release her." He took a step into the house, his focus never wavering from whoever he was watching out front.

Sabine had no idea how he knew she was in trouble. The man who held her smelled like fish, making her want to gag.

"Everyone in town has been offered a hefty reward for capturing this woman," the man holding her said.

Horror filled Sabine. This man planned on selling her to the assassin who in turn would kill her.

"Do you have any idea who this woman is?" Evander said, enunciating each word carefully as he took another step into the house, his attention now divided between the man holding her and the person outside.

The man shifted on his feet, but he kept her firmly in his grip.

"The woman you have the audacity to touch is the queen of Lynk. I'm fairly certain if you turn her over to an assassin and she ends up dead, her husband—the king of Lynk—will hunt you down and kill you himself. If I were you, I'd release her."

The man chuckled. "For the amount of money I'm gonna get, I don't care who she is."

Sabine didn't even come up to this man's chin, so she couldn't head-butt him. Thankfully, her brothers had taught her a thing or two growing up. Moving her hand out from under her cloak, she angled her body to the side and reached back, grabbing the man between his legs and squeezing as hard as she could.

The man yelped and released her. She immediately lunged away from him, but he grabbed hold of her cloak and she fell on the floor. When she scrambled to her feet, she saw a dagger protruding from the man's chest. She hadn't even seen Evander throw the weapon. She looked at him, her eyes wide with horror. Not only had Evander killed the man, he'd done it without hesitating. She had no idea how someone could kill so easily when there were other options like injuring him instead.

Evander stepped farther into the house, kicking the door shut. "Are you okay?"

"Yes."

"Grab the dagger."

Knowing time was of the essence, she did as he said and rushed over to the dead body, pulling the weapon free and wiping the bloody blade on the man's pants. Clutching the dagger, she stood and followed Evander deeper into the house. "How are we going to get out of here?" she asked.

Instead of answering, he entered a bedroom, glanced about, then exited.

"If everyone in town is looking for me, we're never going to make it out of here alive." Panic took hold, and her body started shaking.

He peered at her. "Have you so little faith in me?"

She had no idea how he could joke at a time like this. Lifting her arm, she wiped the sweat from her forehead, her stomach queasy.

In the next room, he went over to the window and opened it. "Perfect," he whispered. He climbed out. "Let's go."

Sabine hoisted herself up and through the open window. Evander reached forward, grabbing her waist and setting her on the ground. They were in a narrow alleyway between two houses. He put his finger to his lips, and she nodded. He waved for her to follow him as he headed toward the back of the house.

Clutching the dagger, Sabine stayed close to Evander, constantly glancing over her shoulder to see if someone was coming after them. So far, no one else had entered the alleyway. At the corner of the house, Evander peered around the side of it. Satisfied with whatever he saw, he reached back, taking hold of Sabine's hand. He squeezed it and led her onto the walkway that wound between the houses.

It felt as if they were going away from the canal instead of toward it. Evander kept turning, taking different walkways, making it difficult to know where they'd been and where they were going. They went over bridges, along various pathways, and between houses and stores. She was so turned around, she had no idea where they were.

Just when Sabine was about to ask if Evander knew what he was doing, they rounded a building and the walkway abruptly ended. A forest of thick trees stretched before them.

Without hesitating, he pulled her along, into the forest, ducking under a low-hanging branch.

"Is this a good idea?" she whispered. The trees were so close together that the foliage blocked most of the daylight, making the area not only dark, but cold and eerie. This felt like a place where one went to die, not hide.

Instead of answering, he pulled her along, his warm hand holding hers. After about twenty feet, he stopped and cocked his head to the side, his brows furrowing.

A twig snapped and Evander released her, slowly turning to face the way they'd come from. He reached down and pulled a knife out of his boot. With a weapon in each hand, he widened his stance.

Shock rolled through Sabine. She couldn't believe Evander was willing to fight for her. The easiest solution would be for him to kill her, bury her body here in this forest, and no one would ever know what happened to her. Instead, he stood before her, ready to kill.

Sabine's heart pounded so hard she swore she could hear it in the quiet forest. And then she noticed the birds had stopped singing—just as Evander said would happen when a threat neared. Which meant they weren't alone. The hairs on the back of her neck stood on end as she realized they were about to be attacked.

Clutching the dagger in her hand, she remained behind Evander, his back to her. She held her breath, too afraid to make a sound.

Movement to the right caught her attention. She glanced that way and spotted a man dressed in solid black creeping toward them with a small sword in hand.

Evander's head turned the other direction.

Sabine couldn't help it, she had to know. "How many are there?"

"Five," he responded. "Can you climb?"

"Climb?"

"I want you up in a tree, out of the way."

The tree beside her had branches low enough that she could grab hold of one and hoist herself up. However, if she was up there, then she couldn't help Evander down here. While she didn't think these men would kill him since he was their prince, she couldn't be certain. Regardless, he couldn't take on five men and keep her safe, even if she was up in a tree. Eventually, these men would tie Evander up or knock him out. Then they'd take her to the assassin. Evander wouldn't bother coming after her because it would be too late by the time he managed to find her.

"If you can climb, get up there now," Evander said, his words harsh and snapping her into action.

She did as he said and took hold of a lower branch, pulling her body up. She held onto the trunk while she carefully stood. Then she grabbed the limb above her and climbed higher, hoping no one would be able to strike her from this high up.

Once she was safely perched on one of the larger branches, she glanced down and spotted five men nearing Evander.

"You good?" he called up to her, not once looking her way.

"Yes."

Quicker than lightning on a hot summer night, Evander simultaneously threw two knives in different directions, each one embedding into a man's chest. Both men dropped to the ground with a soft thud.

One of the other men charged at Evander, knocking him over. When the man landed on top of Evander, Sabine spotted a knife sticking out of his back. She hadn't even seen Evander use the man as a shield before he'd allowed himself to be tackled. Evander shoved the dead man off him and jumped to his feet.

The fourth man attacked. Evander swiped the man's legs out from under him, threw a dagger at the fifth person, and then produced another knife and rammed it into the fourth man's neck as he tried to stand.

Sabine counted the dead men just to be sure and confirmed all five were accounted for.

Evander stood there, not even winded.

The entire ordeal had lasted only seconds. "Is it safe to come down?" she whispered.

"Yes." He glanced up at her. "You made it higher than I thought you would."

She started to reach forward to grab hold of a branch when she froze.

"What's the matter?" Evander peered behind him and then back up at her, his brows pulling together with confusion.

She couldn't move or even talk. Directly in front of her—only a foot away—a large black snake had wound itself around the branch. The head of the snake was focused on her as it slowly moved the bulk of its body into a coil atop the branch. Somehow she knew if she moved, it would strike.

"Stay very still," Evander said, his voice deep and low. "When I tell you to, fling your body backward, away from the snake."

She started shaking, unable to fathom moving. Not only was she paralyzed from fear, but she was certain the snake would jump right along with her and when she landed, it'd be on top of her. She'd seen enough snakes attack and eat small creatures like rats and bunnies. She would end up in the belly of that thing. A meal. And after Evander had gone through all that work to keep her alive.

"Sabine," Evander said, his deep voice now behind her. "I want you to let go and fall back. I'll catch you."

She couldn't move. Death by an assassin seemed better than death by snake. It would probably be less painful.

"You have about a minute until that thing strikes. When it does, you'll be paralyzed instantaneously. Then it'll eat you while you're alive. It's one of the most venomous snakes there is. Without turning your head or making any sudden movements, let yourself fall back."

Cold, hard fear gripped her. She knew she needed to do as Evander said, but she couldn't force her body to move. A tear slid down her cheek.

"Now, Sabine!" Evander said, his voice firm and laced with a hint of panic.

The image of the snake flinging itself forward gave her the incentive she needed to launch herself backward off the branch. She flew through the air, screaming. The snake lunged after her just as a dagger cut through the air, impaling the snake and pinning it against the tree trunk. Sabine crashed into Evander, and they landed together in a heap on the ground.

"I imagined that going much smoother in my mind," he said.

She rolled off him, shaking, unable to believe he could make a joke when she'd almost been eaten alive. She stood and looked at the tree trunk where the snake was impaled. The creature was longer than her and its body as wide as one of her arms.

"Are you okay?" Evander asked as he stood and brushed himself off.

She nodded, still speechless. Her stomach felt queasy, and she wanted nothing more than to lie down. Preferably in her childhood bed back in Bakley where it was safe from assassins and snakes. A hug from her mother sounded really good right about now.

"We need to be on our way," Evander said, his voice all business.

She wondered if nothing phased him...killing people, venomous snakes. He acted as if this were like any other day.

Not touching the five dead bodies, Evander headed back toward the town. Sabine hurried after him, ready to be out of this forest. When they reached the walkway, Evander slid his arm around her shoulders, tucking her into his side. She wondered if they should be traveling out in the open like this. However, the crowded streets felt safer than the forest. It wasn't even noon and she'd already been attacked by assassins and almost eaten by a snake. Perhaps she should just call it a day before she wound up dead.

"I always thought women from Bakley were prudes," Evander whispered in her ear. "But you just climbed a tree, faced a seven-foot snake, and survived a kidnapping attempt. All in all, not what I expected from someone who hails from a kingdom known for sitting around drinking tea and knitting all day."

She glared at him.

He chuckled, the sound deep and throaty. "There she is," he murmured, nudging her stomach with his free hand. "Glad to have you back."

She almost rolled her eyes but didn't want to give him the satisfaction. At least her body was starting to calm down and no longer shook from fright.

They quickly reached the docks along the canal with ease. Glancing about, Sabine thought this was a different location than the one they'd arrived at yesterday.

Evander withdrew his arm and nodded to one of the boats. Without questioning him, Sabine stepped in, taking the front bench and noting this was indeed a different boat.

She made sure to keep her hood low so no one could see her face as she sat with her arms on her legs, hunched over, trying to look like a man under the cape.

Evander stepped in after her and untied the boat. He shoved them away from the dock, and they made their way toward the center of the canal where they immediately caught the current, heading south. Evander sat on the bench behind her.

After a few minutes, she turned around to face him. "You just killed five men." Six if she counted the one from the house. It had been terrifying and mesmerizing to see. Evander had moved as if a brush stroke from an artist's hand —smooth and unwavering.

He kept his focus on their surroundings, not bothering to respond. While Sabine knew he was an assassin and the leader of an assassin guild, seeing him in action was very different from knowing it. She had no idea if this was the sort of thing he did daily, weekly, or monthly. While killing those men seemed like nothing to him, it was something to her. He'd saved her life. But was her life worth those six men?

Shifting the topic, she said, "I want to thank you for the, uh, snake thing." She scratched the side of her neck.

At that he looked at her, his green eyes dark under the hood of his cloak. "I didn't think you were going to jump in time. That's why I killed the snake."

Interesting that he justified the snake's death but not the men. "I assumed killing the snake was your plan all along." She clutched her hands together, playing with the ring on her finger.

He shook his head. "I was afraid if I missed, I'd infuriate the creature and we'd both wind up dead."

"It doesn't seem to me that you're the type of man who ever misses." He had to have spent an inordinate amount of time honing his skills in the art of killing. She'd never seen anyone fight the way he did or throw a dagger with such precision. If she were a betting person, he was a man she'd never bet against.

"I don't," he said, confirming her suspicions. His piercing gaze remained on hers.

"What was your childhood like growing up?" she asked, genuinely curious how he'd spent his days. While he didn't have the large muscles Rainer did, Evander was lean and toned, indicating a different sort of fighter.

A wry smile slid across his face, softening his features. "I have three older sisters," he replied. "I think that explains enough."

She couldn't help but laugh, trying to imagine a younger Evander being fussed over by a handful of women. While Sabine had grown up chasing after her brothers with a wooden sword, Evander had probably played with dolls.

"What about you?" he asked. "I've heard some scandalous stories about the wild princess from Bakley."

"All lies, I'm sure," she said, appalled that she'd been hailed as wild. As the sixth born, she doubted anyone cared enough about her to investigate the sort of person she was.

Evander scanned their surroundings, not looking at her as he said, "When my father began looking for a proper wife for me, he considered you."

Shock rolled through Sabine. Until Rainer had inquired after Alina, she never thought her or her sister would marry someone from another kingdom. She'd mistakenly assumed they weren't important enough. Now, she realized how naive she'd been. "I had no idea," she replied, dumbfounded by his admission. Her parents had always made it seem as if she didn't matter, which was why she'd always thought she'd marry for love. How wrong she'd been.

"Once my father learned you ran wild with barnyard animals, were rude, and what was the word he used? Oh, yes, you behaved barbarically, he deemed you an unsuitable match." Evander chuckled.

"Are you serious?" How ironic that they should consider her the barbaric one when Evander was the one running around killing people. This assassin-pirate-prince. She folded her arms, irritated. "I don't recall your father ever sending a delegation to Bakley to meet me."

"He didn't. He sent a spy."

She raised her eyebrows at that. "And your spy determined all of this about me?" She found that hard to believe. Granted, she liked to ride her horse, run through the fields barefooted, and help feed the animals in the barn by their castle.

"He did. At first, my father assumed he was joking because it is well-known that women from Bakley are proper, refined, and generally prudes. But when he sent a second spy who confirmed what the first spy said, we knew it had to be true. You were deemed unfit to marry into our family. I think my father said you were clearly a farmer's brat."

Sabine's eyes widened as embarrassment set in. Yes, her father was the king of a kingdom of farmers. Yes, she tended to do as she pleased. But she knew how to behave. At least, when she wanted to. "Maybe he should have investigated my sister, Alina. Had he done so perhaps you would have been engaged to her since she is—was—a proper woman. Maybe then she'd still be alive and my family not tied to Lynk."

"I think I was ten when he sent his spies to Bakley."

She wanted to hit him. Here she'd been thinking all of this had recently transpired. If he'd investigated her character when she was only ten, then yes, she was a wild child.

"Today, when you took hold of that branch and pulled yourself up, I knew, without a doubt, that all the stories were true."

"Why's that?" she asked.

"Because you were strong enough to climb a tree and you didn't hesitate to do it." He glanced at the shoreline.

She had no idea what to say to that.

"Not many women can do what you did today."

"Then you're lucky I spent my younger days roaming wild," she said, trying to make a joke of her upbringing.

He looked her right in the eyes and said, "You showed bravery today. Something I did not expect."

His compliment made her face warm, and she broke eye contact.

Up ahead, the canal split into two, each waterway going a different direction. Evander reached back, turning the lever and steering the boat toward the leftward one. "We're going to stop soon," he said. "We'll go into town, sleep for a bit, and then I want to travel at night."

They hadn't been on the waterway for long, and she didn't understand why they wouldn't travel longer, at least until dusk. If it were up to her, she'd put as much distance between them and the assassin as possible. "Won't it be easy for someone to track us at night if we're the only ones out on the water?" And navigating at night would be difficult since the clouds were so thick they covered the moon and stars.

He smiled. "No. It'll be harder. You'll see."

After a couple of miles, Evander steered the boat to a dock. Sabine didn't know how he could tell where one town ended and the next began since the entire canal was lined with structures on both sides. To her, it was one big town that didn't end. Perhaps it was.

Evander tied the boat up and got out, stretching. Sabine joined him.

"I'm starving. Let's eat then find an inn." He took her hand, leading her from the dock into town.

Since it was midday, the walkways were crowded with people. Here, all of the structures were built next to each other leaving no room between them. Waterways crisscrossed through the area and dozens of bridges connected the narrow pathways together. All of the signs above the stores and shops were in another language, making it impossible for Sabine to read any of them.

Evander pulled her to the right and opened a door, revealing a small tavern. There was a bar with a counter in the middle and about a dozen tables around the perimeter. He chose a table in the back corner.

"I'm surprised everything is made from wood," Sabine commented as she removed her cloak and sat down. "Especially since it rains so much."

"It's what's available," Evander said as he hung his cape over the back of a free chair. "We don't have a lot of stone around here to use for building."

A man wearing an apron approached. He looked between the two of them before speaking to Evander in another language, his voice a near whisper.

Evander nodded and flashed the man his tattoo, replying in another language. The man bowed then went into the kitchen.

"I'm assuming you ordered us food?" she said, feeling like there had been more to the conversation than that.

"I did." Evander pulled Sabine's chair—with her sitting on it—closer to him.

"What are you doing?" she hissed.

He smiled and said, "It seems everyone is looking for a man and woman traveling together who *aren't* married." He put his arm around her shoulder. "Therefore, I informed that man that we *are* married. You're even carrying my child."

"You've got to be joking," she mumbled. Her situation kept getting more and more complicated. She had no idea how she would explain any of this to Rainer. Hopefully, she would never have to.

"Are you feeling unwell?" Evander asked.

"Yes. It must be because I'm pregnant." If she was forced to play this ridiculous role, she would go all out.

Her brother, Rolf, and his wife must have had their baby by now, and Sabine didn't know if they had a boy or a girl. She hadn't even asked Otto when she saw him. Leaning her elbows on the table, she covered her face with her hands.

"I didn't think you'd play the role so seriously," Evander said. His free hand came up and cupped her cheek, turning her head to face his. He was only inches from her. "What's the matter?" he whispered. "I can tell something is bothering you, and I don't think it's the ruse."

Her mind was a jumbled mess right now. She not only missed her family, but her relationship with Rainer was non-existent.

"Sabine," Evander said, his brows pulling together. "What's wrong?"

She shook her head, not wanting to confide in him. Not wanting him to know her marriage to Rainer wasn't consummated which meant it could be annulled. If that happened, any protection she might have would cease to exist.

"You have a lot going on in that pretty little head of yours," Evander muttered. "Your eyes..."

The man returned, setting two plates of food on the table before leaving.

Evander didn't move. He still had one arm around her shoulders and the other on her cheek. He patiently waited for her to answer his question.

But she couldn't. "Everything from this morning is catching up with me," she lied.

He slowly released her and nodded.

She didn't think he believed her. Part of his assassin training had probably been how to tell if someone was lying.

Now she felt guilty for not being honest with him. But she didn't owe him anything. He probably had plenty of secrets he kept from her. After all, they barely knew each other. Yet... somehow she felt safe with him at her side. She took a deep breath, needing to clear her head.

Evander pulled one of the plates closer to him and started eating.

Sabine reached for the other one. "What is this?" she asked, eyeing the entire fish—head and all. "And why is it on a stick?"

"The stick is so you can pick it up." He didn't look her way as he spoke.

A pang of regret filled Sabine. She wanted Evander to look at her and smile. She wanted him to tease her. Something. Anything. It felt as if a wall had gone up between them. She wanted to tear it down.

The man approached, placing two bowls of soup on the table. He said something in a language she didn't understand before bowing his head and leaving.

"Does he know who you are?" she asked. Evander had shown the man his tattoo, so he obviously knew what assassin guild he belonged to. She suspected Evander only ate at establishments he had some connection to. But she wondered if anyone knew he was also their prince.

"No. It is customary for people to bow their heads as a sign of respect. That's all."

She wondered what they did for royalty.

Since the fish didn't look particularly appetizing with its head still attached, she decided to start with the soup. "I don't have a spoon."

"Just pick it up and drink it."

With a shrug, she lifted the bowl and took a sip. The warm soup tasted decent. When she set the bowl down, Evander reached over and took hold of her hand.

"Keeping up the ruse," he mumbled with a forced smile.

It was time to take him down a notch. "Oh yes." She batted her eyes at him. "My doting husband, whom I adore." She lifted her hand to the corner of his lips. He stilled. She wiped the area with her thumb. "You had a little something there."

His eyes narrowed, as if he didn't quite believe her.

She puckered her lips and blew him a kiss. He'd told her to play the part, so she was. And she was very good at flirting. She'd had lots of practice. And, for some reason, it was easy and fun to be this way around Evander. With Rainer, she'd always felt as if he had the upper hand. Perhaps it was because he was older than her. Or maybe it had something to do with him being overly sensual. With Evander, she could just be herself, and she found it refreshing.

Evander leaned closer, pushing her hair behind her ear and whispering, "Well played, Sabine. Well played." His breath sent a shiver through her. "See, all you have to do is pretend I'm Rainer."

It felt as if a bucket of cold water had been dumped on her. "Who said anything about me being in love with Rainer?" It was an arranged marriage, nothing more.

"Aren't you?" His brows pulled together in confusion.

She didn't know why she felt the need to defend herself, but she did. "I only met the man a few weeks ago. Love cannot grow in so short a time." She focused back on her food instead of the man beside her.

As she sipped her soup, she couldn't help but think about Rainer and what she did—and didn't—feel toward him. From the first moment she saw him, she'd been attracted to him. He was by far the most handsome man she'd ever seen. When he touched her, she wanted to melt into him. Devour him. But that was simply because of his dark hair and eyes, the curve of his mouth, and the feel of his hands on her body. Having flirted with plenty of young men in her days, stealing a kiss or holding hands, she knew her body craved Rainer, but her heart and head didn't care for him. There was nothing about his personality that drew her to him. She was coming to understand that to love someone, she needed both —the attraction and the friendship.

"You seemed quite in love with him when I watched the two of you together. I'd say you are besotted with the man."

She didn't know why he continued to push the matter. Perhaps she needed to show him something in order for him to understand. Of all people, she thought Evander would be able to easily spot a lie. He seemed to earlier when they were talking.

Trying to keep a straight face, she bit her bottom lip and peered at him through hooded eyes. "You think I'm in love with Rainer because we danced together a certain way?" she said, her voice low and sultry. Leaning toward him, she brushed her nose along the side of his face, breathing him in. He stilled. "You say you watched me with him?" She moved so her lips hovered at the corner of his. "I thought you were a trained assassin. I thought you'd know an act when you saw one." She gently kissed his jaw and then moved back, unable to help the smirk on her face as she watched him blink several times.

"You're not in love with him?" he asked, his voice slightly off.

Sabine knew she'd affected Evander, and somehow that made her feel powerful. "No, I don't love Rainer, and I'm not sure I'll ever be able to." The truth slipped out before she realized what she'd said. She needed to be careful what she shared with this assassin-pirate-prince. "Every time you saw the two of us together, it was all an act. Rainer expected me to dress a certain way, behave a certain way. It was all about perception." She felt the need to diffuse the tension building between them, so she decided to make a joke. "Just like now." She reached over, placing her hand on this thigh. "You do understand I'm not in love with you, don't you?"

He shook his head, his features softening. "You're a handful."

"Thank you." She smiled.

"It wasn't a compliment."

"To me, it was," she said as sweetly as possible.

"Are you done slurping down that soup?"

"I think the baby and I have had all we can handle," she teased, knowing he was going to regret this little ruse of theirs. She never did anything half-way.

"Then come on, wife," he said, pulling her to her feet. "Let's go find a room for a few hours since I can't seem to keep my hands off you." He tossed some money on the table, then the two of them exited the tavern. It seemed he didn't do anything half-way either.

Outside, a light rain had started to fall. "Do you ever get sick of it?" she asked as they headed along a narrow walkway and across a bridge.

"The rain?"

She nodded.

"No. Never."

"At first, I couldn't figure out why you have these wooden walkways everywhere," she said. "But now that I see how much it rains, it makes sense. No one would want to be covered in mud all day long."

"And some of them are built right over the water," he said, taking her hand.

"How do you know where we're going?" He couldn't possibly be familiar with every single town up and down the canal.

"How do I say this," he mused. "The more reputable inns,

such as one a husband and wife expecting a child would stay at, are a few blocks from the canal. The ones along the waterway are for single men traveling for work." They went down another road, this one less crowded. "See that sign ahead?"

"The one with the square symbol?"

"That's the one. The square with the angled line above it and the three dots in the middle indicates a family-friendly inn."

She thought it sort of looked like a house. "And if it isn't family friendly?"

"Then it would only have one dot."

She made a mental note in case she ever found herself needing to find a place to stay in Avoni.

They went into the inn. Evander spoke with the woman at the front counter, telling her that his pregnant wife needed a bed to rest for a few hours. He handed over some money.

Evander turned to Sabine. "Let's go, honey." He held out his hand.

She slid her hand into his, and he led her down a hall, opening the second door on the left. The tiny room had a single bed, only large enough for one person.

"I apologize, but this is the only available room."

"I'll take the floor," Sabine said.

"You'll take the bed. I'll prop myself up against the door." He pointed to it. "No lock."

"Do you want to look for another inn?"

He shook his head. "It would be suspicious if we left."

She removed her cloak and bag.

"We'll leave in five hours," Evander said as he sat on the floor, leaning his back against the door.

After taking off her boots, Sabine climbed into bed. She laid on her side, facing Evander.

He closed his eyes, and she watched the soft rise and fall

of his chest. A few days worth of stubble covered his chin, giving him a harder edge than before. It made him look slightly older. His hands rested at his sides. While he appeared innocent, he'd killed several men today. Originally, she assumed it was to protect her. But really, he did it to keep her alive so he wouldn't wind up in a war with Rainer. Evander hadn't saved Sabine because he cared about her in any capacity. They weren't even friends. Not really. She barely knew him. Yet, for some strange reason, she wanted to. Every little thing he revealed about himself was like peering behind the door in a great castle. The more glimpses she got, the more intrigued she became. She wanted to see it all.

And that scared her more than knowing an assassin was hunting her.

Chapter Six

Sabine and Evander left the inn at dusk. The streets remained crowded, even more so than before. The two of them kept their ruse up by holding hands, hoping not to attract any attention. While Evander wanted the assassin to be able to track them as they made their way to the palace, he hoped to stay a day or two ahead of him.

At the dock, dozens of people were haggling, trying to acquire a boat for the evening. Evander quickly led Sabine to where they'd tied theirs up. She stepped in, getting settled on the front bench while Evander untied the knot. He shoved the boat away from the dock, and they set out. He expertly navigated them between several boats until they were in the middle of the canal, once again heading south.

The majority of the boats had two passengers with a raised pole at the front with a lantern hanging from it. Sabine hadn't noticed that yesterday—and she'd been paying attention. "Why are there so many out on the water at this hour?" she asked, trying to determine the reason for the change from the day before. Perhaps something was going on that she was not aware of.

"You'll see." Evander scooted over on the rear seat and patted the spot next to him.

Since they were pretending to be a married couple, she moved to sit beside him.

As they floated along the canal, the sky darkened and more and more boats joined them. Sabine continued to take in her surroundings, diligently observing. Evander had to be impressed she'd remained quiet for so long. However, with several boats so close by, she didn't want to point it out by talking and attracting attention.

A light flashed to her right. She blinked, wondering what it had been. And then another light flashed right in front of her. She watched as tiny bursts of light appeared all around. Her eyes widened, and she turned to Evander. "What's going on?"

"Lightning bugs," he said. "Have you never seen them before?"

She shook her head, marveling at the idea of bugs producing light.

"They only come out at night," he explained.

"Is that why there are so many people on the water?" It truly was a sight to behold. It felt almost magical witnessing the tiny flashes. Like fairies if fairies were real.

The corner of his lips pulled into a wry smile. "Sort of. It's Lovers' Night. Since we're newly married, it's only appropriate we're joining in."

"Lovers' Night?" She'd never heard of such a thing.

"The story goes that Princess Kalina fell in love with a young man named Lakin from a warring family. The two managed to secretly marry on this day almost two hundred years ago."

"That sounds romantic. Did the two families stop fighting and become friends?" she asked, watching the lightning bugs all around her in a beautiful display of nature.

"No. When her parents found out, they killed Lakin and his entire family. They burned Lakin's village to the ground. No one survived."

She looked at Evander. "That's horrible." And violent.

He turned to face her. "It is. Kalina took her own life when she discovered what her parents had done."

"I hope that taught them a lesson," she replied.

"Unfortunately, it did not. However, the king and queen declared today a day of mourning. On this day each year, no fighting is allowed in order to pay respect to the princess. However, it has turned from a day of mourning to a day of love."

"But not by royal decree?"

"No." He smiled, the look both mischievous and thoughtful.

Sabine found herself leaning toward him, wanting to hear what he said next.

"The people decided that since they couldn't fight, they'd make love. Through the years, the day became known as Lover's Night."

She laughed, enjoying the idea that something beautiful could come from a tragedy.

Evander reached out and took hold of her hand, bringing it to his lips and kissing it. "In case anyone is watching us," he murmured.

"Is this dead princess your ancestor?" she asked. She recalled the story Markis had told her about the warring families and one managing to assassinate the others in order to gain control of the land. She didn't know the timeline of these events.

"She is not." His attention went to the shoreline. "My ancestor is the young man she married."

"I thought you said the royal family had Lakin's entire line killed."

He looked at her. "Everyone except his unknown twin brother who wasn't home at the time. When he returned and discovered what had been done to his family, he swore revenge. He eventually got it. It took decades of planning. But he got what he wanted."

Which must have been the throne. Sabine shivered.

Evander wrapped his arm around her shoulders, pulling her closer to him.

"Avoni's history is very…colorful," she said.

"It's complex. A delicate balancing act."

Curious to know more about Evander and Avoni, she asked, "Besides being your family's representative to the League, what are your responsibilities as a prince?"

He peered at her. "That is a complicated answer that I do not feel like discussing tonight."

As the only male son, she wondered if he was involved with the army. But then she remembered Avoni didn't have a standing army. Obviously there were sentries at the royal palace, but other than that, she couldn't be sure what the kingdom and royal family had in place for protection.

Sabine eyed Evander, wondering if he had a lover. It was Lover's Night, and he seemed a little off, almost wistful. He'd told her brother he would marry Lottie, but that didn't mean he didn't have someone at home that he loved. She had so many questions for this man beside her. However, now was not the time to ask them. Some of the answers she wasn't ready to hear. Not tonight with the lightning bugs floating around them as they drifted along the canal, Evander's arm on her shoulders.

Neither of them spoke as they passed town after town. The night wore on, and the boats gradually lessened. Since they'd slept during the day, Sabine didn't think they'd stop tonight. Not tired, she remained at Evander's side until the lightning bugs faded away, the boats around them docked, and they were the only two people on the canal. At some point, one of them reached over and took the other's hand.

Hours passed, and Sabine and Evander continued to float along. With the thick cloud cover, no moon or stars shone above. Sabine tried to remain alert, watching for hidden threats. The buildings on either side of the waterway ended, replaced by a thick forest. The trees made it impossible to see what dangers could be lurking behind them. The only sounds were crickets and the occasional owl.

Sabine moved and sat across from Evander in order to keep an eye on one direction while he watched the other. At first, the darkness had been scary. However, after so many hours of it, it now offered a sort of comfort. Like a blanket.

Neither of them spoke as they continued to make their way south. Sabine focused on listening and watching, as Evander had taught her to do. The skin on the back of her neck tingled when she realized it had gone quiet. Too quiet. No crickets or any other creatures made any noise. The only sound was the occasional lap of water hitting the boat.

Sabine looked at Evander, about to say something when he pulled out a knife from his boot and handed it to her. She took the weapon, clutching onto it. He continued to scan the area around them as he slid another knife from his sleeve and a third from his back somewhere. With a weapon in each hand, he motioned for Sabine to get down.

Her heart pounding from fright, she slid from the bench and laid in the bottom of the boat, hoping she wasn't visible from the shoreline.

The boat drifted along in silence.

She didn't like the idea of Evander remaining upright and

unprotected. If someone shot an arrow at him, he'd be hit. Thankfully, he joined her a moment later.

"I'm glad you finally saw reason and decided to get where it's safe," she whispered.

He wedged himself between her and the side of the boat. "There's a rope across the canal up ahead. I'm hoping we pass right under it."

A chill slid through her. "Is that rope always there?" she asked, already knowing the answer.

"No."

"Do you think it's the assassin?" she asked, wondering how he'd caught up with them already.

"Yes."

"What's the plan?" she asked, assuming the assassin had to be close by watching. When he saw an empty boat, he'd probably be able to figure out they were hiding in it. Her body began to shake from the thought of being attacked. Her hands were sweaty, so she wiped them off on her cape. At least she had the weapon. Holding it helped her feel as if she had something to protect herself with.

"Can you swim?" Evander whispered, reaching out to tuck a strand of her hair around her ear.

The simple gesture startled her. "Yes, but not well. Why?" Why had he done that? No one could see them, so they didn't need to keep up the ruse of being a married couple right now.

"I may have to flip the boat. If you hold onto the side there," he pointed to the rope handle nailed on the edge, "you can keep your head in the air pocket so you can breathe."

Blinking, she thought through all he'd said. The idea of being under a boat, in the water, when it was dark out and she wouldn't be able to see anything, scared her. She really hoped he didn't have to flip the boat. But seriously, why had he tucked her hair behind her ear like that? Perhaps it was a nervous gesture on his part. Regardless, he didn't need to touch her so intimately.

"We're coming up on the rope. Get ready."

"For what?" she asked.

"I don't know. Something."

She looked up and saw the boat pass under the rope. If either of them had been sitting, they would have been knocked off.

Something thudded against the side of the boat.

Evander cursed and sprang to his feet, searching the water for threats.

Sabine sat up, peering over the side and not seeing anything.

She heard a slight whoosh, and then the boat shook. She swiveled around and saw a man had jumped into their boat, landing on the rear bench seat.

Evander lunged forward, tackling him over the side and into the water with a splash. The two men grappled as the boat continued floating along the canal, leaving the men behind.

Having no idea how to make the boat stop, Sabine grabbed the long pole attached to the side and shoved it in the water, trying to get it to do something. When nothing happened, she reached for the steering handle at the back of the boat. Turning it, she managed to angle the boat toward the shoreline. Once the front of the boat struck land, she stuck the pole in the water until it hit the bottom. She held it there, trying to keep the boat in place.

While she hadn't gone that far, she no longer saw the men fighting. She scanned the canal, searching for Evander, and not seeing him anywhere.

Terror sliced through her like lightning through a tree trunk. If the assassin had killed Evander, she'd be at a serious disadvantage. Not only would she have to face the assassin alone, but Avoni was a strange kingdom with odd customs. And Evander...the mere thought of him being injured made her feel ill. Staring at the dark water, she didn't understand why it became hard to breathe or why her vision blurred.

Sabine gripped the side of the boat. If Evander died trying to protect her, she'd never forgive herself. He didn't deserve to die on her account.

The crickets began chirping again as if everything were fine. As if a fight hadn't happened only moments ago.

Something appeared in the water several feet away, heading toward Sabine. Clutching onto the boat, she leaned out, trying to get a better look as a body lying face down drifted past. The person was too far away to tell if it was Evander or the assassin. Her stomach cramped with nausea.

She scanned the canal again, looking for the second person. Squinting, she spotted someone swimming directly toward her. Her heart thudded in her chest. "Evander?" she whispered, moving backward, away from the edge of the boat. She spotted the dagger Evander had given her on the bench but decided against it. She'd rather not let anyone get that close to her. Grabbing the pole, she used it to shove away from the shoreline. The boat immediately got caught in the current, putting space between her and the assassin.

"Sabine," Evander called out. "It's me."

Relief filled her. She turned the lever again, steering back toward the shoreline where she used the pole to hold the boat in place.

Evander swam over and grabbed onto the side of the boat, hoisting himself out of the water and collapsing onto the floor, soaking wet, his chest rising and falling.

Sabine looked him over, trying to determine if he'd been hurt. "Are you injured?" she asked, not spotting any blood.

"Of course not." He glanced at her. "You know it's not

safe for you in Avoni if you don't know what you're doing or where you're going."

"I know." Tears filled her eyes. Evander was here, with her, unharmed. He was alive. It had been the assassin's body she saw floating by. "I would never leave without you." She hooked the pole back onto the side.

Evander sat up. "Really? Because you sort of left me back there which indicates otherwise."

She didn't know how he could joke at a time like this. "I didn't know if it was you or not," she said, trying to explain.

He wiped his face off with the edge of Sabine's cloak. "Your lack of faith in me and my abilities is astounding." He stood and grabbed the pole. "We need to get going." He moved to the rear bench seat and shoved the boat away from the shore.

She got the impression that she'd upset him. Or disappointed him.

Now that they were back in the middle of the canal floating along with the current, Evander set the pole aside and reached into his bag, taking out a dry shirt. He pulled his wet one off, tossing it on the floor.

Sabine sat there staring like a teenager who'd never seen a man without a shirt on. Evander's muscles were well defined, and there was something about his sleek elegance that made her want to run her hands over his chest. He was all lean muscle, not an ounce of fat on him. His shoulders had a slight dusting of freckles over them.

She turned on the seat, facing forward, away from him. Her ogling must be because of the attack they'd just experienced. It was irrational to be attracted to this man in the boat with her. He'd kidnapped her. She was married. He wasn't her type. He killed people. Rubbing her hands over her face, she tried clearing her thoughts.

There was something about Evander's kindness toward

her, the way he joked with her and made her laugh. She needed to snap out of it. She was here for one reason and one reason only—to get rid of the assassin so she could return to Lynk—to her husband. She had a war to stop.

The sound of water falling came from behind her so she twisted around and saw Evander wringing his shirt out over the side of the boat. At least he was clothed now.

He hung his wet shirt to dry over the seat beside him. "I guess there's not much I can do about my pants except sit here and be uncomfortable." He looked her right in the eyes. "Unless you're good with me taking them off?"

If he wanted her to say it was okay for him to change his pants in front of her, she wasn't going to. He'd have to sit there and suffer. "I think you'll manage just fine." She'd never been so thankful for it being dark out as she was now. Under the night sky, there was no way to see her blush.

Wanting to change the subject, she asked, "Was that Ex you killed?"

"No, unfortunately it wasn't." He scanned the shoreline. "It seems news of his reward for your capture has not only spread to other towns, but most have figured out where we're headed now."

"Thank you."

"For what?" he asked.

"Keeping me alive." While she knew he did it to save his own skin and keep his family and kingdom protected, she still wanted him to know she appreciated his help. "Does it bother you?" she asked, curious to know more about this man before her.

"Does what bother me? Sitting here in wet pants? Yes."

She shook her head. "Killing people."

He didn't answer right away, and she thought perhaps he wasn't going to. "If I think of them as people, yes," he said, his voice soft. "But you have to understand, there is a code. We live and die by that code."

She didn't understand what he meant by code and was afraid to ask.

"Sometimes it's better to be proactive." He ran a hand through his wet hair. "I didn't set out in life to be the head of the Crimson Cloaks."

Her eyes went to the tattoo around his wrist.

"I'm the youngest person ever to lead them."

She imagined it wasn't an easy position to earn or maintain.

"But my family...they're the most important thing to me. If being the leader of an assassin guild keeps them safe, then it's worth it."

Sabine had no idea how any of this worked. "I thought your family was head of one of the guilds?"

He nodded. "My father was. Traditionally, it passes to his first born son. But after three daughters, people started to question him. By the time I was five, there had already been attempts on my father to take his place. My parents started training me even more. I shouldn't have had to take over until my thirties, but we knew my father wouldn't make it that long."

"So you took the position from your father?"

"I had to pass a series of tests, but yes, I took the position from my father. He is now just a king. Nothing more. Sometimes I think he resents me for it. But he's alive." His focus went back to the shoreline.

Sabine could feel the conversation was over. She didn't think Evander had ever shared this with anyone else.

The sky started to lighten. Dark clouds, a constant here in Avoni, promised rain. The forest along the canal ended, replaced by two and three story buildings, jammed close together.

Evander steered the boat toward a dock.

"Are we stopping?" Sabine asked, wondering how far they were from the palace.

"I need to change out of my wet pants and sleep for a few hours." When they neared the dock, Evander reached out, tying the boat up. He got out and extended his arm.

Sabine grabbed his hand, letting him pull her up and out of the boat.

He wrapped his arm around her shoulders, tucking her into his body, as they made their way from the dock into town.

Sabine tried to act normal, as if they were married and behaved this way all the time. However, the nearness of him felt different today than it had yesterday.

"Are you doing okay?" Evander mumbled in her ear, sending a ripple of pleasure down her spine.

"I'm fine."

He chuckled and slid his arm from her shoulders to her hand. They entered an inn, and Evander went over to the woman at the counter, inquiring about a room for the night. After paying and obtaining a key, he led Sabine up a staircase and to the end of the hallway to the last door on the right.

She stepped inside and removed her bag and cloak. The bed was large, big enough for the two of them to sleep without touching. She was just about to crawl under the covers when Evander took hold of her arm, stopping her.

"I'm famished," he said. "Let's grab food first."

The last thing Sabine felt like doing was eating some gross fish this early in the morning, especially at a tavern.

"I'll stay here. You go and eat. I'm not that hungry." She pulled back the blankets.

"Sorry," he replied. "It's too dangerous for you to remain here alone. You need to come with me." He went to the door, opening it, and motioning for her to join him.

Sighing, she followed him downstairs and out of the inn. They made their way along a crowded walkway.

"I'm surprised your parents allow you to leave the palace at all seeing as how dangerous your kingdom is," she mumbled.

"It's not that bad." He grabbed her hand, and they took the path to the right.

"We've been attacked more times than I can count," she said. It seemed to be a daily occurrence here, and it was exhausting.

"Then you can't count very high," he teased, poking her in the ribs. "And there's a hit on you. Otherwise, you would be safe here. Well, *safer*."

"I'm not sure anyone is ever safe in a land filled with assassins and warring families."

Evander eyed her sidelong as he led her into a small store filled with all sorts of baked goods.

Everything smelled divine, and Sabine wanted to sample it all. She noticed Evander speaking to the man behind the counter, and she got the feeling they knew one another. The man ended up packing a variety of pastries in a basket for them to take back to their room.

"This is convenient," she said as they exited the store.

"You look like you're about to fall over, so this seemed the better option."

"Me? You still have wet pants. In Lynk they would have dried by now."

His eyes narrowed. "I can't believe you just said that. You really are tired if you're complimenting Lynk." Since he held the basket with his right hand, he slid his left around Sabine's fingers, pulling her closer. "We're being followed," he whispered near her ear.

She groaned. "I don't have the energy for another attack. This is getting ridiculous." And with so many people around, being attacked would cause a massive scene which in turn would only attract more people to them. Unless the person followed them back to the inn, waited for them to fall asleep, and then broke in and kidnapped her.

"You don't have the energy?" Evander said. "I don't recall you jumping into the canal and fighting the last one." He shoved her in front of him and into a narrow alleyway. "This way," he mumbled, handing her the basket.

"Am I supposed to hit my attacker over the head with this basket full of food?" she asked, wanting to instead whack him over the head with it. She didn't want a basket—she wanted a weapon.

"I need my hands free so I can face whoever is going to come up behind us."

She glared at him.

He rolled his eyes and pulled out a knife, flipping it and handing the hilt to her. "Better?"

"Much." She took it, glad to have more than a basket to defend herself with.

"Get moving." Evander put his hand between her shoulder blades, pushing her forward.

She thought she heard footsteps behind them; however, she didn't dare look back to see. Just when she was about to reach the end of the alley, a man stepped into it, blocking the path.

"Duck," Evander said.

As Sabine squatted, she felt something move above her head. The man in front of her flew to the ground, a dagger protruding from this chest. The sheer quickness, brutality, and precision Evander killed with sent a wave of unease through her. Not having time to think too much about it, she dropped the basket and stood, holding the knife out before her. If anyone came too close, she would defend herself. Twisting to face the other end of the alley, she spotted a man rushing toward them.

The attacker lifted his arm and threw a knife aimed right for her.

Evander shoved Sabine against the wall. The knife flew by, only inches from her chest.

As the man neared, he withdrew another weapon, throwing it at Evander. Evander deflected it, then threw his dagger at their attacker. The man dodged it, producing another knife and tossing it at Evander. Evander twisted, and hurled a knife at the man who managed to move out of the way just in time.

The man stopped about five feet away, a smile on his face. "I have one weapon left. Do you?"

Evander's hands were empty. "I thought you were supposed to take her to Ex alive, not kill her yourself."

The man shrugged. "As long as I take her body to Ex so he can see she's dead, that's all that matters." He lifted his arm, about to throw his last weapon right at Sabine's chest.

Evander stepped in front of her, blocking her from the assassin.

Sabine couldn't let him die on her account. His life was no less important than hers. Besides, both her brother, Rolf, and her guard, Markis, had taught her how to throw a knife and since she had one in hand, she would use it. Readjusting her grip on the weapon, she leaned to the side, aimed, and Evander shifted just as she threw it, knocking her to the ground. Something metal clanked against the wall above her. Evander kicked his leg out, tripping the assassin. Then he lunged to the side, picked up a dagger lying on the ground, and plunged it into the man's chest.

Sabine shoved the hair from her face, trying to get a better look. The assassin laid in a pool of blood, lifeless. Evander's chest heaved up and down as he sat there, looking winded.

"What's the matter?" Sabine asked, coming to his side, immediately knowing something was wrong.

He reached down, pulling his shirt up and revealing a slash on the side of his torso.

Horror filled her. "How did that happen?" she asked, covering her mouth with her hand.

"I thought you were handing me the weapon, not throwing it." He examined his wound.

"I did that?" Her hands started shaking. "I'm so sorry."

"It's just a nick," he gritted out. He tore off a piece from her cloak, balling it up and shoving it against his side to stop the bleeding. "It's not that deep."

"Let's get you back to the inn," she said as she wrapped an arm around him, helping him to his feet. She couldn't believe she'd injured him by accident. "I'm so sorry," she said again as they rounded the corner, joining the throng of people on the walkway. Blood began seeping through the cloth and onto Evander's fingers. It had to be worse than he was letting on.

"Turn here," he said, nodding his chin.

When they reached the inn, she opened the door, letting him lean on her as they went inside.

Evander went to the desk, reached over and grabbed a quill and paper. He scribbled a few things down. Tearing the paper in half, he gave one to the woman working there and then shoved the other in his pocket.

"Your face is looking rather white," Sabine said. If it truly was a slight nick, he shouldn't be losing so much blood or have such pasty skin.

"Let's go to our room," he said, looking at her pointedly.

She nodded and wrapped her arm around him, helping him up the stairs. In their room, he sat on the edge of the bed. Sabine removed his shoes then lifted his legs onto the mattress. "What can I do to help?"

He handed her the paper he'd written on. "I made a list of what I need. You will take it to the apothecary's where he will give you everything. When you get back here, I'll need you to help close my wound." He reached in his pocket, pulling out several coins and handing them to her. "I'm losing a lot of blood, so I need you to hurry."

"Where's the apothecary?" she asked, trying to remember if she'd seen one around.

"Exit the inn. Turn right. Go two blocks, then turn left. It'll be another block down on the left. Look for a circle with a flame around it."

She clutched the paper, nodding.

"Sabine," he said, regaining her attention. "Put this on." He removed his bracelet and handed it to her. "Keep your hood up and don't talk to anyone other than the apothecary. Show him that bracelet. After he reveals a red mark on his inner right wrist, give him the list."

"Okay." She repeated everything he'd said in her mind, trying to commit it to memory. After the bracelet was hooked on her wrist, she folded the paper and left the room, running down the stairs and out of the inn.

On the walkway, she tried to keep her head down as she took note of the streets she passed, being sure to turn at the right places. She scanned the signs, looking for the right one. When she saw the circle with a flame, relief filled her.

She threw the door open and burst inside. "I need help," she said even though she didn't see a single person in the store. Then she remembered what Evander had told her about talking to no one but the apothecary. She stood in the middle of the shop, waiting.

Along the walls were several shelves filled with glass bottles, bowls, and plants. A funny smell permeated the room. There was a counter covered with stains in the middle of the shop. Since time was of the essence, she decided to take matters into her own hands.

"Hello?" she called out, louder this time. "Is anyone here?"

A door between the shelves opened and an older man with white hair came out, drying his hands on a towel. "Can I help you?" he asked, squinting at her.

She reached out, showing him the bracelet.

His eyes widened as he leaned closer, examining it. "What do you need?" he asked.

She tapped her right wrist.

"Oh." He lifted his arm, revealing a red tattoo matching the sign out front.

She handed him the paper. "It's an emergency." She dumped the coins Evander had given her on the counter.

The man nodded and got to work pulling several bottles from the shelves. He poured the ingredients into a bowl then mashed them together. Once done, he used a spoon to put the pasty goo into a container, capping it with a lid. "This is for the cut. It will help with infection." Then he pulled out a black rock and put it in a stone bowl. Using a hammer, he beat it into a fine powder. Then he put the powder into another container and capped it. "This is to stop the bleeding. Use this first, then the gel second."

Sabine nodded.

He reached under the counter, withdrawing a bottle. "This is to be taken like a drink."

"Okay."

The man picked up the list, reading it again. He went into the back room and returned a moment later with a needle and thread. Gathering everything together, he put the items in a round basket, handing it to Sabine.

"Thank you," she said, taking the basket.

"Good luck."

She exited the shop and took off running. On her way back to the inn, she got turned around. On the verge of panicking, she took a deep breath and forced herself to calm down. She didn't have time to waste. After going another block, she realized she'd missed a turn. Shaking her head, she backtracked and found the correct pathway. When she reached the inn, she went inside, running up the stairs and bursting into the room. She set the basket aside before closing and locking the door.

"That was quite a dramatic entrance," Evander said, his voice weak. A sheen of sweat covered his forehead.

Sabine sat on the bed beside him with the basket. She withdrew the black powder. Evander reached for it. "Let me," she said.

"Have you ever done this before?" he asked.

"No." She almost lied and said yes but figured he'd know. "Just tell me what to do."

He nodded.

She reached forward, carefully removing the cloth pressed against his wound. The cut wasn't long, just deep.

"Sprinkle the black stuff on it," he ground out.

She uncapped the bottle and shook it, covering his wound with the black substance. The blood immediately stopped oozing out.

"Now use the gel," he said.

She removed its cap, trying not to gag at the smell. "Do I just put it on with my fingers?" She didn't want to hurt him.

"Yes, but only use half. Save the other half for after."

"After what?" she asked, scooping up about half of the contents.

"Don't press too hard," he said. "Just cover the area."

She nodded, gently putting the gooey substance over his wound.

"Now I need you to sew me together."

"You want me to do what?" The only thing she'd ever sewn was a pillow.

"Don't overthink it," he said. "Pick up the needle and thread."

With shaking hands, she found the needle and thread.

"Push my skin together and sew. Pretend it's fabric."

He had to be joking.

"Hand it to me. I'll do it."

"No." She would fix him up. After all, he was in this mess because of her. Once she had the needle threaded, she placed it at the tip of the wound.

"I'm only going to be numb for a few more minutes," Evander said. "I'd like to have the wound closed before feeling returns to the area."

That gave her the strength to begin. She used one hand to hold the skin together and the other to push the needle through his skin. She quickly sewed the skin closed and tied off the thread. "Now what?"

"Did the apothecary give you something for me to drink?"

Sabine reached into the basket, pulling out the other vial and handing it to Evander.

He took it and quickly drank the contents, handing the vial back to her when done.

"Now what?"

"We wait." He laid his head back against the pillow. "In a couple of hours, I'll have you put the medicine for infection on the wound again."

After placing everything back in the basket, she set it

aside and stood. "Let's get your shirt off." Not only did they need to keep the wound clean, she didn't want it rubbing against the cut and making it bleed again.

"I don't want to move and reopen it."

Since his shirt was pretty much ruined, she took hold of the bottom of it, tearing it in half. Then she carefully pulled it from him without moving him too much.

"I've always envisioned a woman doing that to me but under very different circumstances." The corners of his lips rose in a slight smile.

"If you can joke at a time like this, then I know you're going to be okay." She tossed his shirt in the corner of the room and left.

She heard him calling out after her, but she ignored him. Downstairs, she went to the young woman working behind the counter. "May I please have a bowl of water?" She had no idea if this was a strange request or not.

The woman nodded and left the room. She returned a minute later with a bucket filled with water and a small towel.

"Thank you." Sabine carefully carried the bucket upstairs. Back in the room, she set the bucket next to the bed.

"I thought I made you mad, so you left."

"Have you so little faith in me?" she asked, using the same words he had earlier. She sat on the edge of the bed and dipped the towel in the water. Then she used it to gently wipe the dried blood from Evander's torso, being careful to avoid the area around the cut. She noticed goosebumps covered his skin as she wet it.

"You don't have to do this," he said, his voice soft.

"I know. But I want to." She continued to wipe him off until most of the blood was gone. "Now let's clean your hands." After she re-wet the towel, she wiped the blood from his hands, noticing the calluses on his fingers.

When she finished, she tossed the towel in the bucket.

Evander reached out, taking hold of her hand. "Thank you."

"It's the least I can do. You've saved me countless times."

Sabine remained beside him, sitting on the bed, holding his hand. His breathing became steady, and his coloring slowly returned to normal.

The room began to darken. She carefully slid her hand from his and stood. Taking her discarded cloak, she rolled it up and stuck it under the door as Evander had done. After making sure the door was locked, she laid on the other side of the bed, as far away from Evander as possible so she wouldn't accidentally touch his wound.

Lying there, she watched his chest rise and fall as he slept. At some point, she reached out and took his hand, holding onto it, wanting to comfort him in any way she could.

Chapter Seven

Sabine awoke and glanced outside, spotting thick, dark clouds. Without seeing the sun's placement in the sky, she had no idea what time of day it was.

Peering over at Evander, she examined his cut. While the wound itself was red, the area around it didn't look nearly as puffy and swollen as it had yesterday. Relief filled her. And her sewing job wasn't half bad either.

Smiling, she remained lying there, watching the rise and fall of Evander's chest. She needed to wake him so they could be on their way. Staying in one place too long wasn't a great idea. However, he looked so peaceful. She was just about to say his name when he mumbled something. She leaned in closer so she could hear him.

"She said no one could ever love someone like me," he murmured.

"Evander," Sabine whispered, trying to rouse him without startling him. That was the last thing she wanted to do to an assassin. He'd probably flip her over or put her in a choke hold.

"So beautiful," he mumbled. "The most beautiful woman I've ever seen." He sighed. "But it can never be."

Sabine wondered who he spoke of. While she knew he'd agreed to marry Lottie, she hadn't asked if he was in love with someone. The mere thought of him having a lover didn't feel right. Whoever this beautiful woman was who'd told him she couldn't love him was a fool.

Propping her head on her hand, Sabine examined Evander in greater detail. He really was a handsome man. She didn't know why she hadn't seen it before back in Lynk. The curve of his face, his strong jawbone, and his eyes. Even though she couldn't see his piercing green eyes at the moment, it didn't mean she couldn't picture them perfectly in her mind. The way they sparkled when he teased her, the seriousness in them when danger lurked close by.

She allowed herself to look at his body. At his toned shoulders and the curve of his upper arm. The slight dusting of freckles on his skin especially near his elbows. Her hand reached out of its own accord, tracing a line from his shoulder down to his hand. He was the opposite of Rainer in a lot of ways, and she found that appealing.

Evander mumbled something incoherent.

Scooting closer to him, Sabine gently pressed her stomach against his arm and placed the palm of her hand on his chest, not wanting to startle him and wind up dead. "Evander, it's time to get up." She gently patted his chest.

He reached up, wrapping his fingers around her hand. Peeling his eyes open, he peered over at her. "Morning," he said with a small smile, his voice gravelly. "I haven't slept that well in a long time."

"It's probably from the medicine." Speaking of which, she needed to give him the second dose.

"And here I thought it was because of you," he teased. He

slowly sat up and examined his wound. "Not bad." He reached for the basket of medicine beside the bed.

"I'll get that for you." She sat up.

"I can do it." He lifted the vial and ingested the rest of the medicine. Then he spread the gooey substance over his cut. "Looks like it's already healing."

"I'm so sorry I stabbed you. I really meant to throw the knife at the assassin." She covered her face with her hands. The entire ordeal had happened so quickly. Next time, she'd have to be more careful. Hopefully, there wouldn't be a next time. She dropped her hands and looked at him to see if he believed her.

"I know it wasn't your fault," he replied. "I'm just embarrassed you had to help me back here and sew me shut." He ran a hand through his messy hair.

He was kind of adorable in the morning. Sabine found herself wanting to run her hands through his hair, too.

Evander swung his legs over the side of the bed.

"Are you able to stand?" She hurried and got out of bed in case he needed her help.

"I'm fine. I could use some food, but other than that, I'm good." He stood and stretched. "We need to be on our way. It's only a matter of time until someone else finds us here."

Trying not to stare at his sleek back, Sabine went over to their bags and put them on the bed. "I'm assuming you'll want a clean shirt." Her face warmed just thinking about how she'd torn off his shirt last night.

"Yes, thank you. Whatever is on top will be fine."

She reached into his bag and pulled out a black shirt.

"I hate to ask this of you," he said, his voice sounding unsure, "but can you help me put it on?" He kept his eyes focused on the floor. "I don't want to tear a stitch." A tinge of red spotted his cheeks.

He was embarrassed to ask for assistance. Sabine smiled.

She loved when she had the upper hand. "Evander, the great and mighty assassin-pirate-prince needs my help?" She batted her eyelashes at him.

"Assassin-pirate-prince?"

"That's my nickname for you." She came and stood before him, the shirt clutched between her hands.

"That's some nickname." He finally looked her in the eyes.

Her breath caught at the sight of his mesmerizing eyes.

"Maybe start with the sleeves?" he suggested.

She cleared her throat. "Good idea." She slid the shirt on his arms, then pulled it up to his shoulders. He lowered his head, and she put the shirt over it. Once his head was through, she carefully lowered the fabric, brushing her fingers against his skin as she did so. "Hopefully, the medicine will prevent the shirt from sticking to your wound."

Evander pinched her chin, forcing her to look at him. "Thank you for everything."

"My pleasure." Her chin felt as if it were on fire.

He smiled. "Let's be on our way."

She grabbed both their bags, hoisting them over her shoulder, her stomach growling as she did so. They hadn't eaten in over a day. She'd have to make sure they got something on their way to the canal.

Evander opened the door. "I can carry my bag."

Sabine refused to hand it over. "I got it."

"Honestly, it's not that bad. I feel fine."

She shrugged. "Regardless, I'm perfectly capable of carrying two bags." She stepped around him and hurried down the steps. He followed at a much slower pace.

At the bottom of the staircase she turned to face him. "Are you sure you're ready to go out there?" If someone attacked them, she wasn't sure he could hold his own in a fight.

"We can't stay here," he said as he joined her.

"Can you defend yourself?" she asked as politely as she could.

He nodded. "I can even defend you." He poked her in the ribs.

She folded her arms, not convinced.

"I've trained to fight while injured. I can do it if I have to. The worst that can happen is I rip my stitches open and you have to tend to me again." He smiled, holding her gaze.

"Fine." There was no use arguing with him. Sabine turned and grabbed the door, swinging it open. Stepping outside, she stumbled to a halt. She stood there, frozen, not knowing what to do.

Dozens of men dressed in black surrounded the inn effectively blocking any chance Sabine and Evander had of escaping. "You've got to be kidding me," she mumbled, trying to think of how to get them out of this. They didn't have enough weapons to fight their way through and, quite frankly, as talented as Evander was, even he couldn't take on this many people at once.

She took a step back, bumping into him. Maybe she could just lock herself in the inn and remain in there forever. Eventually she'd starve and die, but it seemed she was going to die regardless. Right now, that seemed a better option than being taken by these assassins and murdered.

Evander put a steady hand on her shoulder, holding her in place.

She was about to tell him they should take their chances inside rather than fight all of these people when Evander said, "It's about time you show up."

Confusion filled her. There was no need for Evander to goad these men into attacking them.

"Glad to see you're still alive, brother," the one front and center said, coming forward and pushing her hood back, revealing a rather pretty, womanly face—not a man.

"What's going on?" Sabine asked.

"This is my sister, Princess Gemma, and this is a unit of her best fighters." Evander moved his hand from Sabine's shoulder to her lower back, stepping beside her and smiling.

Sabine knew Avoni didn't have an army in the traditional sense of the word. "Her best fighters?" she asked, wanting clarification that these people who were dressed and looked like assassins were on their side and wouldn't be attacking them.

"Yesterday, when we returned to the inn, I had a message sent to the palace. I was afraid with my injury that I wouldn't be enough protection for you, and I requested help." He dropped his hand from her back and stepped forward, wrapping his arm around his sister and hugging her. "It's good to see you. Thank you for coming."

It would have been nice if he'd mentioned this to Sabine before now. She tapped her foot, thinking about how her brothers hated to ask for help. The fact that Evander had swallowed his pride and did this revealed a lot about him. Another curtain he'd pulled back for her to see behind.

Gemma came and stood before Sabine, her face unreadable. The young woman had beautiful dark red hair pulled into a bun. Her hazel eyes glistened, reminding Sabine of Evander. Both brother and sister had the same skin tone.

"Gemma," Evander said, "may I introduce Queen Sabine Manfred." Evander extended his arm to Sabine.

Sabine smiled at Gemma, for some reason wanting the woman to like her.

"I have a lot of questions for the two of you, but I suspect that is a conversation for us to have in private." She glanced between Sabine and Evander, neither one of them responding. "We must get moving—especially since there is a large bounty on your head." She focused her attention back on her brother. "You look awful."

"Thanks."

Gemma made several hand gestures to the members of her unit and as one, they turned, facing out, making a pathway down the center between them.

"Let's go," Evander mumbled, taking Sabine's hand.

The two of them followed Gemma as they made their way between the assassin-soldiers. When they reached the middle of the group, the unit closed in around them, effectively blocking them from an attack.

The urge to tease Evander about this being a bit excessive and the fact that his sister had come to their rescue was almost too great to pass up. However, with so many people around, she didn't feel comfortable joking with him. It seemed best to keep her mouth shut for now. While she probably shouldn't be holding Evander's hand in front of others, it at least afforded her the opportunity to make sure no one bumped against his side where the cut was.

As a group, they made their way through the town and to the canal without incident. Based on Sabine's estimates, there were fifty people which meant they were going to have to take at least a dozen boats. Instead of stopping at the dock as she thought they would, they traveled a few blocks south along the canal until they came to a longer dock that had a large, flat boat with a roof. Gemma and her soldiers began boarding.

"Are we taking this?" she asked.

"We are." Evander helped Sabine step into the boat.

She led him to the back so he'd be out of the way. With so many people on board, she didn't want him to be jostled or hit on his side.

Once the rest of the unit had boarded, the boat slowly pushed away from the dock, heading south along the canal.

Evander sat on the floor, pulling Sabine down with him. "It's safer," he said.

Sabine leaned her back against the side of the boat, watching everyone else stand around.

"Sorry," he said, recapturing her attention.

"For what?"

"At first, I was afraid the wound was deep and I wouldn't be able to defend you properly. I thought asking my sister for help was the best course of action. But now that she's here, I regret doing so. Not only does it seem excessive, but you appear overwhelmed and uncomfortable. I thought she'd send one or two fighters. Not come herself with her *entire* unit. For that, I apologize." He rubbed the back of his neck, avoiding her gaze.

"There's no need to apologize." She'd rather have more protection than not enough. She had no doubt Evander would have fought to protect her if necessary, even if that meant he got hurt in the process. Having reinforcements here was a good thing.

He tilted his head to the side, looking into her eyes. "It seems the tables have turned and you have become my protector. Thank you for stitching me up and administering the necessary medicines."

Her face warmed from both the compliment and the intensity of his attention. "It was the least I could do." She reached out and took hold of his hand, squeezing it.

"Here," Gemma said as she squatted before Evander holding a bottle. "You need to take a swig of this medicine to make sure you don't get an infection." She handed it to Evander. "And make sure you see the healer when we get there."

"Where are we going?" Sabine asked as Evander took a drink from the bottle.

"We are headed to the main palace." Gemma stood,

looking at her brother. "I hope you know what you're doing." She folded her arms.

"I do," he replied, tucking the bottle in his bag.

Gemma raised a single eyebrow, her glance going between Sabine and Evander. "I sure as hell hope you have your story straight because they are going to grill you." She turned and joined her fighters who all seemed to be giving Evander and Sabine some space.

Evander sighed, resting his head against the side of the boat and diligently looking at the ceiling.

"Is everything okay?" Sabine asked, wondering about Evander and what sort of relationship he had with the rest of his family.

"You know how sometimes you get these grand ideas and you're so sure they'll work just as you imagined?" He tilted his head, looking her in the eyes.

She laughed because she understood exactly what he was talking about. "Yes, only you know things never go as planned."

"Yes, I'm learning that." He smiled an adorable half-smile.

Sabine leaned her head on Evander's shoulder. "Your sister looks pretty intimidating dressed in those pants and tunic." There had been a couple of women in the Avoni delegation and they had worn something similar.

"Please don't tell her that. Her head is big enough already."

She laughed again. "Are all women in Avoni, regardless of station, allowed to fight?"

Evander drew little circles on the back of her hand. "Of course. Why wouldn't they?"

"I don't know. Because they're women?"

It was his turn to laugh. "You Bakleys are so backwards sometimes."

Sabine had never thought much about the way women

were treated until she'd left Bakley and saw vastly different behaviors and customs in other kingdoms. She had a lot to learn. "Why did your sister give you that ominous warning a few minutes ago?"

"Because I sort of wasn't supposed to go with the delegation to Lynk. I'm sure my parents are going to be furious with me."

That surprised her—both that he wasn't supposed to go in the first place and that he'd gone without permission. "I thought you are your family's League representative?" And a representative had to be there to approve of her marriage to Rainer.

"I am," he admitted. "But I only took up that role a few months ago. Prior to that, I...uh...had been too young."

"You're eighteen?" she asked.

"Yes."

He was the same age as her then. "So your sister is concerned your parents will be upset that you went against their wishes?"

"Yes. Their direct orders, actually." He rubbed his face. "I'm the only son. They thought my sister, Carin, should go instead. She's twenty and apparently since she's third born, they can spare her." His voice dripped with sarcasm.

"Why'd you do it then?"

He shrugged. "Carin didn't want to go, and I was curious to see Lynk and meet King Rainer." He peered down at her, his brows drawing together ever so slightly.

"What's that look for?"

He sighed and glanced about the boat. Anywhere, really, but at her.

"Evander?"

"I watched the two of you together," he whispered. "I assumed he seduced you to get what he wanted from you and your kingdom. You seemed so taken with him. As if he had you under his spell."

Sabine's face warmed thinking about her time with Rainer. Whenever she'd been with him, she'd felt a physical connection between them, but that was all. She suspected he was that way with most everyone since he was such a sensual person. He had been in a relationship with Heather for years and that was the woman he loved, not Sabine. When Rainer and Sabine were together, it was all for show. A performance to make sure the people of Lynk thought they were in love to strengthen Rainer's position as their new king.

She hated that Evander thought her so naive. She especially hated that he assumed she was taken with Rainer but Rainer wasn't taken with her. It made sense since she was so much younger than the king. And she wasn't nearly as beautiful as Heather. Yet, the thought of someone else seeing it so easily embarrassed her.

"I guess it doesn't matter," Evander said. "You're married to Rainer, and you are the queen of Lynk." He leaned his head back against the side of the boat again. "My parents are going to be furious with me."

"For going to Lynk and disobeying them?" Her parents would be livid with her if she had gone against their wishes.

"That. And for snatching you away from Rainer and bringing you to Avoni." He looked sidelong at her. "I need to ask a favor of you."

"Anything."

"Can you please not mention to anyone that I kidnapped you?"

She thought about that. At this point, she no longer considered herself kidnapped. She'd chosen to come here to escape her assassin and to remain alive. "You didn't kidnap me."

"I took you from the palace."

"To see my brother. There was no kidnapping involved. If I had to go back and do it all over again, I'd go willingly with you."

He reached out and took a strand of her brown hair, wrapping it around his finger and watching her. "Are you sure?"

"Yes."

He released her hair. "You know King Rainer can't be trusted, don't you?"

Staring into his green eyes, she wondered how long he'd wanted to say that to her. "I know." She wasn't some lovesick, besotted young woman who didn't know any better. She was married to a man who didn't love her and probably never could. She barely knew him and wouldn't even consider them friends. She was more comfortable around Evander and knew more about him than she did her own husband. But that was on Rainer. He'd kept her at arms length, not wanting to get to know her. Not even trying. She was a means to an end for him. Nothing more. A pang of sadness filled her—not over Rainer but over the thought of not marrying someone she loved and respected. Shaking her head, she tried to clear it. Thinking of what could have been would do her no good.

"What's the matter?" Evander asked, his finger tracing a line on the side of her cheek.

"You know how you said that thing about making plans and them never going the way they're supposed to?"

He smiled. "Unfortunately."

"Well, the same can be said for my life." She closed her eyes, not wanting to cry. It had been a long, emotional few days, and everything was starting to catch up to her. "I always thought I'd marry a man I loved. I never thought I, the sixth-born child, would be sent off for a political match of such importance." And she never thought her one and only sister would be murdered.

"I suppose that's an issue with being born into a royal family—even one like mine. We have influence, wealth, power, but we also never get to do what we want, especially if we plan on keeping the throne. If we were selfish and always put our own needs first, we'd be happier. But then we'd be killed and someone else would lead the kingdom." He shrugged. "Would you rather be poor, untitled, and marry for love?"

"I don't know." She'd never really thought about it. Prior to coming to Lynk, her days had been spent doing what she wanted. She hated to admit it, but she'd been selfish. Now, she looked at things differently. She was glad she was in the position she was so she could help her kingdom and right the wrongs committed. "Let me ask you this," she said. "If you could do anything you wanted right now, what would it be?" From the limited time she'd spent with him, he seemed to have a tremendous amount of freedom to do as he pleased. But did he enjoy the life he led? Perhaps there were things missing that he longed for.

His eyes darted to her lips and then back to her eyes. "Anything?" he asked, his voice suddenly husky.

She nodded, a warm feeling spread through her body.

"I don't know," he said, his eyes searching hers. "What about you? What would you do?"

It felt as if something inside of her was caged and needed to burst free. "I don't know, either." Maybe she'd scream. But letting the scream out meant the emotions would come flooding out with it, and right now, she needed to keep it together. That thing caged inside of her needed to stay caged. She was on a boat filled with fighters, and they were headed to the Avoni palace where she would meet the king and queen. It wasn't about what she wanted or needed. It was about saving the Bakley children, protecting her family's kingdom, stopping a potential war, and trying to make it out of this alive.

Staring into Evander's eyes, everyone and everything faded away as he reached forward, placing his hand on her cheek, his thumb gently wiping a tear away. She hadn't realized she'd shed it.

"You're not at all who I thought you were," he whispered.

These past few weeks, she'd learned a lot about herself. She wasn't the same person she was prior to her sister's murder. And sitting here, with Evander's hand on her face, she wanted nothing more than to lean into him, reveling in the feel and warmth of this man beside her. This assassin-pirate-prince. He was not at all the person she thought he was when they'd first met.

"Evander," Gemma called out, her voice cutting through their moment.

He flinched.

"Come here." Her voice was curt and demanding.

Evander slowly got to his feet and went over to his sister.

Sabine watched the two of them arguing in hushed whispers, looking her way every few seconds.

An overwhelming sense of sadness filled her. Evander was a good man, and he deserved to marry someone better than Lottie. He was kind, caring, funny, and he'd make an excellent husband. He was the opposite of Lottie, and the princess didn't deserve him.

Sabine rubbed her face. Everything was becoming more and more complicated. She longed for a simpler time. As she sat there, she didn't understand the pain she felt in her heart.

A few hours later, the boat turned into another canal that jutted off from the main one. After about a mile, the canal ended at a dock with a couple dozen boats tied to it. After their boat was anchored, everyone began disembarking.

Since Evander had never returned to sit with Sabine, she stood and went to find him. He was standing at the other end of the boat, his back to her as he leaned on the railing, staring at what was probably the palace not too far away.

Sabine placed her hand on his back. "Is everything all right?" she asked.

He nodded.

"Is that your home?" The land surrounding the canal was flat and covered with bright green grass. In the distance, roughly ten miles away, a forest started. However, directly in front of them, a little less than a mile away, a large wall stood, concealing what she assumed to be the palace. Sentries patrolled along the top of the wall.

"It is. Home sweet home. Well, one of them anyway." Evander led Sabine off the boat.

Those who'd accompanied them now marched in two single file lines directly toward a gate in the wall. Gemma turned back to face Evander. "I must get my people inside. I'll leave you to handle this."

"I have it all under control," he replied.

Gemma turned back around, marching along with her unit.

"What's your sister's role?" Sabine asked, wondering if her job was simply to command these soldiers. For a female member of the royal family, Sabine thought that odd.

"She doesn't have one."

"She's not an officer in the military or anything?"

"We don't have a military in the traditional sense of the word." Evander took her hand and helped her step off the dock and onto the thick grass. "Gemma loves to fight, so she joined a security unit when she was fifteen. She's since risen in the ranks. However, she holds no special position other than being a princess. For the royal family, my eldest sister, Lyra, is first in line and has two children of her own, making Gemma fourth in line. Therefore, Gemma is just Gemma."

"Is she a member of your assassin guild?"

He eyed her. "That's not something you speak of in Avoni."

She nodded, understanding the warning as they approached the wall. "How did you end up being a League member then?" It seemed as if that duty should have fallen to Gemma.

"The League meets in secret and prefers that the members be male if possible." He shrugged. "Since I'm the only man, once I became old enough, the position went to me."

"Other than that, you don't have any special job for your family?" What she really wanted to know was if the royal family employed him to be an assassin on their behalf.

He smiled at her. "Other than being their favorite son? No, I don't."

"Since my sister died," she said, her voice soft, "I'm now the only female sibling." She had four brothers, and Evander had three sisters.

They walked in silence for several minutes. "How's your side feeling?" she asked.

"About that." He pulled her to a stop and glanced up ahead at the wall. "I don't think you should tell anyone that you stabbed me. Since I technically kidnapped you, it could give the wrong impression, and I'd hate for my parents to put you in the dungeon."

Her heart started to beat faster. "You don't think I tried to kill you, do you?" she asked, panic rising.

"No, not at all."

Maybe she shouldn't enter through the gate and into the compound. Especially if she might be thrown into the dungeon. She glanced about, looking for a place where she could run to and hide. "You don't think your family will believe me?"

"No, I don't."

Terror filled her. She hadn't realized she'd be entering a hostile environment.

"You need to understand that everyone in Avoni learns to use a weapon at a young age. My parents would find it hard to believe that an eighteen-year-old woman would accidentally stab someone. It's just not done. They'd assume you were trying to kill me for kidnapping you."

"But you didn't kidnap me," she said, taking a step back.

"Regardless, my parents aren't stupid. They're going to question how and why you're here with me. I don't want to give them any reason not to trust you." He resumed walking. When he realized she wasn't alongside him, he stopped and turned around to face her. "Are you coming?"

"Into a fortified compound where I might be accused of attempting to murder you and be thrown into the dungeon?" She folded her arms. Maybe she could just sleep on the boat. It wasn't that cold out. Right now, she'd take her chances with a couple of assassins hunting her rather than an army of them behind that wall.

"Come on," he said. "It's not safe out here."

"I'm not sure it's safe in there."

He rolled his eyes. "Sabine." He waved her toward him. "I won't let anything happen to you. You'll be safe so long as you don't tell them I kidnapped you or that you stabbed me with a knife." He came back to her, took hold of her arm, and dragged her along the path toward the wall.

"Fine," she grumbled. "But if I end up in the dungeon or

dead, I expect you to save those Bakley children and protect my family and kingdom."

"And which family and kingdom would that be? Lynk?"

She shook her head. "Bakley."

"Then you have yourself a deal."

At the gate, they were granted passage. On the other side of the wall, Sabine stopped, her eyes widening at the sight before her. It was as if she'd entered another world. The entire wall had been built around a lake. The palace had been constructed in the middle of it, not on an island, but right on top of the water. Bridges and wooden walkways connected dozens of beautiful wood buildings.

The unit of fighters that had accompanied them went along the wall to the right. About a quarter of a mile away, there were several small structures built near the wall. That must be where the sentries were housed.

Evander and Sabine walked across the clearing toward an archway that led to the main bridge connecting the land to the palace.

"I like that you don't have guards following you," she said.

"I'm perfectly capable of taking care of myself."

Of that, she had no doubt. They passed under the archway and onto a bridge leading to the palace.

At the other end, she stepped onto a wooden platform built over the water. She jumped to see if it would move. It did not. However, it looked as if it were floating on the water. She wondered how all of this had been built.

"You okay?" Evander asked, eyeing her with amusement.

She straightened. "I'm fine." She gestured for him to lead the way.

He took her along the wooden pathway to the first building which was a tall, skinny structure four stories tall.

"Ready?" Evander asked, pulling his bottom lip between his teeth as if nervous.

She'd never seen him act nervous before. "Ready for what?" To be thrown in the dungeon? For someone to jump out at her? To face a squad of knife throwers?

"To meet the king and queen of Avoni."

She shook her head. "I look terrible and haven't bathed in days. I'd prefer to freshen up first." And calm herself down so she could speak intelligently when introduced to them as the queen of Lynk. If she met them right now, she was pretty sure she'd stumble over her words and admit to stabbing their son who'd kidnapped her. Overall, it wouldn't be a good first impression, and she had no desire to be thrown in a dungeon or start a war.

"You don't look terrible," he said. "But I should probably speak to them first before I introduce you to them." He bit his bottom lip again.

Sabine tried not to smile at his nervous habit.

"What are you grinning about?" he asked.

"Nothing." She smiled, batting her eyelashes at him.

His eyes narrowed. "I have a feeling you're silently laughing at my expense."

At that she laughed.

"You're infuriating sometimes," he said, shaking his head. "Come on, I'll show you to a guest room." He resumed walking.

Chuckling, she caught up to him, bumping her shoulder against his. She was just about to ask him to give her a tour of the palace later when they rounded the corner and Evander bumped his shoulder against hers just as her foot caught on something. She was right at the edge of the walkway and lost her balance.

It felt like slow motion as she stumbled, about to fall into the water, when Evander caught her around the waist, pulling her back up. They stood toe-to-toe, her breath heaving as she stared into his wide green eyes.

Chapter Eight

"I'm sorry," Evander whispered. "I didn't mean to knock you into the water." His grip on her stayed strong and firm.

"My foot got caught. Between that and the shoulder bump..." She blinked, her breathing coming out harder as she stood there with Evander's arm still wrapped around her, her torso pressed against his.

He cleared his throat and removed his arm. "Sorry." He took a step back.

"You already said that." She suddenly felt awkward and didn't know what to do with her hands.

Evander rubbed the back of his neck. "Um...this way." He resumed walking, not bothering to see if she followed.

Taking a deep breath, Sabine headed after him, wondering why she felt so inept and off kilter simply by touching the man. Over the years, she'd flirted plenty and never had her body react this way before.

Evander led her down another walkway and to a building on the right. She didn't know why they referred to this compound as a palace when it consisted of dozens of individual buildings connected by bridges and walkways all situated over a lake.

He opened the door and motioned for her to enter first. She stepped into a small, square room bathed in natural light from several windows. Off to the left was an opening in the floor revealing the water below. She peered at it and saw several fish swimming.

"This way." Evander headed to the hallway at the back of the room. He led her past several doors, finally stopping at the last one on the right. "This will be your room while you remain here with us." He opened the door but didn't step inside. "I am not permitted to enter."

She nodded, moving around him and into the room. The first thing she noticed was the stark contrast to Lynk. Since the Lynk palace had been built atop a mountain, her room was at the edge of a cliff and her balcony stuck out over the side. While the views were breathtaking, she'd always been nervous being so high up.

Here, the room wasn't even built on land but rather over water. A large bed was on the floor as seemed to be the Avoni custom. Behind the bed, on the wooden wall, were archways with colored glass in them. To the left, the same shaped arches but with clear glass, displaying a view of the lake outside. Several potted plants softened the room. A small fireplace was situated across from the bed. To the right, she found a dressing closet and a small bathing room with a low wooden tub.

"A servant will be along shortly with some clothing for you to wear," Evander said. "She will also assist with anything you may need."

"Thank you." The large bed welcomed her, and the thought of being able to get a good night's sleep without worrying about being attacked or accidentally cuddling with someone sounded divine. However, first she needed to be introduced to the king and queen of Avoni.

"I am going to inform my parents of your arrival and let them know you'll be staying here with us. Assuming everyone is amiable, we'll dine together this evening. That is if I'm still alive." The right corner of his lips rose in a wry smile. "I'll be back in an hour or so." He closed the door and left.

Sabine put her bag down and removed her cape. She went over to the windows, gazing outside at the lake.

A soft knock sounded on the door. Sabine called out for the person to enter.

A middle-aged woman came in wearing red pants and a matching long-sleeved tunic. "My name is Naya," she said. "I am here to help with anything you may need." She set the armful of clothing she carried on the bed.

Sabine thanked her for her kindness. She eyed the clothing, curious as to what had been brought. So far, she'd only seen Avoni people wear long sleeves and pants, usually dark colors, and nothing at all what she would consider beautiful or exciting.

"Shall I draw a bath?" Naya asked.

"That would be wonderful."

Naya went into the bathing room and pressed a lever. Water cascaded out from a spout and into the tub. She knelt and lit a fire beneath it. "That'll take a bit to fill and warm. Would you like for me to start a fire in the hearth in your room?"

"Please."

Once the fire got going, Naya went over to the door. "This string here is attached to a bell. If you need anything, pull the string and someone will immediately attend to you."

"Thank you."

Naya left so Sabine could bathe and dress in private.

After peeling off her dirty clothes, she climbed into the tub, trying not to moan from the glorious heat. Leaning back, she soaked in the water until she became sleepy. Sitting up, she grabbed the soap, washing her skin and hair. She rinsed, then got out and dried off.

Going back into the other room, she examined the clothes Naya had brought. There were a couple of pairs of pants and several long-sleeved tunics similar to what she saw the women in the Avoni delegation wear. All rather plain and simple. Since nothing stood out to her, she randomly picked a pair of pants and one of the tunics, putting them on. She managed to comb her hair, getting all of the knots out from her journey.

Someone knocked.

Sabine went over and answered the door, finding Evander standing there with his hands behind his back. He had on black pants and a tunic made from silk with gold buttons down the center. His hair was washed and combed back, his face shaven. He looked rather handsome.

"Hmm," he said, his eyes scanning her from head to toe. "Did Naya not give you anything nicer to wear?"

"No," Sabine said, looking down at her outfit. She rather liked the pants since they were comfortable and easy to move in. However, she didn't think they were queenly. And since she was going to meet the king and queen of Avoni, she wanted to present herself as a royal and on equal grounds.

A smile spread across Evander's face as he pulled a box out from behind his back. "Then it's a good thing I borrowed this from my sister. Change and meet me out here once you're ready."

She took the box and closed the door. Setting the box on the bed, she opened the lid and sucked in her breath at the sight of a beautiful red and black silk outfit. She quickly put it on and went over to the mirror to see how well it fit her.

The red long-sleeved top was form fitting while the black skirt had red stitching up the side in a pattern of leaves. She'd never worn anything like it before. She ran her hand over the material, reveling in the softness of it. While she was fairly certain the shirt should be tucked under the skirt as she had it, she had to be sure.

Sabine went over to the door and opened it. "Do I look okay?" She turned in a slow circle before Evander.

His eyes widened.

"Please tell me what needs to be fixed." The last thing she wanted to do was make a fashion blunder when meeting the king and queen.

"Nothing." He cleared his throat. "Nothing at all. You look…you look nice."

"Am I wearing this correctly?" she asked, gesturing at the outfit, wanting verification.

"Yes." He held out his arm, so she took it. "We need to be on our way."

"You look nice as well," she said, trying not to stare at him. While they'd been traveling, he'd been more pirate and assassin. Tonight, he was all prince.

Walking along the hallway, Sabine felt a strange awkwardness between them. Wanting to diffuse it, she said, "I'm glad to see you're alive."

Evander chuckled and Sabine relaxed, a calmness extending through her. Even though she was about to meet the king and queen of Avoni and be introduced as the queen of Lynk, she knew she could do this. She would be regal, witty, and gain this kingdom as an ally. She'd met Evander and his sister, Gemma. Both seemed like nice, normal royals. Granted, they were also assassins. The king and queen were trained assassins as well. Everyone in this entire palace was probably an assassin. Even the servants. She was going to die.

"Why'd you stop walking?" Evander asked.

She hadn't even realized she'd stopped. "No reason," she lied as she resumed walking.

Evander opened the door, and they exited the building.

"We'll be dining with my parents and siblings this evening. They are all anxious to meet you." He spoke rather formally, as if nervous.

If he was nervous, then she had reason to be as well.

They started to cross one of the bridges when Sabine stopped, this time to take in her surroundings. Oil lamps hung on the outside of the various buildings while lanterns lined the bridges and walkways, the water reflecting their luminance.

"Is everything all right?" Evander asked.

"It's beautiful here." She let go of his arm and turned in a slow circle. "I've never seen anything like this." Sabine looked up at Evander. This strange man with red hair and green eyes. Her assassin-pirate-prince. She smiled at him. When she had first woken up aboard his boat, she never guessed they would become friends. The more time she spent with him, the more handsome he became.

"Evander!" a woman called out as she joined them on the bridge. She wore an outfit similar to Sabine's, only her top was olive green and her skirt dark brown. When she reached them, she wrapped Evander in a hug and kissed his cheek.

Sabine took a step back, startled. Evander had never mentioned anything before about being attached. She should have known. Someone like him would have to have many women vying for his affection.

The beautiful woman with dark hair and eyes looked at Sabine.

"I'd like to introduce you to my sister, Carin," Evander said.

A strange relief filled Sabine. "You two look nothing alike."

"I'll take that as a compliment," Carin said with a smile. "It's nice to meet you. I'm glad the dress fits, though I think it looks much better on you than on me."

"Let's go to supper together," Evander said, offering Sabine his arm again.

Sabine took it, and the three of them headed across the bridge.

"How long will you be staying with us?" Carin asked.

"I'm not certain. There are a few extenuating circumstances we are dealing with." She didn't know how much Evander had told his family about her situation. "Once everything is settled, I shall return to my home in Bakley."

"Wait," Carin said, moving to stand in front of them and blocking the pathway. "Are you *Princess* Sabine Ludwig of Bakley?" She raised her eyebrows.

"Oh, I'm sorry." It was still hard for her to think of Lynk as her home and not where she'd grown up. "I meant Lynk."

"Technically, she's Queen Sabine Manfred now," Evander said, speaking to his shoes and rocking back on his heels.

Carin hit her brother. "You didn't tell me you brought someone of such importance home to meet the parents," she chided him.

Sabine had been under the impression Evander had at least told his family who she was.

"Wait, you're married?" Carin folded her arms and eyed Sabine.

"Yes," Sabine replied. She decided to not say anything else on the matter until she'd been formally introduced to the king and queen.

"I do remember receiving an announcement that Rainer wed and declared some woman his wife and queen," Carin said. "That's you?"

Sabine didn't know why this was so difficult for her to grasp. "Yes."

"I plan on explaining everything over supper when the family is together," Evander said, waving his arm for Carin to get out of the way.

"You married King Rainer without the League's permission?" Carin asked, raising her eyebrows.

"I did," Sabine replied.

"Huh." Carin glanced between the two of them. "And you're here unaccompanied with my brother?"

"Your brother is my escort. Again, we'll explain everything over supper."

"Just get out of the way," Evander mumbled.

Carin raised her arms in placation. "I'm impressed." She stepped aside, and they resumed walking.

"Impressed?" Sabine asked.

"Like you said, we'll wait until my mother and father are with us. This should be good." She smiled and sped up.

"This supper is going to be a disaster," Sabine said.

"It'll be fine." Evander reached out with his free hand, placing it over her hand that held onto his arm. "Besides, I'm here to protect you. I'll make sure you're not dragged to the dungeon and put in chains."

She rolled her eyes. "You need to stop bringing that up." She realized how ridiculous it was now that she'd seen the palace. Clearly they didn't have a dungeon. If someone wronged them, the king and queen probably just killed them on the spot. Threw the body in the water for fish food.

He chuckled. "I love watching you get all uncomfortable when I do. It's hilarious."

"It's so hilarious I can't stop laughing," she deadpanned.

Carin glanced over her shoulder at the two of them before she pulled the door open to one of the larger buildings.

Sabine stepped inside.

"Excuse me," Carin said, "I need to speak privately with my brother for a moment." She closed the door, remaining outside with Evander.

Startled, Sabine stood there, wondering what was so important that Carin had to talk with Evander right this moment and why it couldn't wait until after they ate. The king and queen were expecting them.

Mumbled voices came from the other side of the door. Glancing around, Sabine didn't see anyone, so she leaned against the door, trying to hear what they were discussing. She couldn't make out any of the words. Afraid someone would catch her eavesdropping, she moved away from the door and tried to at least pretend to be patiently waiting for them.

She found herself standing in a square room similar to the one in the building where her room was. There were three hallways that jutted off of this room.

The door swung open and Carin and Evander entered.

"Shall we?" Evander said, not meeting her eyes as he gestured to the hallway at the back of the room. Carin headed that way, so Sabine followed, noticing Evander fold his hands together behind his back.

They went down a short corridor which opened to a dining room. A rectangular table, with six place settings, was situated in the center of the room, taking up a majority of the space. Several round lanterns hung from the ceiling, casting the room in a soft glow. The wall across from where Sabine stood was lined floor to ceiling with windows, showcasing the glassy lake outside. Four potted trees, one in each corner of the room, added to the ambiance.

Going farther into the room, Sabine said, "I see why you found Lynk such a strange place."

"What do you mean?" Carin asked.

"Lynk is hot, humid, open, and bright," Sabine explained.

"Most of the cities are built on mountains." Here everything was green, it rained constantly, the air was chilly, and the buildings were more closed and contained. "At least here in Avoni, I never feel like I'm going to tumble to my death if I lean out of a window." She smiled, trying to keep the mood light.

Carin raised her eyebrows. "That is…interesting."

A door to the left opened, and three people entered the room. The first was an older gentleman in his late forties with dark brown hair and eyes. Evander introduced him as his father, King Kai Botoko. At the king's side was a woman of similar age though she had auburn hair and bright blue eyes. Evander introduced her as his mother, Queen Serilda Botoko. The other person Sabine recognized as Gemma.

"My eldest sister, Lyra, lives at a different palace with her husband and two young children," Evander said. "Everyone, this is Queen Sabine Manfred of Lynk."

"It's a pleasure to meet you," Sabine said, with a slight tilt of her head, as she'd seen her mother do when royals from other kingdoms came to visit. She realized she should have asked Evander if there were any particular customs she needed to be aware of.

"Welcome," Kai said. "I must admit I was surprised to receive King Rainer's declaration that he'd married you and crowned you queen."

"Were you?" Sabine asked. "I thought you sent the delegation to Lynk to approve of our wedding. I should think me marrying the king, as planned, wouldn't come as a surprise." She knew the statement was bold, but she wanted to assert her position here and let them know she couldn't be pushed around easily.

The king and queen exchanged a look that Sabine couldn't decipher.

"Let's all take a seat," Kai said, gesturing to the table, and not acknowledging Sabine's comment.

Evander pulled out a chair for Sabine. When she sat, he whispered, "Bold. Well done."

"I was afraid it was dungeon worthy," she whispered back.

He chuckled and took the seat next to her. The king and queen sat at either end of the table while Gemma and Carin sat directly across from Sabine and Evander.

Several servants entered carrying plates, setting one before each person.

Sabine reluctantly peered down and was disheartened to see several things on her plate that she didn't recognize. She was starving and could really go for some meat and potatoes instead of…whatever this was before her. It looked like some sort of fish and several vegetables.

Once the servants left, the king started eating and everyone followed suit. "Tell us, Queen Sabine, how you came to be in Avoni with Evander."

A loaded question, and one that needed to be answered carefully. Evander and her should have discussed all of this ahead of time. However, she'd been so focused on meeting the king and queen that she hadn't stopped to consider what she should specifically say to them. She knew what she *shouldn't* say.

"The League was gathering, and Sabine wanted to meet with her brother. I offered to escort her," Evander said.

Under the table, Sabine folded her hands in her lap. Evander reached over and took hold of her hand, squeezing it once before releasing it. She had to trust him to lead this conversation. Forcing herself to appear relaxed, she lifted her fork and picked at her food.

"I didn't know the League was meeting here in Avoni," Queen Serilda said.

Sabine felt her face heat up. It was clear they had some explaining to do and couldn't gloss over the situation. Evander's parents were intuitive. She'd need to not only watch what she said but how she behaved around them.

"We met at the usual place," Evander said, taking a bite of his food.

"Can you please explain to us why the two of you are here then?" Kai said, taking a drink from his cup.

"If I may?" Evander said to Sabine.

"Of course," she replied, trying to figure out why he was asking her permission to tell the story.

He proceeded to explain how he'd escorted her to Nisk where she met up with her brother. Then he said that when she went to return to Lynk with Prince Anton, they discovered an Avoni assassin tracking her. "I offered to escort her back to Lynk to ensure she made it there safely."

"I'm still not understanding why the two of you are here in Avoni," Serilda said. "It seems an odd way to return to Lynk."

"Ex is tracking us," Evander said. "We've led him here."

The king set his fork down, sitting back in his chair and watching his son.

Not wanting anything else to eat, Sabine pushed her plate away.

"If you have something to say, Father, just say it." Evander took another bite of his food.

"Do you want to go first or shall I?" Serilda asked her husband.

Kai took a deep breath, rubbed his face, and took a drink of wine. "Evander, do you realize the position you've put us in? King Rainer has every right to question our intentions. Escorting the queen back to Lynk is one thing, luring an assassin here is another. The two of you have been traveling alone. It doesn't look good. King Rainer has every right to raise his sword against us now." He glanced at Sabine, as if not sure how much to say in front of her.

"We were on our way to get guards to accompany us," Evander said. "Then we got sidetracked with the attacks." He took another bite of food. "Oh, and I, uh, agreed to marry King Rainer's sister, Princess Lottie." He shoved more food in his mouth.

The room went uncomfortably silent. Sabine knew everyone was trying to process what Evander had said. While sitting there waiting for them to respond, she tried not to squirm in her seat. This felt like being back home and having to explain something she'd done to her father and awaiting his verdict.

Sabine decided it was time for her to speak. "Once the assassin who's after me is dealt with, I plan on returning to Lynk and doing everything in my power to make sure there is peace among all our kingdoms." She tried to look reassuring as she sat there before the king and queen of Avoni. Truth be told, she felt weak. Insignificant. But she knew Rainer needed her and she was tied to him for life now. She would do everything she could to maintain peace. Her own wants, desires, and happiness no longer mattered.

"How do you plan on accomplishing that?" Kai asked.

A good question and one Sabine had been considering. She had a couple of ideas but didn't want to share them with anyone. "The less you know, the better," she responded.

"Is my son involved in whatever plan you've concocted?" Kai asked.

"No, he's not." And her plan was only an idea right now. She hadn't figured out anything specific and didn't know if it would even work. She'd have to either ask Anton to help or investigate the written laws on her own to be sure before she did anything.

"I don't know how your husband will respond when he

learns you're here in our palace. I don't want him to think we've kidnapped you," Serilda said, looking at her son as she spoke as if she knew what he'd done.

Sabine understood her concern.

"His army is large enough to invade our kingdom," Gemma commented.

"I think the goal here is to prevent any sort of a war," Sabine said.

"Then you should leave and go home," Gemma muttered, her voice low and soft.

"She will," Evander said. "I just have to take care of Ex."

"Why?" Gemma asked.

"Because if an Avoni assassin kills her, Rainer will invade our kingdom. Taking care of Ex ensures Avoni's safety."

"And what of Rainer's…other activities?" Kai asked.

"I have no intention of going to war with any other kingdoms," Sabine said with as much conviction as she could muster.

"I'm not sure you speak for your husband," Serilda said.

Sabine felt her face warm. "I understand." And she did. "But I see a way to avoid Rainer going to war." She hoped. She liked that the queen interjected her thoughts on the matter. Kai and Serilda seemed to be true partners both in marriage and in ruling. However, that was only the impression she'd gotten from her brief interaction with them.

"I will think about the matter," Kai said. "We'll talk more later. For now, you are allowed to remain here under our protection. The assassin, Ex, will be dealt with."

"Thank you." It felt as if the tension in the room eased and Sabine could relax.

"I have a question," Carin said. "Why do you trust my brother to keep you safe? Are you friends?"

Sabine peered over at Evander and found him watching

her. She smiled at him. "Friends?" she said to Carin, not looking at her. "You think I actually like your brother?"

He raised a single eyebrow. "Of course she likes me," he responded, keeping his focus on Sabine and not once looking at his sister. "How could she not? I'm an excellent conversationalist with a witty personality."

Sabine chuckled. "That is debatable." She looked away from him and reached for her cup of water, taking a drink.

"Forgive me for saying this, but you have quite the reputation for being a flirt," Gemma said. "Now that you're married, I hope that is no longer the case."

Sabine blinked, heat searing through her as she looked over at Gemma, confirming that Evander's sister was indeed talking to her. She didn't know why Gemma felt the need to bring it up. She pursed her lips, knowing she had to respond. If this were her family, she'd push right back and not cower. She had to behave the same now.

Sabine looked at Gemma. "Why? Are you afraid I'm going to flirt with you?" She batted her eyelashes.

Evander burst out laughing.

"No," Gemma responded, looking from Evander to Sabine. "I was just concerned about my brother."

"Good grief," Evander said as he stood. "I'm going to take my leave before this gets any more embarrassing." He pulled Sabine's chair out. "I'll escort you back to your room," he said to her. And then to everyone else, "It's been a long day, and we're both exhausted."

"It was a pleasure to meet you," Serilda said.

As Sabine stood, she smiled sweetly and said, "Thank you all for a lovely evening." She bowed her head, showing respect for the king and queen, before following Evander from the room.

Outside, the wind blew softly. Sabine folded her arms, trying to stay warm.

The two of them walked along a pathway and onto one of the many bridges.

Halfway across, Sabine stopped to admire it all. Leaning her arms on the railing, she took in the glowing lanterns reflecting on the water, the bright moon, and the twinkling stars. "This may be the first time I've seen the sky here in Avoni." Granted, there were still some thick clouds here and there.

When Evander didn't respond, she glanced over her shoulder. He stood behind her, leaning against the railing, watching her. "What is it?" she asked.

He shrugged. "Nothing."

Not believing him, she went over and joined him, leaning her back against the railing and imitating his stance. "Is everything okay?" She looked at his torso as if she could see the cut through his tunic. Maybe the exertion of the day had taken its toll on him.

"Everything is fine." He tilted his head back, looking up at the sky.

"Can I ask you something?"

He peered at her, his green eyes almost glowing under the moonlight. "You can ask me anything." His voice rang with sincerity.

"Are your sisters normally this overprotective of you?" What she really wanted to know was what Carin had said to him before supper. However, coming out and asking seemed impolite and nosy.

He reached back, placing his hands on the railing. "I'm the youngest. I'm sure you know what that feels like with older siblings, even when you're old enough to take care of yourself."

"I do." Sabine turned and faced the water, sliding her hands over the railing. Her left hand extended toward Evander's but not quite touching his.

"Gemma...well, she was interested in a man who my parents didn't care for. His skills weren't as honed as one would expect. I expressed my concern over the match. I think she was just trying to get me back at supper. Don't take anything she said too seriously."

Sabine nodded. "And Carin?" She looked at Evander's long fingers curled around the railing. She wanted to trace her finger over the back of his hand but didn't dare touch him.

"She just wanted to know what was going on before supper." He shifted his hand and his finger touched hers.

Neither of them moved.

"I should get you to your room," Evander whispered.

Sabine nodded. Needing to distract herself from the man standing at her side, his finger touching hers, she asked, "Is there a chance the assassin could get past the wall and sentries?"

Evander shook his head. "It would be suicide for him to try to even approach the wall. He will wait for us to leave, then he'll strike."

"I don't want you getting hurt protecting me." She couldn't live with herself if he died because of her. He didn't owe her anything, and yet, he'd become her protector.

He nudged her with his shoulder. "Don't forget you asked me to train you. How about tomorrow morning we work together after breakfast?"

"I'd like that." She looked up at him. With them each facing a different direction, shoulder to shoulder, his face felt close to hers. His lips were right there. If she leaned in ever so slightly...

Evander pushed away from the railing and straightened, breaking the connection that had been brewing between them. He reached out, taking her hand, and gently leading her from the bridge. They walked in silence to the building where she was staying.

Sabine wondered if it only housed guests or if it was where the royal family had their bedchambers as well. She hadn't slept on her own in several nights, and the thought of being away from Evander made her feel strange.

Inside, he led her down the hallway and stopped at her door. "Goodnight, Sabine," he said, his voice husky. Reaching out, he cupped her cheek, rubbing his thumb against her skin. "Sweet dreams." His eyes searched hers a moment before he suddenly turned and left.

With her breathing unsteady, Sabine went into her room, odd feelings inundating her. Excitement, happiness, longing, and fear all bombarded her. She had no idea why she felt this way.

Chapter Nine

Sabine awoke in a cold sweat. Feeling a sense of wrongness, she sat up, glancing about her room. Nothing seemed out of place, and no one else was in the room. She missed her dog, Harta. Whenever the animal was near, she felt safer. She laid back down, her heart beating erratically. Unable to relax, she got out of bed and padded over to the window, looking outside. The clouds had covered the moon and stars, making it hard to see anything. Her hands shook, and a light sheen of sweat covered her forehead.

Naya had said if she needed anything—no matter the time—to ring her. Sabine went over to the rope and pulled it. She stood there, waiting. For some strange reason, she hoped Evander came. His presence would ease the tension building inside of her.

A soft knock came from her door.

"Come in," Sabine said.

Naya entered, wearing a sleeping gown. "What can I do for you?" she asked.

"I don't know," Sabine admitted. "Something feels wrong. Maybe a cup of tea will help?"

"Of course." Naya left the room.

Sabine went back over to the windows, staring outside. A light rain started to fall. It felt as if she stood there for quite some time—far longer than it should to make a cup of tea. Worry filled her, and she began to pace about the room. Something was wrong.

A soft knock sounded on her door again. She rushed over and opened it to find Evander standing there, his hands on either side of the doorframe. Shirtless, his pants hung low on his hips. Even in the dark lighting, she could see the curves of his torso and the bandage across his wound.

She took a step back, forcing her eyes to focus on his face. "What's going on?" she whispered, noticing his wet hair.

"Naya woke me and said you told her something felt wrong. I went out and spoke with the sentries on duty. Ex was spotted nearby. We think he's surveying the area. He won't come near the palace. Not only are there traps, but to make a move against my parents is treason. He wouldn't survive." Water dripped onto his face, running down the side of his cheek.

"I didn't know Naya would tell you."

"You need to learn to always trust your instincts," he replied.

She moved closer to him. "Regardless, I'm sorry I woke you."

He ran a hand over his face. "I was up."

"Couldn't sleep?"

He shook his head.

She reached up, placing the palm of her hand on his cheek, as he'd done to her earlier tonight.

He closed his eyes. "I was…trying to think of a way to get rid of Ex." He opened his eyes, looking directly into hers.

"Will you come in?" she asked, needing the comfort of his presence. Without him, she'd never be able to fall back asleep.

"I can't," he whispered. "But if you want, I can remain out in the hallway as your guard."

She couldn't believe he'd be willing to do that for her. "That's not necessary," she said. "Go back to your room. You need to sleep."

He nodded but didn't move. "Do you still want that tea?"

"No." She needed to let him sleep. He was still recovering from the injury she'd caused him.

"Goodnight, Sabine." He tapped the door frame before turning and walking away.

She watched his retreating form until she could no longer see him. Then she closed her door and climbed back into bed, knowing sleep would not be coming anytime soon.

—

The next morning, Naya arrived with a tray of food for breakfast, surprising Sabine since she'd assumed she'd eat with Evander. After she dressed and ate, Naya led her to an empty room where she was asked to wait.

Alone, Sabine surveyed her surroundings, wondering when Evander would arrive and what they would work on. She wiped her sweaty palms on her pants, hoping he still planned to train her. To the right, a handful of floor to ceiling windows overlooked the lake. Thick clouds covered the sky, and a light rain fell outside. As she meandered around the room, she estimated it to be forty feet by thirty feet. While no furniture adorned the room, there were a few potted plants in each corner. No rugs covered the smooth, dark wood floor.

"Good morning," Evander said.

Feeling a sense of relief, Sabine turned and found him standing just inside the room, leaning against the wall, watching her. "It's about time you showed up," she said, trying to keep the mood light. After last night, she had a surge of emotions raging through her that she didn't want to acknowledge or even consider.

He pushed away from the wall and came farther into the room, his focus solely on her.

Warmth spread through Sabine, and she felt her face heat up. Ignoring her body's reaction to Evander, she asked, "What's on the agenda for today?"

"Same as last time," he said, his voice sounding husky. "I want you to rely on and use your senses."

"Okay." She couldn't look away from him. Something about the intensity of his gaze, the smooth way he walked, the confidence he gave off, pulled her in.

Evander placed his hands on her shoulders. "I'm going to blindfold you." He turned her so her back was to him. He let go and then reached in front of her, revealing a black silk scarf. He placed it over her eyes, tying it at the back of her head. With the fabric secure, he put his hands once again on her shoulders. "I want you to focus on your surroundings," he whispered in her ear. "Take a deep breath, and let me know what you see and feel."

She shivered from the warm caress of his breath and the nearness of him. "Obviously, I see nothing." Her voice came out breathy, so she cleared her throat, not wanting him to know he had any effect on her.

Evander chuckled, making her toes curl.

She could feel the heat of his body behind her, hear the gentleness of his breathing, and imagine the grin on his face. It annoyed her that she could be so in tune to him. However, it had to be because they'd just spent so many days alone together—nothing more. It couldn't possibly be anything else.

"I want you to see without looking," Evander whispered next to her other ear. "Use all your senses because your eyes can deceive you. Being blindfolded will force you to focus on what you hear and smell. Trust your instincts." He squeezed her shoulders.

She took a deep breath, clearing her mind and trying to focus. The first thing she noticed was Evander. "I smell you," she admitted.

"How do you know it's me?"

A good question and an answer she didn't want to give. She'd recognize his scent anywhere. "I don't know," she lied.

"I think you do," he whispered, his chest pressing against her back. "You need to learn how to identify various scents so you know who or what they belong to. I'm sure it's nothing you've ever had to pinpoint before, so take your time."

She breathed in Evander, trying to put into words what scents were uniquely his. "You smell like..." She hadn't really thought about it before and found it difficult to formulate the right words. He didn't have strong, distinguishing smells— probably on purpose—but there was something that was distinctly him. "I don't know. Sweat maybe? It's just the smell of you."

His nose glided along her neck as he breathed her in. She held perfectly still, afraid to move.

"And you smell like a hint of rosemary. It's hard since these clothes don't belong to you, but I can smell it on your skin."

She'd never considered how she smelled before. Or ever thought Evander would have smelled her like that. Being blindfolded only enhanced the feeling of his touch, making her skin tingle.

Evander released her shoulders and stepped away from her. "What else do you sense?" he asked.

Her back suddenly felt cold without him touching her. She stood there, listening, trying to figure out where Evander had gone or what was happening. Something shifted in the air in front of her; however, she was certain Evander was still standing behind her. She couldn't say how she knew other than instinct. "Is someone else in the room?"

"Why do you think that? Put it into words." His voice still came from behind her.

The air smelled fresher. "I think a door opened because of the smell."

"Good," Evander said. "What else?"

She tried to focus on the room again. "I think someone is in here."

"Why?"

"The air shifted." It sounded dumb to say, but it was the only way she could express her thoughts. "And...I think I smell jasmine." She couldn't be certain, but there was definitely a light floral scent that hadn't been there before. A soft patter, like footsteps, came from Sabine's right. She reached out, her hand touching a narrow, boney arm. "Are you a woman?"

"I am," Gemma said.

Sabine hadn't realized Gemma would be aiding in the training today.

"Now listen for a moment, then tell us what you think is happening in this room," Gemma said. It sounded as if she'd stepped a few feet away.

Utter silence greeted Sabine. She strained to listen, not hearing a single thing. She no longer felt either Evander or Gemma nearby. Even though she had the blindfold on, she closed her eyes and took a deep breath, forcing herself to relax. An odd smell filled the room—barely there but there nonetheless. A hint of food and soap. Then she heard the soft pitter-patter of feet followed by people breathing.

She wiped her hands on her pants. "The room is filled with people." She was certain of it.

"Astute," Gemma answered. "It has been a pleasure assisting you this morning."

Sabine heard the sound of footsteps on the floor again, this time heading toward the door, and she assumed everyone was leaving the room. When it became silent again, she asked, "Are we done?" She reached up, removing her blindfold, expecting to be alone with Evander.

Serilda stood before Sabine, startling her.

"Forgive me, Your Majesty, I didn't expect to see you here." Sabine clutched the blindfold in her hands, wondering where Evander had gone.

The queen smiled. "I want to speak with you." She wore a long-sleeved black top with a matching skirt. No crown adorned her head, and if Sabine hadn't known this was the queen standing before her, she never would have guessed.

Glancing about the room, she didn't see anyone else. "I was just training with Evander and Gemma," she said, as if she needed to explain why she was in the room.

"Let's take a walk." Serilda gestured toward the door and headed that way, the expectation for Sabine to follow clear.

Suddenly nervous, Sabine trailed after the woman. They exited the building and went along one of the wooden pathways. She had no idea what the queen wanted to discuss with her and hoped it wasn't about Evander or the kidnapping.

Serilda led the way across one of the bridges and to a large gazebo.

Sabine wanted to ask how all of this had been built over water but knew now was not the time for that conversation.

"No one will be able to overhear us here," Serilda said as

she entered the gazebo furnished with two cushioned benches and a table.

The gazebo was situated over the water, and no other buildings or walkways were nearby—just the bridge they'd taken to reach it. The roof offered protection from the rain though the air remained chilly. The queen sat on one of the benches, so Sabine sat on the other.

There was something peaceful and serene being out on the water like this. "Your kingdom is beautiful," Sabine said, gazing out at her surroundings. Several large trees lined one part of the lake, their branches hanging low over the water.

"I've heard the palace in Lynk is beautiful as well," the queen said as she folded her hands on her lap.

Sabine felt as if this conversation were a test of sorts. As to what she was being tested on, she had no idea. However, she knew she needed to tread carefully. They were both queens of kingdoms capable of causing great harm. She smiled and replied, "I suppose it depends on what your definition of beauty is." The Lynk palace had always scared her since it had been built so high up. It always felt as if she would tumble to her death at any moment.

"Very true." Serilda watched Sabine for a moment before saying, "I'll get to the point of this conversation since I have a lot to do today. My son is very important to me and to this kingdom."

"I'm sure he is." So this was about Evander. Sabine clutched her hands together, preparing herself to answer as vaguely as possible.

"He cares for you. I can see it."

An interesting way to start this conversation. "We have become friends." Though friends didn't feel like quite the right word.

"I'm concerned that when you return to Lynk, your husband will question your time with my son."

A valid concern. "I've already written to Rainer letting him know the situation. I'll be frank with you." She took a deep breath and continued, "My husband needs me alive in order to maintain his position as king. Your son is doing everything in his power to keep me alive. Rainer will be grateful, I'm sure."

The queen crossed one leg over the other. "If I can see your *friendship* with my son, so will King Rainer."

"I think Lynk having a strong connection to Avoni will benefit both kingdoms in the long run. If that can come from my friendship with your son, then that is a good thing." It would hopefully allow their two kingdoms to work together—especially if Lottie was to marry Evander.

Serilda raised a single eyebrow, the look condescending. "You clearly do not know your husband well."

"We haven't known each other for very long."

"You haven't known my son for very long either and yet, you seem to know him."

A point well made and taken. Sabine didn't have an answer for Serilda. The men were so vastly different that she couldn't even compare the two.

"Rainer is a jealous man."

Sabine remembered how Rainer had reacted to Markis. However, given that his mother had had an affair with one of her guards, she understood his behavior on the matter.

"I can tell by the look on your face that you know exactly what I'm talking about," Serilda said. She stood and went over to the railing, gazing at the lake surrounding them. After a minute, she turned and faced Sabine. "I need you to be completely honest with me right now. Your life depends on it."

"How so?" Sabine feared the queen would ask if her son kidnapped her. Because if Rainer found out that Evander kidnapped Sabine, he would unleash his army against Avoni. The queen had a right to be concerned.

"As long as you answer truthfully, you will live." Serilda's eyes narrowed. "And trust me when I say I'll know if you're lying to me."

A sheen of sweat covered Sabine's forehead. She would have to be honest with the queen—and she'd promised Evander she wouldn't tell them he'd taken her. "What if I can't answer your question without breaking a promise?"

"Then tell me that, and we'll go from there." She folded her arms.

Sabine nodded. "Okay."

"Did you know about Rainer's plans with regards to the Avoni delegation?" Serilda asked, her eyes intently watching Sabine.

She wasn't sure if the queen was referring to the night of the masquerade ball. "Do you mean about him and your ship?"

"Yes." Her eyes narrowed slightly.

"He didn't tell me anything if that's what you're asking."

"But clearly you know something. Tell me what you know and how you came to know it."

Sabine swallowed, trying to recall everything. She didn't want to get a detail wrong and be put to death for it. "When I was searching for my sister's killer, I came by some palace gossip. A few of the women thought the masquerade ball Rainer was throwing was as a distraction so he could have the Avoni ship searched."

"Why would he have the ship searched?"

"To see if there was evidence someone from Avoni killed my sister." But by that point, her and Rainer were married, so he knew the assassin was hired by someone in his inner circle—if he hadn't already discovered it was Lottie. Knowing this, she didn't understand why he'd search the Avoni ship...

unless it was to plant evidence. The night she'd discovered her sister's killer, the assassin had been doing that very thing —planting evidence to make it look like someone in the delegation had killed Alina. Sabine wiped her forehead.

The queen's eyes narrowed even more.

Sabine needed to be totally honest. "Now that I'm thinking it through, I see he couldn't have been searching it. He had to have been planting evidence." Wanting to pin the assassination on Avoni so he could say he solved the murder, strengthen his position as king, and have a reason to attack his neighboring kingdom.

"Is there anything else?" the queen asked.

"I already told your son Lottie is the one who hired the assassin, Ex. I saw her and Ex in the rooms the Avoni delegation was staying in. They planted evidence there. However, I took it on my way out. I couldn't read it since it was in another language. It got destroyed."

"And that's everything you know?" The queen pushed off the railing and came closer to Sabine. "There isn't anything else you need to tell me?"

Sabine wiped her sweaty palms on her thighs, trying to think through everything to see if she missed something. Other than the kidnapping, she thought she covered it all. "I don't think so."

Serilda nodded slowly. "I want to reiterate that there isn't anything else that you know about the delegation I sent to Avoni?"

"I can't think of anything." Rainer hadn't let her join in on any of the talks the two kingdoms had, so she hadn't interacted with them much.

Serilda patted Sabine's shoulder before sitting beside her on the bench. "You are not aware that King Rainer killed my entire delegation before they left Lynk?"

"What?" She must have heard the queen incorrectly.

"Everyone in the Avoni delegation, except Evander, was murdered."

It felt as if Sabine had just been tossed off a cliff. She couldn't breathe. She bent forward, resting her elbows on her thighs and gripping her head with her hands. "When did this happen?"

"The night of the masquerade."

The night Evander had kidnapped Sabine. "How?" she asked, unable to believe that Rainer had managed to murder a dozen assassins on his own. He had to have used his army to accomplish such a feat. But perhaps it was a mistake. However, she couldn't turn a blind eye to the facts. She'd seen with her own eyes Lynk soldiers escorting Bakley children north toward Lynk. She'd read Rainer's mother's journal revealing his father had abused and eventually killed his mother. When she saw Rainer fight, she'd seen brutality in him. Again, just because she didn't want to believe it didn't mean it wasn't true.

"From what we've gathered, King Rainer had holes put in the bottom of the ship. When my people left, his soldiers on land shot fire tipped arrows at the vessel. There are also rumors he had some sort of poison on board, but I can't verify that."

Which meant the people in the Avoni delegation had either burned or drowned. What a horrible way to die. "Why would he do something so awful?" She couldn't think of one rational reason for him to murder them.

"That is a very good question." Tears filled the queen's eyes. "Is there anything you haven't told me?"

Sabine rubbed her face. The queen had to have known and been friends with the people who were killed. Her grief had to be immense. "There is one thing I haven't told you," she whispered. "One thing I promised Evander I wouldn't reveal."

Serilda's shoulders sagged, as if she knew. As if Sabine's words had confirmed her suspicions.

Panic gripped Sabine. "It can't have anything to do with me being here in Avoni or with Evander."

"Are you certain?" Serilda asked.

"Rainer's plan had to have been in place long before I left Lynk." She'd known he'd planned to do something with the Avoni ship—she just hadn't thought he'd destroy it along with the delegation.

"The reports I'm receiving indicate Rainer retaliated against the delegation because one of its members took you." Serilda stood.

"That's not possible," Sabine insisted. "Both events happened simultaneously."

"Did my son kidnap you?" Serilda asked point blank.

Sabine nodded.

The queen sighed. "This complicates things," she mumbled.

"Rainer never has to know," Sabine insisted.

"Possibly. But what you should be asking yourself is if Rainer thought you were on board that ship he destroyed."

A wave of dizziness came over Sabine, and she bent over. "He needs me. He'll lose his throne if I don't give him an heir by the time he turns twenty-five." Her voice sounded lifeless, monotone. How she felt right now. But she knew there was more to it than that. Rainer had a backup. However, she was under the impression the backup child only worked if it was passed off as hers. But if Rainer had purposefully killed her and then didn't tell anyone she was dead…Sabine rubbed her face then looked up at the queen. "I'm so sorry for your loss. I didn't know any of this would happen." And now that she'd written that letter to Rainer, if he thought he'd killed her— which she didn't think he'd do—now he knew she was alive.

"Oftentimes our actions have consequences we don't

anticipate." The queen leaned against the railing, observing Sabine.

"Are you going to retaliate?" she asked, wondering if there was more to this conversation than the queen trying to discover Sabine's involvement in all of this.

"I haven't decided what we're going to do." She folded her arms.

"Evander agreed to marry Princess Lottie," Sabine said. "That might help relations between our kingdoms."

"Possibly. Or when he agreed to marry her it only confirmed Rainer's suspicions that Evander was the one who'd taken you. After all, Evander is the sole survivor—which I am grateful for."

Sabine felt sick to her stomach at all the queen had revealed.

"I know my son brought you here for an important, valid reason. However, I think your stay here should be short. Avoni families will be asking questions. You will be seen as the enemy, and you're in a land of assassins. I can only guarantee your safety for one week. That is all. I suggest you find somewhere else to hide, or return to your husband and leave my son out of this." And with that, she turned and left the gazebo, not giving Sabine a chance to respond.

Stunned by all that had been revealed, her eyes filled with tears. Sabine couldn't believe Rainer had killed the entire Avoni delegation. She truly did not know the man she'd married. It seemed with each passing day, things only became more and more complicated. She blinked the tears from her eyes and stood, about to head back to her room, when she realized she had no idea how to get there. If she wandered around the compound, she was bound to run into someone who'd help her—unless word about the delegation had spread. In that case, she could cross paths with someone who'd lost a loved one. The people who lived here in Avoni had to hate Lynk, and now that Sabine was the queen of that kingdom, they had to hate her by extension. Being here in the land of assassins no longer seemed like a wise idea since she was their enemy.

Feeling exposed out in the open, she slid to the floor and leaned against the posts of the railing, curling her legs to her chest and wrapping her arms around them. Everything was a mess, and she didn't know how to fix any of it. If she went walking around here, someone could kill her out of spite. The worst part was she couldn't even blame them. Her *husband* was responsible for killing the entire delegation. She wondered if Evander knew.

Leaning her cheek on her knee, she tried not to cry, but the tears came of their own accord. Right now, she really needed her sister to talk to. Sabine had married a monster—a man who wanted to take over all the kingdoms, wage war against thousands if he had to, and for what? Power? Money? Why couldn't he be happy with what he had? And her role in all of this was to simply be a breeder. She was expected to have his children and then be gone—like Rainer's own mother. Sabine was a means to an end.

Her life suddenly felt rather bleak. If only there was a way to change the course of it.

Footsteps sounded on the bridge. Sabine peered around the post and spotted Evander approaching the gazebo. His face remained blank, unreadable. If he knew about the delegation, he would hate her. Maybe he'd kill her himself and be done with her. He'd save himself the trouble of dealing with the assassin, and he'd have retribution for all of those families who'd lost a loved one.

Evander stepped into the gazebo.

Sabine refused to meet his eyes. Embarrassment, horror, and sadness all warred within her. She had no idea what to say to him. She couldn't be the queen of a kingdom responsible for such atrocities. And yet, she was. She held some responsibility for what had happened. Maybe she could have stopped it if she'd been more involved, had pushed Rainer to tell her his plans, or even if…well, she didn't know. But she could have and should have done more.

Evander squatted before her. "I've been looking for you," he said, his voice soft and gentle, almost caressing. "When you didn't return to your room, I got worried."

She shrugged, still not looking him in the face. She had no idea what to say or how to apologize for something Rainer —her husband—had done. She didn't want to be associated with him. However, it was too late for that. She was his wife and the queen of Lynk.

"I take it my mother told you," Evander murmured, moving to sit beside her.

"How long have you known?" she asked, needing to know.

"I just found out last night."

"You must hate me." Her voice cracked.

"Why would I hate you?"

She wiped her tears with the edge of her sleeve, unable to speak. She didn't know the right words to express her sorrow or how to tell him how sorry she was for what had happened.

"You had nothing to do with their deaths," he said, wrapping his arm around her shoulders. "It's not your fault."

As the queen of Lynk, she was responsible. The tears kept falling.

Evander sat there holding her, not bothering to say anything else.

There was nothing he could say.

Sabine stood in front of the windows in her room, staring outside, as a light rain fell. She'd been standing there most of the day. Thinking. After Alina's death, she'd jumped headfirst into agreeing to marry Rainer without fully understanding the consequences of her choice. All she'd thought about was revenge. Now, all she wanted to do was to return to Lynk and demand Rainer make Lottie pay for having Alina murdered. She wanted Rainer to be held accountable for killing the delegation. She wanted the Bakley children returned to their families. But she held no sway with the king, and he would not listen to her. To outsmart Rainer, she would have to come up with a plan. She had a few ideas, and one in particular that she thought might be crazy enough to work. But she wasn't ready yet. She needed some more information before she could do anything.

A soft knock sounded on her door. "Sabine?" Evander called out.

"Come in." She didn't hear the door open and close but rather saw Evander's reflection in the window as he came up behind her.

He stood there, his arms folded, watching her. He lifted his right hand, rubbing his jawbone. "I wanted to check on you," he said, his voice soft.

"I didn't think you were allowed in my room," she whispered.

"I'm not."

"Then why are you in here?"

He took a step forward, coming to stand at her side. "Everyone already thinks we're having an affair."

"Why do you suppose that is?" She'd been wondering what it was about her and Evander's friendship that gave his family pause. At first, she thought they got along like brother and sister. But deep down, she knew that wasn't the case. She no longer thought of Evander that way.

"They're just being overly cautious," he said, not meeting her gaze in the reflection.

"You being in here won't help the situation."

"Then no one can know I'm in here."

She turned toward him but he remained facing the window, not meeting her eyes. "Is something bothering you?" He wasn't acting like himself. After she asked the question, she wished she could take it back. The entire delegation he'd traveled to Lynk with had been killed. Of course he was upset. She reached out and rubbed his arm. "I'm sorry." There was nothing else she could say.

"We need to deal with the assassin," Evander said, still not meeting her eyes. "He's been spotted outside the wall again."

She moved to stand in front of him. "Are you mad at me?" She wouldn't blame him if he was.

"No." He finally looked at her.

The more time she spent with him, the more handsome he became. She took a deep breath, letting the air out slowly. "Then what's the matter?"

His focus went back outside the window to the lake, not looking at her. She wanted him to turn his beautiful eyes her way again. When he looked at her, she felt like she was home.

He shook his head. "Honestly?"

"Please."

He glanced at her. "I spoke with my parents. They're not happy with me. I've been reprimanded for kidnapping you."

"I'm sorry I told your mother." In her sorrow, she'd forgotten she told the queen about what really happened. "She said my life depended on telling her the truth, so I did."

He closed his eyes. "And...they're not happy about our... relationship."

"Our friendship?" she asked. "Isn't us being friends a great benefit to both our kingdoms?"

He peered at her. "My family feels I've formed an unhealthy attachment to you, and you're skewing my thinking and reasoning."

Taken aback, she didn't know what to say. She wasn't manipulating Evander. She truly cared for him.

He ran a hand over his face. "Sabine."

She loved the way he said her name. She smiled at him. When he looked at her, a warmth blossomed inside her.

"Sometimes I can't figure out who you really are," he mumbled.

His words hurt her. "What's that supposed to mean?" They'd spent enough time together that he should have a good idea of her character.

"All our spies say you're a flirt, you have suitor after suitor, and take nothing seriously."

Something unpleasant formed in the pit of her stomach. "Is that so?" The fact that he was even bringing this up and asking her to defend her actions spoke volumes. She would not dignify it with a response.

"But the Sabine I know is none of those things."

The unpleasant sensation in her stomach evaporated as quickly as it had formed.

He reached out and took hold of her hand. "I can't help but wonder who the real Sabine is."

"I ask myself that question all the time." The rain started coming down harder.

"You don't know who you are?" he asked, his voice laced with skepticism.

"No. Do you know who you are all the time?"

His brows drew together.

"Let me put this another way," she said. "When I was in Bakley, living with my family, I was one person. I'd never traveled or been on my own. I was a little spoiled. I was a flirt. Then my sister died, and I went to Lynk. I changed. I had no choice but to become the person I needed to be to survive. You can't tell me you're so old and wise as to know exactly who you are and what you're supposed to do all the time."

The corners of his lips pulled into a smile, and the lines around his eyes softened. "No, I suppose not." He squeezed her hand then released it.

Sabine wasn't sure what exactly was going on between them, but she had a feeling their friendship was teetering on something undefined. She needed to diffuse whatever was building between them. "Good. I'm glad you don't think yourself overly wise," she teased, nudging him.

He chuckled, the sound like honey.

"Now let's figure out what we're going to do about this assassin. Your mother wishes for me to leave within the week, and I think that wise. We can't have rumors spreading about our friendship. I'm sure my husband would be insanely jealous to learn I'm consorting with his enemy."

"Enemy?" he said, his brows raised. "I'm going to be your brother-in-law."

His words repeated over and over in her mind. The thought of him marrying Lottie didn't sit well with her. And Sabine didn't want Evander to be related to her that way. It felt wrong.

Chapter Ten

Sabine silently followed Evander from her room. As he led her through the compound, she didn't pay attention to where they were going since she was lost in her thoughts. Thoughts regarding her relationship with Evander. Ever since that time he jumped on her balcony back in Lynk, she'd felt he was on her side, trying to warn her, not hurt her. Strange how she went from being mad he'd kidnapped her to understanding and trusting him. She even liked spending time with him because he made her laugh. She found herself wanting to be around him since she enjoyed his company. Craved it even.

"In here," Evander said, holding a door open for her. "This is our war room." As she moved past him, his hand brushed her lower back and a tingle of warmth jolted along her spine. Interesting that her body responded to him like that. He was just a friend—nothing more. Even though her marriage hadn't been consummated yet, nothing could happen between her and Evander. And it wasn't like she *wanted* something to happen. She shook her head, trying to clear her thoughts and wishing everything wasn't such a jumbled mess.

Inside the middle of the square room, there was a single table. No chairs, no maps, no papers, nothing. If this was where they planned missions and wars, it didn't feel like it since it was so empty.

Gemma entered from a side door. "I'm glad you're both here." She went to the empty table and stood there, waiting for Evander and Sabine to join her. Once they did, she continued, "We've spotted Ex on the south side of the lake. We never would have seen him had we not been specifically looking for him."

Sabine wondered why this was called the war room and why they were standing at an empty table.

"Is Ex alone?" Evander asked.

Sabine wondered what the laws were here in Avoni with regards to killing people. She assumed Ex was allowed to hunt a target he'd been commissioned for so long as it had nothing to do with the royal family. As to whether he was allowed to assassinate a royal from another kingdom, she didn't know—especially since she was on Avoni soil. It could change things. She suddenly wondered if she should have returned to Lynk. She shook her head. If she'd gone with Anton, she'd be dead already.

Gemma reached beneath the table and withdrew a scroll, setting it on the table and unrolling it, revealing a map of the surrounding land. A few words were scribbled on it, but Sabine didn't recognize the language.

"Is the plan to kill Ex?" Sabine asked, staring at the map as if it held the answer.

"Yes," Gemma said. "However, there's more at stake than just a man's life."

Meaning the political ramifications that went along with killing one of their own to protect someone from Lynk, especially when an entire Avoni delegation has just been slaughtered by the king of Lynk. If anything, the king and queen of Avoni should be seeking retribution, not killing an Avoni assassin to protect an enemy. But again, Sabine didn't know how things worked here, and these were thoughts she didn't want to voice in case Evander changed his mind and no longer wished to help her.

"We are in a bit of a situation," Evander muttered as he set his hands on the table, observing the map.

"That we are," Gemma said. "You're going to have to find a way to get rid of Ex quietly." She folded her arms. "And I have no idea what you're going to say to his family when they inquire. You'll also need to deal with whomever hired him."

The irony was that Sabine had been trying to deal with Lottie all along. The problem was that they couldn't just get rid of Lottie since she was a member of the Lynk royal family. It would take something more creative.

"It's my future bride," Evander said.

"What?" Gemma asked.

"The person who hired the assassin to kill Sabine is Princess Lottie, my soon-to-be wife."

Gemma's eyes narrowed as she studied her brother for a minute. "Did you agree to marry her to protect Sabine?"

"No," he replied. "I agreed to the marriage to protect Avoni. If Rainer invades the other kingdoms, I'm hoping he'll leave us alone or at the very least, it'll buy us time to come up with something."

"Let me ask you this," Gemma said. "What's Lottie's goal? To kill her brother and take the throne?"

"No," Sabine answered. "Lottie wants the throne, but she's not going to kill Rainer to get it. She's trying to get rid of me so he loses the throne by not producing a child by the time he turns twenty-five." Out of the corner of her eye, she caught Evander flinch. "However, now that I'm married to Rainer, she can't have me killed."

"But isn't that exactly what she's doing?" Evander asked.

"She hired someone to take care of it for her so she can keep her hands clean." She recalled what she'd heard back in Lynk. "He said he'd do it in such a way that blamed Avoni for my death and that it wouldn't be traced back to Lottie." Thinking over the conversation, she wasn't sure it was Ex Lottie had been talking to. It could have been someone from Lynk.

Evander tapped the map, examining it as if it held all the answers he sought. "This person could have hired Ex so it would be traced to Avoni." He leaned over the map. "I think we should take Ex out. We hide the body so no one finds out. That will buy Sabine time to make it out of Avoni safely and…return home." He glanced up at Sabine. "But you still won't be safe. If Lottie hired someone to orchestrate it all, you're still going to be in danger."

She nodded, wondering how they could stop it for good since marrying Rainer hadn't done the trick.

"I'll take care of Ex tonight," Evander said. "I want to do it before he leaves the area or gathers reinforcements. Then Sabine and I will leave in a day or two."

"Where will you go?" Gemma asked.

"I'll escort her back to Lynk."

Sabine pinched the bridge of her nose. She was in way over her head. Staying alive in Lynk would be infinitely more difficult since she didn't know who Lottie had doing her dirty work. At least here they knew Ex was after her, and she had Evander to protect her. In Lynk, she'd be all alone.

The two siblings kept staring at one another. Sabine got the impression there was more going on between them than she was privy to.

"What about the kidnapped Bakley children?" she asked,

wondering how she could live with a man who was capable of such things.

"When you return, discuss the matter with Rainer. Hopefully, he will release them as a gesture of goodwill," Gemma answered.

"And if he doesn't?"

"Sometimes you have to choose the lesser of two evils," Gemma said, her focus returning to the map before them on the table. "Back to Ex." She pointed to the map. "What are you thinking?"

"I can't involve the family," Evander replied. "I'll have to deal with him on my own."

Cold terror filled Sabine. "I don't think that wise. What if something happens to you? I can't let that happen on my account."

"The second Evander stole you," Gemma said, "he set this in motion. He must finish it."

It seemed everyone knew he'd kidnapped her. "The assassin would be after me regardless of whether Evander took me or not. He doesn't need to be solely responsible for keeping me safe. Let me help."

"No," Gemma and Evander said at the same time.

"You'll stay here where it's safe," Evander said.

"And my brother brought you into Avoni," Gemma said. "He is responsible for your wellbeing. If something happens to you here, Avoni will pay the price."

It didn't seem fair since the person responsible for her situation was Lottie.

"We're both trained, and it will be an equal matchup," Evander mused.

"Which is why it's important you have a plan," Gemma said. "The sooner you face him, the better. Try and have the element of surprise."

"I agree," he mumbled, observing the map.

"Am I the only one who thinks this is a bad idea?" Sabine asked.

They both looked at her. "Yes," they answered together.

She rolled her eyes. "I don't want Evander hurt. I'd rather you take a unit of men with you."

"He can't involve the family, our assassins, the sentries, or anyone else for that matter," Gemma said. "He has to do this alone and quietly. No one can know." She looked at her brother. "You'll have to clean this one up as well."

"I know."

"I don't want you to put your life at risk for me," Sabine said, clutching onto his arm. "If something happens to you, I'll never forgive myself."

He turned and faced her, his eyes intense with emotion. "I have to return you to Lynk," he said. "Agreed?"

She nodded.

"The only way I can do that is without Ex tracking us or sending more men after you. As my parents so bluntly stated, I put you in this mess, I must fix it. If I'd left you at the Lynk palace, you'd be protected. I've put you in danger. This is my fault, and I'll make it right."

She slid her hand down his arm to his hand. Twining her fingers with his, she squeezed. "I can help."

"Yes, you can," he answered. "I need you to stay in your room where I know you'll be safe. I can't deal with Ex if I'm worried about you."

That wasn't the answer she wanted.

Gemma cleared her throat. "I need to return to my unit," she said. "I'll make sure everyone is busy between three to four in the morning. That's your window to enact your plan. If you need anything else from me, you know where to find me."

"Thank you," Evander replied.

Gemma exited the room.

Evander peered down at their joined hands.

"This plan is too dangerous," Sabine whispered. She'd already lost her sister to an assassin and couldn't stand the thought of losing another person she cared for.

"I have to." He leaned his forehead against hers. "It's what I'm trained to do."

She took hold of his other hand as well, as if she could keep him there forever. "Please don't go alone."

The corners of his lips rose. "Have you so little faith in me?"

Tears filled her eyes. "I can't lose you." She leaned back so she could see him better.

"Sabine." His green eyes bore into her as he let go of her hand and reached up, cupping her cheek. "Let me do this for you." He ran his thumb over her bottom lip, sending a jolt of warmth through her.

"It's too dangerous," she insisted, grabbing hold of his upper arms, trying to hold him in place.

He slid his hand from her cheek to the back of her head. His eyes kept searching hers. "Have you ever wanted something so badly but knew you could never have it?" he whispered.

"Yes." She swallowed, staring at his lips. She'd never before felt an intense desire to kiss a man because of their connection. She'd only done so for fun, curiosity, or to even make her brothers mad. But this, this was something else entirely. She *wanted* to kiss Evander. Leaning toward him, she placed her lips next to his right ear and whispered, "I want something that I can never have." She squeezed her eyes shut then forced herself to move back, away from him.

Only he didn't let go. He was staring at her lips. His hands now cradled either side of her head, just below her ears, holding her in place. He leaned forward, inches from her.

She moved her hands to his waist.

Then, ever so gently, he kissed the edge of her lips. It was tender, careful, and not nearly enough. If something happened to him, this would be their last time together. She wanted him to know what he meant to her. Not having the words, she turned her head, leaning into his kiss and deepening it.

Her body felt as if it had been engulfed in flames. The smell of Evander filled her. His lips moved over hers but it still wasn't enough. She parted her lips, craving more of him. His tongue slid into her mouth, touching hers. All thoughts escaped her as she only felt this man in her arms. His right hand slid to her waist, up under her shirt, pressing against her back.

And then he leaned away, his eyes widening. "I'm sorry," he whispered, his chest heaving up and down.

She didn't want him to stop. Clutching onto him, she tried pulling him closer.

He took a step back, breaking their contact. "I didn't realize I..." He ran a hand over his face.

The reality of the situation came crashing down upon Sabine. She was married to the king of Lynk and in Avoni kissing the prince who was engaged to her husband's sister. If anyone found out they'd kissed, she could be killed for treason. "I'm sorry," she whispered. This was her fault. She never should have acted on her feelings for Evander. Especially when she didn't fully understand them herself.

"No," he responded. "I'm sorry. This is my fault, not yours."

"I think we're both complicit." She turned, facing away from him, trying to regain her wits. She couldn't afford to act on her own feelings, wants, or desires. It had just been the thought of something happening to him that had scared her. With her hands on her hips, she forced herself to walk a few feet away from him, still not daring to look at his face. She'd just thrown herself at him like a harlot.

"Sabine," Evander said, his voice soft and gentle. "I—"

She couldn't bear to hear him explain away what had just happened between them. When she was alone she would examine it, think about it, and feel it. Right now, she needed to lock it away before it became overwhelming and she did something stupid. "No," she said, interrupting him. "I just... do you ever wish you could go back and redo something in your life?"

"All the time." He sighed. "But I wouldn't take back that kiss," he whispered.

She pinched her eyes shut, forcing herself to ignore his comment. She couldn't let it affect her right now. She'd digest it later, when she wasn't standing in front of him. Wanting—needing—to change the focus of their conversation, she said, "I would go back and not take my sister's place." She wouldn't have married Rainer.

"Don't you want revenge?" he asked.

"I do. But I'm not sure I went about the right way of getting it." And it seemed all she'd done was get herself into a situation where she could very well end up dead. She'd been dealt an awful hand and now she had to play it, regardless of what she wanted.

"I may be able to help you there," he mumbled. "Especially if I marry Lottie."

"I don't think you can assassinate your future wife." Even though Sabine might want her dead. "And what if she catches wind? She might try to kill you."

He chuckled. "I'm a trained assassin. Have a little faith." He shook his head.

Sabine folded her arms, wanting to shield herself from this dangerous man before her. She almost laughed at the irony. A couple weeks ago, the danger was from him being an assassin. Now, the danger lie in the way he made her feel when she was near him. She took a deep breath, letting it out slowly. "Speaking of which," she said, "do you still plan on trying to kill Ex tonight?"

He ran a hand over his face before folding his arms, mimicking her stance. "No. The plan *is* to kill him tonight. There's no trying here."

Part of her wished she could help. However, she understood why she couldn't. In order to beat the assassin, it would take a man of equal or better skill. "Does that mean we'll leave tomorrow?"

"No," Evander said. "We'll leave the day after. I need to gather provisions and pack." He ran his hand through his hair.

"Will we have time for some more training?" She wanted to learn a few more things before they set out. She didn't know when she'd ever have another opportunity to be trained by someone like him. While Rainer had shown her some physical maneuvers, he hadn't once hinted at teaching her techniques like stealth, listening, smelling, or any of the things an assassin did. Things that could not only save her life, but allow her to snoop and be invisible in a palace full of busybodies.

The door opened, and King Kai entered. Evander didn't respond and instead, greeted his father.

"I'd hoped to find you here," Kai said.

"I'm actually leaving in order to prepare for my mission tonight," Evander said.

"I didn't come here for you," the king replied. "I must speak with Queen Sabine."

Evander glanced at her. "Very well. I'll leave the two of you alone." He bowed his head before departing from the room.

Sabine turned to face King Kai, not knowing if she should say anything or wait for him to speak.

"Let's take a walk," he said, tilting his head toward the door. "This room usually puts me in a bad mood since when I'm in here, it means I'm planning someone's death or a battle."

Sabine smiled. "I can understand that." She followed him from the room, wondering how often the room was used considering this kingdom preferred stealth, not outright fighting. Besides, the surrounding lands hadn't seen a war in decades. She supposed the League was doing its job then.

Kai clasped his hands behind his back, walking at a slow, leisurely pace.

"The grounds here are beautiful," Sabine said as she came to walk alongside him.

"That they are."

A light rain fell. He led her across a single pathway hovering just above the water, like a bridge but without a railing. It took them to the center of the lake to a squared platform with a roof. Each corner post had curtains tied to it that could be slid closed, giving the illusion of privacy. On the platform were a handful of sofas and a low table in the center.

"I love to be outdoors," Kai explained. "Since it rains so often here, I had this built so I can be outside and not get wet." He smiled and sat on one of the sofas.

Sabine sat across from him. "I assume there's something you wish to discuss with me," she said, noting they had no guards and no one was around. Due to the platform's positioning in the middle of the lake, no one could overhear their conversation. Folding her hands on her lap, she knew she needed to tread carefully—he'd brought her here for a reason.

He crossed his legs, watching her. "Firstly, I'd like to

apologize for my son kidnapping you. He should not have done so. I want to be clear—he did that on his own. He wasn't even supposed to be a part of the delegation."

"I understand," she said carefully. While she didn't mind her current predicament, she was married to Rainer and had to return to Lynk. The situation would need to be handled delicately so as not to add more problems to the ones already mounting.

"I want your assurance that you will not seek retribution," Kai said.

Sabine didn't know what authority she had to make such promises. While she was the queen of Lynk, women seemed to have little power there, and she had no idea if Rainer would respect any deals she made without his knowledge. "As far as I'm concerned, your son escorted me to meet my brother. I was not taken against my will."

"You didn't answer my question."

"No, I will not seek retribution, but I can't speak for my husband." She decided to be as honest as possible. This man sitting before her was not only a king, but an assassin. If she didn't agree to his terms, he very well might never let her leave here alive.

He nodded, as if he'd expected that response.

"I assume once Evander marries Lottie, that will smooth things over between Lynk and Avoni," she added. "But again, I have no intention of telling anyone I was kidnapped. In my mind, I wasn't."

He nodded. "My wife got it out of you in under fifteen minutes."

He had a point.

"You should know, I will protect my kingdom," Kai said, his voice low but forceful. "Even if it means fighting against Lynk."

"Your wife told me what happened...about the ship." She

had to look down at her hands. Even though she was not responsible for the Avoni delegation's deaths, she was married to the man who'd ordered the attack.

"Then you understand that once you leave my home," he raised his hands to indicate the palace, "you will be my enemy."

Tears filled her eyes. She looked up at King Kai and nodded. "It doesn't have to be that way."

"King Rainer is my enemy. You are his wife. Therefore, you are my enemy."

"I understand." Sabine recalled the night of the masquerade and assuming the party was to keep the Avoni people occupied while Rainer had their ship searched. However, now she understood it was so he could make the holes and plant the poison to kill them.

Kai drummed his fingers on his leg.

"Why don't you just send an assassin after Rainer?" she asked, genuinely curious.

"That would break the treaty," he said. "And I refuse to go against the League. It has kept us free from war for decades. I will be honorable and abide by it. If Rainer chooses not to, that's on him."

"And if he breaks it, what happens then?" she asked.

"The other kingdoms will band together to fight him. He will be stripped of his crown."

"Let me ask you this," she said, trying to sound contemplative and not combative. "Would the other kingdoms be a threat to Lynk?" Rainer's soldiers were well trained. Bakley barely had an army. She knew Avoni didn't have a large standing army but rather assassins. She didn't know the state of Carlon or Nisk.

"That is something you should know. I am neither your ally nor your educator." He looked away from her, gazing out at the lake. "Since it seems you are being honest with me, I'd like to ask you a question." His attention returned to Sabine. "What, precisely, is your relationship with my son?"

"Why do you ask?" she countered, her heart beating loudly as anxiety crept in. She couldn't help but think he might have seen them kiss before he entered the room. The thought sent a shard of terror through her.

"If I'm questioning it, I'm sure your *husband* will as well."

She knew it was going to be an issue—especially since she'd traveled alone with Evander. "We are friends. Nothing more." She made sure to maintain eye contact as she spoke so he'd believe her. "My husband will thank your son for keeping me alive." She hoped.

"When we were looking for a suitable match for Evander, we ruled you out."

His words felt like a slap to her face. Evander had said something about her being considered too wild. After being here and seeing how women were treated equal to men, she didn't know how they could have seen her as such a liability. Granted, if women had been subservient, then she could understand. A small part of her felt regret. She would have liked to live here.

"I knew my son would grow attached to someone like you," Kai revealed.

Shock jolted through Sabine. "What do you mean *someone like me?*" Maybe it was because she didn't know how to fight or protect herself properly, and the king didn't want his son attached to such a liability.

"Love makes people do foolish things. If Evander had married you, he'd lose his ability to think logically and do what needed to be done to strengthen this family."

Sabine had always thought the exact opposite. Love made people strong, not weak. She chewed on her bottom lip, trying to decide how to respond. She wanted to argue with him that love was not a hindrance and that it should be celebrated. However, she honestly didn't know. She'd only ever loved her family and had never formed an attachment to a man. All of her dalliances had been just that—simple fun for the sake of entertainment. Nothing serious. She decided not to argue with him. "Then it's a good thing I didn't marry your son."

"Yes," he replied. "Though I'm not sure I prefer Lottie."

"And why is that?"

"She's untrustworthy."

"That tends to be the case with those you don't know or love."

He smiled. "I can see why my son likes you."

"And I do like him. We are friends—but that is all. I can assure you of that. I am married to King Rainer."

"Good. I'm glad to hear it. Because if there was something untoward going on between the two of you, King Rainer would make it his mission to level my kingdom to the ground."

"While I'm flattered you believe that, and I'm equally flattered you believe your son is capable of loving someone like me, you are mistaken. My husband married me for a political alliance. He wouldn't attack your kingdom on my account."

Kai smiled and leaned forward. "You are Rainer's property, and he isn't one to share. He is just like his father." Kai stood. "After all, why do you think he killed my delegation?"

Everything he'd said grated on her nerves. First, she hated the idea that she was a man's property. When she'd been at the Lynk palace, that was how Rainer made her feel. He wanted her to look and dress the part, but he didn't want her to be his partner or share the burden of ruling. And then for Kai to compare Rainer to his father was equally irritating. She'd found the late queen's journal detailing how her husband, Rainer's father, had hit and abused her. It was almost like Kai knew that somehow.

She was still trying to figure out why Rainer had killed the delegation. The only thing she could think of was that he blamed someone in Avoni for murdering Alina. While he knew Lottie was responsible for hiring the assassin, Rainer had to have figured out that the assassin came from Avoni. However, she thought his actions were extreme. The members of the delegation had been innocent. She clutched her hands together, wanting to push Kai on the matter without upsetting him. She didn't want to find herself dead and tossed into the lake, becoming food for the fish.

Kai went over to the side table, pouring himself a drink. He didn't ask if Sabine wanted anything. He took a sip and sat back down. "Did you know I not only sent a delegation to Lynk, but I also sent a unit of men?"

She'd wondered why they'd arrived on such a large ship. "No, I didn't know that. Why did you send so many people?"

"I heard accusations that Avoni is responsible for taking children from Bakley. I wanted to prove our innocence." He took another sip. "While the delegation was at the palace, my unit searched Lynk for the children." He eyed her. "Before my men could return and report back to me, Rainer blew up my ship and my delegation. But my men, they're stuck in the kingdom. I don't know if they've been taken, if they're hiding, or if Rainer even knows they're there. I've had zero communication." He finished his drink. "So you see, if Rainer finds my men in his kingdom, it would be seen as an attack. He would then be justified to strike against me. He'd have everything he needed to go to war. Especially—*especially*—if he knew you'd been kidnapped and were in Avoni."

"The League would have to side with him," she said, everything falling into place.

"Exactly. The League would see his actions as justified."

Sabine leaned forward, sliding her hands into her hair and gripping her head.

She heard movement and saw the king's boots before her. She dared not look up at him.

"And now I hear my son is off killing one of his own countryman for you."

It wasn't like that. He was killing an assassin. A bad, evil person. A man who'd been hunting her.

"I hope you don't get my son killed." He left, the sound of his steps the only thing she could hear above the soft patter of falling rain.

Chapter Eleven

Sabine paced in the bedchamber, unable to sleep. Not only was Evander about to take on a skilled assassin alone, but the king's conversation with her kept replaying in her mind. For some reason, she thought there was more going on than she was privy to. She hadn't had a chance to discuss it with Evander yet. She chewed on her thumbnail—a nasty habit. Once Evander was back, the sick feeling in her stomach would settle. While this entire mission needed to be a secret from everyone in Avoni, she would have preferred for him to have taken a unit of men with him. Surely he could have sworn them to secrecy. But secrets always seemed to have a way of coming out.

Moving her hands to her hips, she continued pacing. Images of Evander getting hurt or worse, killed, inundated her. Sweat beaded on her forehead and her stomach twisted from nausea. If something happened to Evander, the king would probably kill her as retribution or she'd be thrown out of the palace, forced to survive on her own. If she managed to survive, she didn't know how she'd ever live with herself knowing she was responsible for his death. He wouldn't be fighting Ex if it wasn't for her. Thinking about the future, she couldn't imagine it without him. Somewhere along the line, he'd become a friend she valued. Life without him seemed bleak.

Things had a funny way of turning out. When she'd first met Evander, he scared her. Then her fright turned to annoyance. Somehow after that, she got to know him and began to consider him a friend. Now it seemed *friend* wasn't the right word. If she was being truly honest with herself, somewhere along the way she'd started to care for him as more than a friend. She felt inexplicably pulled to him. And that kiss they shared—the one she'd locked away to think about later—had been intense, sensual, and passionate. It could never happen again. It had been stupid of her to give in to her desire and kiss him since she was married.

How had she allowed herself to fall for an assassin? If only this had happened *before* she'd married Rainer. She'd always dreamed of finding someone she loved, marrying, and having children. With Rainer, she didn't think they would ever have a loving relationship. Especially now that she knew the evils he was capable of. Tears filled her eyes. She could imagine love, children, and happiness with Evander. Which was insane because they'd only just met, and she barely knew him. But deep down, she felt a connection to him she couldn't imagine having with anyone else.

When she'd first met Rainer, she thought him devastatingly handsome. And he was. He was the most seductive and sensuous man she'd ever seen. It would be easy to share his bed. But since they didn't care for one another that way, it would also be awkward.

She leaned her forehead against the cool glass, her thoughts turning to Evander. Being with him would be different than Rainer since they shared a connection. They would experience things in unison. Explore each other. The word *love* sprang to mind.

The rain came down even harder, pinging on the roof above her, drowning out her thoughts of things that could never be. She had been born into a royal family, and that meant she had a duty to her people. It was time she put them first instead of her own thoughts and wants. Bringing her sister's killer to justice no longer mattered. All that mattered was protecting her people. She needed to act like the queen she was and no longer be a spoiled, selfish child. She needed to prevent Rainer from going to war with the other kingdoms, and she needed to insist he return the Bakley children to their families.

She snuffed out the candle and climbed into bed. Lying there, the night wore on. The fire in the hearth slowly died, but she didn't bother to add another log to it. The rain continued to pound against the roof and windows.

Something shifted in the air. Sabine couldn't explain it, but the hairs on her arms rose and her heart pounded. When she'd been in the training room with Evander, he'd told her to use and trust her senses. If it felt like something was wrong, she had to act accordingly. She slid out of bed and glanced about the room, not seeing anything out of place. Even though the palace was always quiet, especially at night, it seemed more so than usual. Something was wrong. Turning back to her bed, she quickly shoved the pillows beneath the covers, trying to make it look as if she were still sleeping there. Satisfied, she withdrew a knife from her bedside table then tiptoed to the bathing room, keeping the door ajar and hiding behind it.

Minutes went by, and nothing happened. Maybe she was being overly paranoid and her imagination was getting the best of her. Given what Evander was up to tonight, that had to be it. This was a fortified compound. No one could get in.

Regardless, she didn't want to go back to bed. Instead, she sat on the floor in the bathing room, still tucked behind the door. The darkness made it harder and harder to keep her eyes open.

Sabine jolted awake, the knife on the floor beside her. She must have fallen asleep and dropped it. Reaching down, she picked it up and readjusted herself against the wall.

Something squeaked, the sound barely audible. She froze, listening. A soft *thump* came from her bedchamber. Forcing herself to breathe slowly and quietly so as not to garner attention, she peered through the crack between the opened door and the wall. In the darkened room, she spotted someone walking toward her bed.

The man leaned over and withdrew the dagger he must have thrown. He cursed and yanked back the blankets, revealing the pillows. He turned and scanned the bedchamber.

Two things became clear to Sabine. One, since this man was in her room, then something must have happened to Evander. Most likely, he was dead. And two, she was going to die because she couldn't defend herself against a skilled assassin. She shouldn't have hid in the bathing room where there was only one exit. She silently cursed herself for being so stupid.

Her entire body started shaking as the man took a couple of steps toward the bathing room. Something behind him moved, and a shadow peeled away from the wall. Sabine squinted, trying to see what was going on in the dark room. A second person appeared. She covered her mouth and nose with her free hand, wanting to stifle the sound of her own breathing as panic set in. She had nowhere to go.

The first man suddenly spun around to face the second person who shifted, revealing a knife in hand. She recognized him as Evander.

The assassin ducked at the same time Evander threw his knife. The weapon embedded in the wall with a *thud*. The assassin rushed at Evander, and the two men began to grapple. Sabine scrambled to her feet, wanting to help.

They slammed into the bathing room door, knocking her over. She screamed, trying to get on her hands and knees so she could stand. Her head pounded from where the door had hit her. Hands grabbed her, yanking her to her feet. She found herself being held by the assassin, her back to his chest, as he clutched a dagger, the tip at her neck.

Evander stood a few feet away in front of them, his eyes wide.

"The only reason she's not already dead is because I need to make it out of here," the assassin said, his hot breath brushing against her ear.

"You'll never leave these grounds alive," Evander said, his voice low and deadly.

"If I don't, then she doesn't either," the assassin said. "Now back away."

"It's not going to happen."

The assassin pushed the tip of the blade into her neck just enough to break the skin. She felt a trickle of blood run down her neck. She closed her eyes and took a deep breath, trying to remain calm, but all she could think about was dying.

The man chuckled, the sound reverberating through Sabine. "It seems we're at a stalemate."

Sabine realized she still held the knife in her hand. While she knew she couldn't move fast enough to kill the assassin before he slit her throat, at least she could do some damage. At least she wouldn't go down without a fight.

The second she rammed her knife into this vile man, he'd kill her. She just hoped it gave Evander enough time to end the assassin before the two could resume fighting. When she died, she'd see her sister again. That was consolation enough.

She just wished she could tell Evander that she cared for him, loved him even, before she died. But with the weapon against her neck, she couldn't speak. It was time for action.

Gripping the knife, Sabine lifted it slightly, then rammed it down into the assassin, striking his thigh. She squeezed her eyes shut, waiting for the pain that would accompany death.

The assassin dropped to the floor, his dagger still in hand.

Evander grabbed her arm, yanking her out of the bathing room. "Are you all right?" He ran his hands over her body before inspecting her neck.

She blinked, trying to understand what had just happened. Glancing behind her, she saw the assassin on the floor, a knife protruding from his chest. "How?" she asked, her voice barely audible.

"I saw you shift your fingers and knew you were getting ready to strike him. The moment you did, I threw my dagger. I'm just glad you moved enough so I could kill him."

"Are you certain he's dead?"

"Yes." He wound his fingers through hers, leading her from the bedroom. "Let's get you out of here."

Dozens of questions filled her mind, like why the two men were in her room in the first place and how had they gotten there?

Evander led her to a room a few doors down. A fire roared in the hearth, but the room was empty. Still too shocked from the events that had just taken place to voice any of her questions, she went over to the end of the bed and sat, staring into the flames.

Evander closed the door before sitting next to her on the bed. "Are you certain you're all right?" he asked.

She felt her neck. It was only a small cut, and the blood had already dried. She nodded.

Evander sighed. "I don't know what I would have done if

something happened to you." His voice came out husky and deeper than usual. He leaned forward, his right hand coming up, gently cupping the side of her face. His thumb brushed over her lips. "Sabine," he whispered.

She clutched onto his shirt, pulling him closer, wanting the comfort of his body against hers. She started to cry.

"Shh," Evander said. "I've got you. Everything is going to be okay. I promise." He wrapped his arms around her, holding her tightly. He kissed her forehead.

But she couldn't focus on him because her skin felt like it was set on fire, as if her flesh were burning.

Sabine screamed.

"What's wrong?" Evander asked, his voice filled with concern.

The fire spread from her neck, down to her shoulders, and to her stomach. She started thrashing, trying to put the fire out, only there was no fire. At least not one she could see. She had no idea what was happening as pain and terror set in.

Evander cursed. "The assassin's dagger must have been tipped with poison."

Poison. She was going to die a horrible, painful death.

Sabine couldn't stop screaming as pain rippled through her, increasing in intensity.

Evander scooped her up, running from the room, carrying her in his arms. He began shouting orders, but Sabine didn't pay attention to what he said. All she could think about and focus on was the excruciating pain. It felt like her skin was being seared off her body. She wanted to pull it away to stop the pain.

They entered a building she'd never been in before. Evander set her on a bed. She thrashed, wanting to put out the invisible fire that engulfed her body. Someone pinned her arms down while someone else tied her wrists to the bed. Then they did the same with her legs.

A piercing scream erupted through her. She was tied to the bed, burning, and she was going to die.

"She needs the antidote," Evander shouted. "Now!"

"We need to figure out what poison is in her system," someone responded.

"She only has minutes left," he said, gripping his hair and sliding to the floor.

An elderly man leaned over Sabine. "Do you feel fire or ice?" he asked.

"Fire," she ground out, panting, sweat dripping down her forehead, arms, and legs.

He nodded. "Vexilun. How long since she was poked?"

"Maybe ten minutes?" Evander said, still sitting on the floor. "We have enough time to save her, don't we Barret?"

"We have roughly twenty minutes. It'll be cutting it close." He barked orders to someone else in the room before tilting her head back, inspecting her wound. "Make that ten. Ten minutes."

People rushed in and out of the room bringing leaves, roots, and vials. Barret stood beside the bed grinding the various ingredients in a bowl.

Someone else laid cool, wet cloths on her forehead, arms, and legs.

"I have enough," Barret announced. He scoped out a spoonful of what he'd made and placed it on her neck where the dagger had pierced her skin. It immediately doused the fire around her head and shoulders.

Another person rushed over with a cup. "It's ready," the woman said.

Barret lifted Sabine's head, placing the cup at her lips. He poured the liquid into her mouth and she swallowed the contents as best she could, coughing slightly at the foul taste.

She could feel her heart beating frantically as the liquid slid down her throat and to her stomach. Then a calmness coated her skin as the fire faded away. Her breathing became steadier.

"How do you feel?" Barret asked.

"Better," she said, her voice coming out hoarse.

"Vexilun is a nasty poison that makes you think your flesh is burning. The pain can be excruciating. After thirty minutes or so, your heart gives out and you die." He reached forward, placing his palm on her chest. "Your heart is still beating too quickly." He shouted something over his shoulder.

Another person approached with a different cup. Barret removed the bindings on Sabine's wrists and ankles and then he helped her sit up. He handed her the cup, and she drank its contents.

"Now what?" she asked.

"We wait and see if you're still alive in ten minutes," Barret said as he took the cup and set it aside.

Gemma burst into the room, the door hitting the wall with such force it made everyone jump. "What happened?" she demanded.

Evander stood. "Queen Sabine has been poisoned. Barret administered the antidote."

"Is she going to be okay?" Gemma asked as she came over and inspected Sabine.

"I believe so," Barret said. "I'm going to make a few more concoctions just in case. I'll be back in five minutes." He bowed then left the room.

"Lucky for you Barret is the best apothecary around." Gemma smiled and patted Sabine's leg.

With each breath Sabine took, she felt better, stronger. Maybe she wasn't going to die after all. Relief filled her.

Gemma eyed Evander, her eyebrows raised as if in

question, but he didn't say anything. Instead, he kept his focus on Sabine.

Now that she was feeling better, she had some questions for Evander, but there were a couple people still lingering around and she didn't want to speak in front of them.

As if reading her mind, Evander put his hands on his hips and ordered everyone out of the room, including Gemma.

Once Evander and Sabine were alone, he came and sat on the edge of her bed. "Are you okay?" he asked, reaching out and taking hold of her hand.

"Yes." Her eyes became heavy. "I'm just tired." And her body ached from all it had been through over the past hour.

Evander nodded. "I'll let you sleep." He made no move to leave.

Sabine closed her eyes, and a sense of calm filled her.

A few minutes later, she heard Barret mumble to Evander about having given Sabine something to knock her out and that she needed to rest. The bed shifted as Evander stood. And then the room went silent. She had to be alone.

Rolling onto her side, she drifted to sleep.

"Father is looking for you," someone whispered.

Sabine could tell she was still in bed, but she was half asleep, unable to open her eyes. Maybe she was dreaming.

"Shh," Evander replied. "Don't wake her."

"You need to deal with the mess you created," Gemma whispered.

"Me?" Evander said. "You were supposed to make sure he was clean before he stepped foot on the palace grounds."

"And you were supposed to kill him quickly," she replied.

Evander didn't respond.

"Let's go," Gemma continued. "You have to face him sooner or later about this."

Evander sighed. "Yeah, I know. I'm sure he already has another plan."

It sounded as if the two of them left the room.

Sabine had no idea what they were talking about or if she'd dreamed the entire conversation. Dreams often didn't make sense.

Sabine awoke and rolled over. She found Queen Serilda sitting next to the bed.

"Good morning," Serilda said. "How are you doing?"

Yawning, Sabine pushed herself to a sitting position, leaning against the headboard. Her neck was sore but other than that, she felt good. "I'm fine." Her voice came out raspy—probably from all the screaming she did last night.

"I'm not sure what happened, but we've never had an attack inside the palace walls before."

Sabine had no idea how to respond to that.

"I would appreciate it if you wouldn't share this incident with anyone. If word got out, others might try to breach our walls as well."

Sabine recalled Gemma telling Evander she would have her guards stationed away from a section of the wall for a specified amount of time so Evander could get out and kill Ex without anyone seeing. She supposed that was how the assassin got in. Instead of mentioning any of that, she replied, "Since you've been so hospitable, I won't say a word." The past few weeks—both here in Avoni and in Lynk —seemed to be filled with assassination attempts. The assassin who'd come after her in the seamstress's room back in Lynk hadn't been as skilled or ruthless as the one she faced last night. Which made her question if he was even an Avoni assassin.

She rubbed her forehead. Before the attack in Lynk, she'd heard a whistle and her dog had run from the room. That made sense if Lottie was involved since she trained the dogs. But her guards had to have seen something and they didn't. That incident seemed like a coordinated attack—from the inside. The person had known how to get out of the palace via the secret tunnels. Granted, Lottie could have divulged that information, but Sabine wasn't so sure she would. If Lottie told an assassin, that assassin would tell others. Lottie had to know that.

"What is it, dear?" Serilda asked.

Sabine glanced at the queen's face. Her brows were drawn together, as if truly concerned. "I don't know," she admitted. "I think I'm just tired from the events of last night." Sabine had been attacked twice—both times by very different men. She knew, without a doubt, that the man last night was an assassin from Avoni. He had been well trained and ruthless. The attack in Lynk hadn't been like that. It had been clumsy.

"Is there anything you wish to discuss with me?" Serilda asked.

Sabine shook her head, wanting to wait to talk to Evander about this.

"Very well." The queen stood then headed for the door where she stopped and turned to face Sabine. "While we might have different methods, we want the same thing— peace."

Sabine didn't respond. If Serilda truly wanted peace, her kingdom wouldn't still be training assassins. And so far, Avoni had done nothing to broker peace. They'd had more than enough opportunities to help Bakley but instead, chose to do nothing. But maybe Sabine was overthinking this. Looking for problems where there weren't any.

Serilda reached for the door handle. "I want you to know that my son cares for you," she said, her voice suddenly soft. "No matter what the future holds, know that he considers you a friend. Maybe something more. Don't forget that." She left the room before Sabine could respond.

Sliding her legs out from under the covers, Sabine stood and stretched, thinking over her conversation with the queen. Her throat was dry, so she went over to the door looking for a string nearby to pull a bell for a servant.

Evander's voice came from the other side. She was about to open the door when she heard his mother say, "You need to fix this."

Sabine had no idea what needed fixing. Then she remembered hearing Evander and his sister whispering about talking to their father.

"I know," Evander said. "You don't need to remind me. I'm painfully aware that I screwed up last night."

Sabine froze, unable to move away from the door.

"What is it, Mother? I can tell you want to say something else."

"You do remember what your duty to this family and kingdom is, don't you?" the queen said.

"Yes," Evander ground out, his voice sounding irritated.

"I don't want to see you get hurt."

"I won't," he replied.

"Just remember what you're doing. Don't get caught up in it all."

"*Mother.*"

"I see the way you look at her."

"You can count on me to do my duty," Evander replied, his voice steely. "Is there anything else?"

"No more mistakes."

Since Evander was probably going to come into the room and Sabine didn't want to get caught eavesdropping, she rushed over to the bed and threw the sheets back, pretending as if she'd just gotten up.

The door opened, and Evander entered carrying a robe. "I

thought you might want to get out of the infirmary," he said by way of greeting. "I brought this for you to wear."

She glanced down, realizing she was still in her nightdress. It was rumpled and torn near her shoulder. She didn't know if she had done that while she'd been thrashing or if it had happened when the assassin had her.

"Thank you." Sabine went over and took the robe, sliding her arms through it and tying it around her waist.

"I'll escort you to a room where you can bathe and change." He opened the door and motioned for her to exit before him.

She stepped outside and squinted from the bright light. Evander led her along the pathway to the right. They walked side by side in silence. There were so many questions she wanted to ask him, things about last night with the assassin, about the conversation she'd overheard him have with his sister, and his mother's comments just now. However, something prevented her from doing so.

Maybe once they left the palace, he'd tell her what was going on. The last thing she wanted to do was to cause problems between him and his family. And she definitely wanted to discuss the assassination attempt back in Lynk.

He led her to the building that housed the royal family. He opened the door and ushered her inside. "Your room is not suitable after the events of last night," he said as he led her down the hallway. "You can bathe and change in here." He stopped before an ornate gold door. "I'll have clean clothes brought for you."

She opened the door and went in, noticing a closet off to the side filled with clothes. "Is this someone's room?" Perhaps his eldest sister who no longer resided in this palace.

"It's mine." He pointed to the door on the left, not meeting her eyes. "The bathing room is through there. I'll be back in a few minutes with clean clothes for you." Without another word, he closed the door.

Standing alone in the room, Sabine turned in a slow circle, taking it all in. It was similar to the one she'd been staying in. A large bed on the floor, a couple armoires, a dressing closet and a bathing room. There was nothing in the room that gave it away as being Evander's. No weapons hanging on the wall…though she supposed that made sense. If Evander's bed was on the floor so no one could hide beneath it, then surely he wouldn't display weapons someone could get ahold of and use. Even though she didn't see anything that resembled Evander, the room distinctly smelled like him.

While she wanted to snoop, she refrained from doing so out of respect for Evander. Instead, she went into the bathing room. The tub had already been filled with steaming hot water. After removing her robe and nightdress, she lowered herself into the tub, allowing the hot water to wash over her. The steam surrounded her face along with a light lavender smell. Evander must have added some oil to the water for her. Then Sabine laughed. It wasn't like Evander had drawn the bath—it had to have been a servant.

After several relaxing minutes, Sabine found soap and washed her body and hair. Once finished, she got out and wrapped the robe around her, peering into the bedchamber. A pile of clothing had been placed at the foot of the bed. Not seeing anyone in the room, she went to the clothes, running her hand over the fabric.

She couldn't help but compare Rainer to Evander, her assassin-pirate-friend. She shouldn't be interested in him in any way, but she was. She couldn't help it. Rainer appeared to be perfect on the outside, luring her to him. But it was just his appearance. Not him as a person. Evander was the one she'd come to know and care for. And through that, she found him more appealing. He made her laugh and feel good about herself. Yet, he was not her lot in life. She was married to Rainer. There was no point thinking about things that could never be. Things she could not have.

She wiped the tears away, not understanding why she was crying. She shook her head, trying to think straight. There were so many more important things to worry about—like stopping a war, returning kidnapped children, and trying to stay alive. Irrelevant things such as her personal feelings shouldn't matter. She rolled her shoulders back, wanting to be strong. She needed to pull it together so she could do what needed to be done to keep her kingdom safe—even if that meant sacrificing her own happiness. It was a small price to pay. Her kingdom deserved peace. Pinching the bridge of her nose, she took a deep breath. She had a job to do. It was time she start doing it.

She lifted the dark purple dress, stepped into it, and slid her arms into the sleeves. Once it was on, she tied the fabric belt around her waist.

A knock sounded on the door. "Come in," she called out.

Evander entered the room, closing the door behind him. He stood there, staring at her, his bright green eyes full of some emotion she couldn't pinpoint.

The air suddenly seemed hot and hard to breathe. Needing to snap the connection she felt pulling her toward Evander, she asked, "Why don't you have anything personal in here?"

He chuckled. "You snooped?" He raised a single eyebrow as he stepped farther into the room.

"No. I just noticed this room is similar to the guest room I was staying in. And there aren't any books, figurines, or letters lying about. There's nothing in here that tells me it's yours."

"My clothes are in here."

She rolled her eyes. "You know what I mean."

"What makes you think I'd have figurines?" He moved farther into the room, only a few feet away from her now.

She shrugged. "You look like the sort of fellow who would have miniature pirate ships."

He laughed, tipping his head back as he did so. "Every time I try to act smooth around you, you go and say something like that." He looked at her. "You make me laugh."

She didn't know how to respond to that. He made her laugh as well, but she didn't want to admit that out loud. It felt too intimate. Especially in the room with the door closed. "You have other homes," she said, thinking out loud. "Do you keep your possessions at another location?" Maybe his main residence was elsewhere because surely he had to have items that were important to him—a favorite book or painting. Something uniquely Evander. She wanted to know what he cherished and why.

He sat on the edge of his bed, looking at her. The wall behind him contained floor to ceiling windows, revealing a handful of trees outside just beyond the water. "I have nothing special to me anywhere," he said matter-of-factly.

"I don't believe that." She fiddled with the tie around her dress, wondering why he didn't want to share this with her. A pang of hurt tightened around her heart. She had to shove it away.

"It's true," he insisted, his voice husky.

"Not even a single wooden pirate ship figurine?" she said, half joking and half serious, trying to keep the heavy mood somewhat light. She couldn't fathom him not having a single prized possession.

"No."

"And why is that?" She tilted her head to the side, watching him.

"Because if I have nothing that I treasure, it can't be taken away or used against me."

The room suddenly felt oddly silent. Sabine blinked, processing what he'd revealed. Sadness filled her. He lived the life of not only a royal, but an assassin. She understood how his enemies would and could use things he loved and cared for against him. Her room in Bakley was filled with items she cherished. Flowers she'd saved, books she'd read, jewelry she owned. Clothes, shoes, letters, rocks, and trinkets. The urge to hug him inundated her, and she had to look away. "I'm sorry."

"It is what it is." He shrugged. "My fate is sealed. There's no point trying to change it. Or be upset."

His statement mirrored her own feelings.

She hesitated a moment before going over and sitting on the bed next to him. "Sometimes I start to think about the *what ifs*...but then I stop myself. There's no point in thinking about things that cannot be." This was the most honest she'd been with anyone since her sister.

He folded his hands, his focus on them as they rested in his lap. He nodded slowly. "Tell me one of your *ifs*."

Thinking over the many *what ifs*, she picked a safe one. "What if my sister never died?"

At that, he turned his head, looking at her. He slid his right hand to her back. "I'm sorry she died."

So was Sabine. "Now tell me one of your *ifs*," she whispered.

His eyes never left hers. "What if I never act on the one thing I'm too afraid to?"

"You don't strike me as the sort of man who's afraid of anything."

With his free hand, he reached up and cupped her cheek. "I'm afraid of losing your friendship."

She didn't think they'd be able to remain friends once she

returned to Lynk. "What's the one thing you're afraid to do?" Her heart thudded in her chest as if she'd just run across the field behind her parents' castle back home.

His eyes focused on her lips. "I wish I'd kidnapped you before you married Rainer."

"That's not a *what if*," she said, her voice coming out all breathy.

"What if I kidnapped you before you married Rainer?"

Even though the ceremony had been performed, Sabine and Rainer hadn't consummated their marriage. She abruptly looked away from Evander, wondering, if only for an instant, if she truly was married. She abruptly stood. These thoughts had no place in her, and they had to stop.

"Sabine?" Evander said, standing and coming up behind her. "Is something wrong?"

She could feel the heat of him behind her. If she tilted back, she would lean into him. Closing her eyes, she imagined all the ways she wanted to be with him. Then she shook her head. "Nothing is wrong," she finally replied. "I just had another *what if* moment." She took a step away from Evander before turning to face him, a forced smile on her lips.

"Care to share?" His eyes kept focusing on her lips.

She knew he felt the same way about her that she felt for him. "I can't," she whispered.

He took a step closer to her, his eyes searching hers. "What if you could? What if we only have this moment in time together?" he asked, his voice coming out soft and husky.

She didn't know how to respond to that.

"What if, just for tonight, we don't think about what we should be doing or what our duties are. What if we just feel?"

Her heart pounded as she searched his eyes, trying to understand what he was suggesting.

Chapter Twelve

"What are you saying?" Sabine asked.

"Maybe we should forego the *what ifs* and just do." Evander slid one hand around the back of her neck, his intense eyes never straying from hers. "Just once in my life, I'd like to do something I want. I want this, and I want it with you." His other hand reached forward, untying the fabric belt around her waist.

Desire bloomed inside her. She closed her eyes, easily imagining him removing the rest of her clothes. The feel of his hand sliding over her skin. His lips trailing along her neck. Her hands exploring his body. She opened her eyes. "It doesn't matter what we want," she said, her voice coming out breathy. "We have a duty that is bigger than us, our wants, and our desires."

"No one will know." He leaned forward, tilting her neck to the side and kissing it just as she'd imagined.

"I'll know." It didn't matter how much Sabine wanted this. She was married and couldn't be with another man. She'd already crossed the line by kissing him earlier.

He stilled. "I...ah...apologize." He cleared this throat and released her, turning his head to the side, away from her.

When she moved to peer into his eyes, she noticed tears in them. Her heart hurt. She pinched her eyes shut, not wanting to see the pain and sorrow on his face. The problem was that she wanted this too. She wanted her first time to be with someone she truly cared for. But it didn't matter what she wanted. And if she gave herself to Evander, Rainer would know. Even if no one found out, Rainer would when they finally consummated their marriage. Evander didn't understand that because he assumed she'd already been with a man before.

"What is it?" Evander asked.

She shook her head, unable to tell him any of this.

"Oh." He took another step away from her. "I didn't realize you were keeping something from me. I thought..."

They barely knew each other. This thing between them had taken her by surprise. "I'm sorry," she said. She didn't know what else to say to him. "I wish things were different, but they're not."

His brows pulled together as he studied her before nodding. "I would have always wondered *what if* if I hadn't tried." He smiled. "There are a few things I need to do to prepare for our journey. You may remain here and rest if you like."

She nodded, exhausted from everything she'd been through.

After he left, she went over and laid on the bed, breathing in the smell of Evander as the tears she'd been holding back finally started to fall.

Someone shook Sabine's shoulder. She peeled her eyelids open and found Evander sitting beside her on the bed.

"It's time for us to go," he said.

She sat up, rubbing her eyes. She must have fallen asleep yesterday and slept straight through the night, having missed supper. She peered through the windows, seeing the dark sky. "Is it morning?"

"It is." He stood and reached out to help her.

She took hold of his hand, and he pulled her up. Two bags were near the door.

"Carin packed yours," he said when he saw her staring at them. Then he pointed to the bathing room. "I put something for you to wear in there. Once you've changed, we'll go."

She stood and stretched before heading to the bathing room where she quickly removed the beautiful purple dress and put on the loose pants and tunic Evander had picked out.

When she exited, she found him standing next to the door holding both their bags.

"Thank you for bringing me here," she said as she joined him. "I'm glad I got to see your palace and meet your family."

The two of them exited the building.

"Even though I managed to get you poisoned?"

"That wasn't your fault. Besides, I stabbed you. I think we're even." She tried to keep her voice lighthearted. "Although you did kidnap me." She poked his side.

He chuckled. "Feel free to return the favor at any time." Using his shoulder, he nudged hers.

Their banter felt like before, and Sabine welcomed it. This is what she wanted—the easy friendship between them. Not the desire and attraction. That was too confusing. Friendship she could handle.

The rain had stopped but the ground remained wet. They crossed over the bridge and made their way to the gate in the wall surrounding the compound. The sentries on duty allowed them through. At the dock, they climbed into a small boat similar to the one they'd previously used when traversing the canal.

Sabine took the front bench while Evander sat on the rear one. After tucking their bags under the seats, he lifted the stick and pushed the boat away from the bank. They quickly got caught in the current, and it carried them along. They traveled in silence, neither one of them speaking. When they came to a split, Evander steered them south.

As the sky lightened, the canal became more crowded with other boats.

"I want to apologize," Evander said. "My behavior yesterday was inexcusable, and I should never have pushed you like that. Please forgive me."

She twisted on the seat to face him. "There's no need to apologize." Nothing had happened between them.

He kept his focus on her. "I want you to know that no matter what happens in the future, I care for you deeply. Regardless of what you hear or what people say. Know my feelings for you are genuine."

She had no idea why he was telling her any of this. "What's the matter? Is there something I should know?"

"The only thing you need to know is that everything I've said to you, I've meant." He clasped his hands together, his eyes never wavering from hers.

Not wanting to push the matter, she nodded, realizing that they were both keeping things from one other. And that thought didn't sit well with her. Wanting to change the subject, she asked, "Where are we going?" They were heading south, not north toward Lynk.

"There's been a change in plans," he said, rubbing his face, seeming unsure.

"You're not taking me back to Lynk?" Now that Ex was dead, they had no reason to prolong her return.

"I received a message from your brother."

"Otto?"

"Yes." His focus went to their surroundings, scanning the shoreline. "He heard what happened and believes it will be best if he escorts you to Lynk."

That sounded reasonable.

"I will no longer be joining you."

"I thought you were going to get Lottie," she said. A strange feeling took root in her stomach. The thought of no longer being with Evander seemed wrong.

"I will. Eventually. But Otto wants to meet with Rainer, and this seemed the best solution."

He still wouldn't look at her.

"Okay," she replied, not really feeling things were okay. There was something he wasn't telling her. She could feel it. Tears filled her eyes. Nothing ever went the way it was supposed to. She twisted around on the bench seat, no longer facing Evander. She sat there, watching the buildings and trees pass by.

Around midday, the rain started. She pulled a cloak out of her bag and put it on, trying to stay dry. When the sky started to darken, she finally turned around to face Evander again.

"Are we not going to stop and eat?" she asked.

He pulled out a loaf of bread and tore it in two, handing her half.

"We're not stopping?"

He shook his head. On both sides of the canal, thick trees lined the water, no town in sight. "We're sleeping in the boat."

She groaned, wanting to stand and stretch her legs. It

seemed that everything was irritating her. The rain was getting on her nerves. She missed her home, her family, and her horse. The thought of returning to Lynk and Rainer made her unsettled. Living with a man she couldn't trust, who wanted to wage war, and who was stealing Bakley children was more than she could bear. But she had to. It was up to her to stop him.

"Where, exactly, am I supposed to sleep on this thing?" Sabine asked, her voice clipped.

"Between the two benches. Just use your cloak for a blanket. I'll keep watch."

Even though she hadn't left Evander yet, everything already felt different. She didn't think it had anything to do with her not spending the night with him. It seemed as if he was purposefully putting a wall between them, preparing her for what was to come.

Since it was getting dark, Sabine decided to curl between the benches, on the floor of the boat, and at least try to get some sleep. While it was completely uncomfortable with her knees up by her stomach, she felt a sense of peace floating on the water with Evander watching over her. She drifted off to sleep.

✦

After traveling on the canal nonstop for two days, Evander finally steered them to a dock where he tied up the boat.

"Glad to see you're not completely insane," Sabine said as she climbed out. "I thought you weren't going to ever stop that boat." Sometimes a woman just needed a moment to herself. She stood and stretched.

"We're short on time," was all Evander said as he grabbed their bags and joined her. "Stay close to me."

"Is there still a threat?" She assumed since Ex had been dealt with, she didn't have to worry about deranged assassins jumping out at her every two seconds.

"I don't think so, but I can't be certain." He led her along a walkway into town.

"Where are we meeting my brother?" she asked. This town looked similar to all the other ones along the canal.

"Not here," Evander replied. "We're just sleeping here tonight. Then we'll travel two more days to a town called Lark which is located near Skyfall River. Otto will meet us there."

"Then I'm surprised you stopped at all. Why not travel four days straight without wasting the time to stop for one night?"

He looked at her sidelong and rolled his eyes. "Don't be so dramatic."

"You're the one who's so eager to get rid of me that we didn't stop last night."

"That's not it." He took hold of her arm and pulled her to a stop, forcing her to look at his eyes. "We shouldn't be stopping at all."

"Then why did you?" she demanded.

"I stopped because you're driving me mad. I thought maybe if you slept in a bed and had a decent meal, you'd return to yourself again."

"I am myself." She folded her arms, glaring at him. "You're not yourself."

He ran his hands through his hair. "You're right." He glanced around before focusing on her again. "I don't want to take you to your brother, and I don't want you to leave. I'm going crazy trying to think of a way to keep you because I'm selfish like that." He heaved in a deep breath, letting it out slowly. "So no, I'm not myself. Because I can't stand the thought of losing you." He stood there with his hands on his hips.

They shouldn't be having this conversation in the middle of a walkway, in the center of a town. "I'm sorry," she whispered. "This is just as hard for me."

He reached out and took hold of her hand, leading her along the pathway again.

Like the other towns Sabine had seen in Avoni, this one had dozens of single story brown structures all with dark green curved rooflines. Since it was getting dark, people were out and about, heading home from work or securing a meal for supper. Hanging lanterns lit the narrow walkways.

Evander led Sabine to an inn. After he secured a room, they headed along the hallway and entered the last room on the right.

Sabine took the bed while Evander stretched out on the floor.

She tossed and turned, unable to get comfortable and fall asleep. She couldn't believe what little time she and Evander had left, they were going to act like this. Two people not talking, as if they barely knew one another. Granted, she didn't want to return to Lynk. To her husband. But she had no choice. She needed to go back so she could save those children and stop a war. Tears filled her eyes. Why did everything have to be so hard and complicated?

"Are you asleep?" Evander whispered.

"No."

"I have an idea." He stood and lit the candle next to the bed. "Make yourself presentable and meet me in the hallway." He exited the room before she could ask any questions.

Curious as to what he had in mind, Sabine slid out of bed and quickly changed into clean clothes and fixed her hair.

When she joined him in the hallway, he folded his hands

behind his back and said, "You're not allowed to ask any questions, and you have to do as I say. Understood?" He lifted a single eyebrow, awaiting her response.

She studied him for a moment, thrilled he was back to his charming self. "Deal."

He smiled and took hold of her hand. "I can't believe you just agreed to that. I thought for sure you'd renegotiate the terms."

They exited the inn and headed along the pathway.

"I'm feeling a little daring tonight," she replied with a smile. "And I could use a challenge." She knew he'd push her to do something out of her comfort zone and for some reason, she welcomed it.

The corners of his lips rose. "Just remember you said that." He smirked.

Growing up the youngest of six and having four of her siblings be brothers, she'd been forced into more dares than she could count. Evander might be surprised and learn a thing or two before the night was over.

After a few blocks, they neared a building with dozens of people standing outside it, laughing and talking. Evander went right past them and opened the door, motioning for Sabine to go in ahead of him.

She stepped into a boisterous tavern. Musicians played in a corner, a long bar took up one wall, dozens of tables were to the left side of the room, and on the right side people were dancing.

Evander poked her side.

"What?" she said, unable to hear him over the people talking and music playing.

He smiled and shook his head, taking her hand and pulling her toward the bar.

About halfway there, a man stepped in front of Evander,

clasping him on his shoulders. They exchanged a few friendly words—none of which Sabine could hear in this loud place.

Evander leaned in close to her ear. "Some friends are here. We're going to sit with them. This here is Gareth." He looked at her, as if asking permission.

"Tonight, I'm at your mercy," she reminded him.

His eyes darkened. "I truly wish that were the case," he murmured.

Gareth ushered them over to a table where three men were sitting. They all greeted Evander like they were old friends.

"Who's the pretty lady?" Gareth asked as he took a seat. He had black hair with dark eyes.

Evander sat on the last empty chair. Since there weren't any other ones available, he pulled Sabine onto his lap. She was about to protest when she remembered their deal—she was to go along with him this evening.

He tucked her hair behind her ear. "This is my special friend," he said with a sly smile.

Sabine rolled her eyes. She had no intention of letting him have the upper hand all night.

The men at the table all laughed.

"I'm Gareth, this is Ian, Mek, and Jeb." All four men had a similar build to Evander, though none of them had red hair. "And you are?"

While Gareth had a friendly smile on his face, it appeared forced. There was something about the way his brown eyes narrowed slightly that made Sabine feel as if she needed to tread carefully. These may be Evander's friends, but they weren't hers.

Since she wasn't sure if she should give her true name, she said, "Lina." Her sister's nickname.

"What are you doing wasting your time with this loser?"

Ian asked, pointing his chin at Evander. Ian had blond hair and blue eyes.

She leaned closer to him, as if about to share a secret, and replied, "That is a question I ask myself frequently."

They all burst out laughing.

Sabine wondered how Evander knew these men. None of them treated him like a prince, which she found interesting. Given that they all had a similar build with toned arms and sharp eyes that seemed to always be scanning the room, she assumed they were fellow assassins. Maybe they were from Evander's guild. None of them exposed their wrists, so she couldn't see if they bore the mark of the Crimson Cloaks.

"I like you, Lina," Mek said as he raised his arm, getting a server's attention. "Our friend Ev here needs someone who can put him in his place."

Sabine looked at Evander. "Ev?"

He shook his head, as if he didn't understand it himself.

A man with an apron approached carrying a stack of cups. He set them on their table along with a jug.

Mek filled each cup with whatever was in the jug before passing them out.

"I don't need one," Jeb said as he stood. "That pretty little woman over there keeps smiling at me. I'm gonna go dance with her." He made his way over to her.

"He shouldn't embarrass himself like that," Mek said, shaking his head. "Jeb can't dance."

Evander chuckled. "I don't think he really intends on dancing." His hand slid around Sabine's waist.

Since there was an empty chair, she peeled his arm back and moved to the seat, glad to no longer be on his lap. She didn't think she could take the heat from his body any longer. It was making her imagine things she shouldn't be thinking about. "How do you all know one another?" she asked no one in particular. Taking a sip from one of the cups, she found the liquid warm, surprising her.

"You never had warm ale before?" Ian asked.

Panic filled her as she realized her mistake. At a table full of trained assassins, she'd just unknowingly shown an expression, giving away a vital piece of information. If this drink was common in Avoni, and she acted as though she'd never had it before, then these men would know she was from another kingdom. It wouldn't take them long to figure out who she was. And that information, in the wrong hands, could be dangerous.

Evander couldn't jump in and cover for her. It was up to her then. "I have a cut in my mouth," she lied, not knowing if they bought it. "Now how do you all know one another?" she asked again, wanting to steer the conversation away from her.

"He didn't tell you?" Ian asked.

These men were far too sharp for her at this hour, and getting them to divulge anything good on Evander wouldn't be as easy as she'd hoped. "Maybe he did and I'm trying to see if your story matches his." She lifted her cup in a silent salute before taking another sip—this time being careful to keep her face blank.

Mek slapped Evander's back. "Finally someone who doesn't fawn all over you. I see you've finally met your match."

These men had to know Evander was their prince. Perhaps they were treating him so informally because they were in a crowded tavern. While her brothers had all been allowed to go to one of the taverns in Bakley, she'd never been permitted to go. This entire experience would be one she wouldn't easily forget. The music was so loud she could feel it vibrating through her body.

Evander leaned in closer to her, his hand going around

her shoulder as he murmured, "Drink up. That's why I brought you here. Two cups of this stuff and it'll knock you out. You'll sleep like a baby."

Liking the sound of that, Sabine finished her drink, trying not to flinch as the warm liquid burned going down her throat.

Jeb returned to the table, mumbling something about women.

Evander pulled Sabine off the chair. "Sit," Evander ordered Jeb. Then to her, "I want you to go and dance with that man over there in the blue top." His chin nodded behind her and to the right.

She twisted around and spotted a man in a blue shirt sitting one table over. Either Evander wanted to challenge her with something silly to see if she'd go through with it, or he wanted her away from the table so he could talk to his so-called friends. She was betting on the latter since he'd ordered Jeb to sit.

"Tell him you're my special friend and that I insist."

"What about my second drink?"

"It'll be here for you when you're done."

She didn't want to dance with some stranger. She'd much rather sit here—even if it was on Evander's lap—and listen to his conversation. By making her dance, she didn't even have a chance to overhear what he said since she'd be too far away.

"Fine." She sighed and went over to the man Evander had indicated. "Let's dance," she said.

"No thank you." He didn't even glance her way.

"Evander insists."

At that, he turned and looked at her. "Then I'm honored to dance with you." He glanced Evander's way, made some sort of sign with his hands, and Evander gave a single nod. "My name is Tad," he said as he stood.

"I'm Lina."

He gestured for her to lead the way to the dance floor.

"Are you with them?" she asked as they made their way toward it.

"Yes."

A man of many words. "I don't want to dance," she admitted. Even though she'd been having trouble falling asleep, she was tired. Her inability to sleep had to do with her discomfort with the idea of leaving Evander and returning to Lynk.

"Neither do I. But orders are orders."

"There's a table over there." She pointed to the other side of the dance area. The table was tucked in the back of the tavern.

"I don't disobey orders." Tad stopped at the edge of the dancing area and held out his hand for her to take.

For a brief moment, she considered telling Tad who she was and that she outranked Evander. But this wasn't her kingdom, and she didn't want anyone to know she was here. The less people who knew who she was and who she was traveling with, the better. Besides, she'd agreed to do whatever Evander said, and she was a woman of her word.

Taking Tad's hand, she allowed him to lead. The song was a fast tune, but he moved slowly, keeping his attention on the table of assassins and not on Sabine. Which was just fine with her. This was some sort of folk dance, and she had no idea what to do. Since they were moving so slow, she could at least pretend like she knew what was going on.

Peering over at Evander, he kept gesturing with his hands, as if trying to explain something. He glanced her way every so often. His face had reddened, and he kept running his hands through his equally red hair. He was sort of adorable when irritated. Not that she knew for sure he was upset, but that was the impression she got.

"Tell me, what do a group of assassins need a bodyguard for?" she asked.

Tad stopped dancing. "You're not from around here." It wasn't a question.

She'd been too formal with her speech. "No. I'm just visiting. I'm on my way home."

His body stiffened. "There's a bounty on your head…" His eyes widened slightly, and he glanced over at Evander.

"What is it?" she asked, trying to decipher his body language.

He shook his head. "Nothing."

"Am I in danger here?" she asked, wondering if the bounty had been called off and if so, by whom.

"This is Avoni," he replied. "There is always danger."

She nodded, as if she fully understood his warning, which she didn't. "How long have you known Evander?" she asked, wanting to see if he'd tell her anything.

"Long enough."

She sighed, realizing she wouldn't be getting anything good out of him.

Evander approached, and Tad released Sabine and walked away without a word.

"Friendly, that one," Sabine commented.

Evander smiled. "Are you getting tired yet?"

"No." She eyed him, noticing his hands in his pockets and the two to three feet of space separating them. "Will you dance with me?"

"I don't think that's a good idea," Evander said.

"Why?"

"I don't know if I can be that close to you and control myself." His eyes focused on her lips.

She poked him in the side, wanting to dissolve the tension between them. "You're an assassin. Your entire life is about control."

He chuckled. "True."

"Now dance with me."

"Why?" he asked, taking a step closer to her.

"I want the experience before we part ways," she said.

"The experience?" He slid his hands onto her hips, pulling her closer.

She rolled her eyes. "You know what I mean."

He shook his head.

"I want to experience what it's like to be at a tavern and dance." She gestured to the room.

"You've never been before?"

"No." Lottie had taken Sabine to the secret tavern below the palace, but she hadn't danced.

"Well then, we must rectify that." A wicked smile slid across his face, and his eyes gleamed with mischief. "Ready?"

Sabine had a feeling she was going to regret this. "Yes?"

He chuckled then stomped his feet to the beat of the drums, bringing her in closer and pushing her away every four beats. When the one instrument made a whirring noise, they spun. After a bit, she started to get the hang of it.

In the tavern, with Evander at her side, she felt like a normal person enjoying an evening with a friend. No one knew she was the queen of Lynk. No one here had any expectations of her, and she didn't have to follow any specific social construct. She could just be Sabine. A young woman dancing with a young man. An assassin-pirate-prince turned friend.

The music and joy swirled within her.

"It's good to see you laughing," Evander commented.

"It's good to laugh." She realized she hadn't been doing it enough these past few weeks. "I feel like I can be myself around you," she admitted. "It's refreshing."

Evander stopped dancing. He stood there, watching Sabine.

"What?" she asked.

He shook his head. "Nothing."

"Liar." She wanted him to tell her his thoughts. When he held things back from her, it felt wrong. It was silly for her to think or feel that way. But she couldn't help it.

"I could see myself loving you. It would be effortless."

The admission tugged at her heart and mirrored her own feelings. She could imagine having a wonderful, happy life with him. They would be both friends and lovers. True partners. Fate could be so cruel.

"Shall we get you that second drink?" he asked.

"Yes." Dancing no longer held the appeal it did a few minutes ago. Not with his admission still fresh in her mind.

Evander led her from the dance area back to the table where his friends were sitting. Jeb pushed a full cup her way. She thanked him and drank the warm ale.

"I want to apologize," Mek said. "I didn't mean to tease you earlier."

"It's fine." She'd enjoyed his teasing and saw no reason for him to apologize. Glancing at Evander, she wondered if he'd told his friends her real identity since they all seemed quiet and reserved compared to before.

She finished her drink. "I find myself tired."

"We'll watch the inn," Mek said. "You both can sleep tonight without keeping watch."

"Thank you." Evander placed his hand on Sabine's lower back, escorting her from the tavern.

When they reached the inn, she spotted Gareth standing outside.

She raised her eyebrows and looked at Evander.

"He made sure the building is secure. My friends will have eyes on all entry and exit points all night."

"And you trust them?" These friends of his. She didn't

understand why he wouldn't tell her they were fellow assassins or whatever they were.

He peered down at her as he opened the door, ushering her inside. "They've all sworn an oath to me and are bound by law."

That didn't really answer her question. However, it was just for one night, and they both needed to sleep.

Back inside their room, Evander lit the candle then turned to face her. "I'll step into the hallway while you change."

"Wait."

Chapter Thirteen

Evander froze, his hand on the door handle. "Sabine." His voice sounded gruff. "What are you saying?" His eyes searched hers.

She blinked, trying to think about why she'd told him to wait and what it meant. She wanted him but couldn't have him. The alcohol was making her bold.

"I…" He left the room, closing the door behind him.

If he'd stayed, Sabine had no idea what she would have done. If she would have kissed him. Covering her face with her hands, she let out a groan. She needed to pull it together. Grabbing her bag, she withdrew her night clothes and quickly changed. She climbed into bed, pulling up the covers and turning her back to the door, not wanting Evander to see the tears in her eyes.

A few minutes later, the door opened and closed. Evander didn't say anything. The room went dark—he must have snuffed out the candle. Then it sounded as if he'd laid on the floor. It was probably best if they didn't share the bed. At least not tonight.

Lying there, Sabine listened to Evander's breathing. She

imagined rolling over and joining him on the floor. Her hands taking the hem of his shirt and pushing it up, running her fingers over his torso, kissing his neck.

His hands gripping her around the waist, his mouth on hers, him flipping her over so he was on top of her…

These thoughts had to be from the strong ale. She pinched her eyes shut, trying to banish the images before she ended up doing something stupid that she couldn't undo.

Sabine awoke. Her arm was extended over the side of the bed, her hand clasping Evander's. His eyes were closed, his breathing even. He looked so peaceful sleeping there. Not wanting to wake him, she remained there watching him sleep.

It was easy to envision waking up to him every day. Picturing their life together, she saw it filled with laughter, talking, and pushing each other to be a better person. It would be a fulfilling life. But that was not her path. Even if her sister hadn't been murdered, Evander's parents wouldn't have chosen her for their son. Their paths never would've crossed.

Pulling her fingers from his hand, she sat up.

A dull light came in through the window, indicating it was time for them to be on their way. Peering back at Evander, she was about to wake him when his eyes opened, looking right at her.

"Morning," he said as he sat up, rubbing the side of his neck. "What's the matter?"

She wanted to say *nothing*, but that would be a lie. "We'll talk on the boat."

He nodded, not pushing the matter.

After they dressed and packed their things, they exited

the inn. Even though Sabine didn't see any of Evander's friends, she noticed him make a few hand signals indicating that at least one of them had to be nearby.

They made their way to the docks, neither one of them speaking. A light rain fell. Evander led her to a boat, and Sabine climbed in, sitting on the front bench.

The boat drifted along, past town after town. Then the scenery abruptly changed. The buildings stopped and trees lined both sides of the canal. Most were so tall and thick that the branches hung out over the water, almost forming a canopy of sorts.

The boats became less and less until they were the only ones out on the water.

"Are you going to talk to me?" Evander asked, his voice gentle.

Sabine twisted on the bench so she could face him. "I want to talk to you about the assassin."

Evander closed his eyes for a minute before nodding.

"In Lynk, a man tried to kill me." She quickly told him about the whistle she heard, the dog running away, the assassin entering, her fending him off, and then the hunt for him which resulted in him escaping.

"I can tell you two things. One—he isn't very good at his job and for that, I'm thankful. And two—he's not from Avoni."

She'd gathered that. "Do you know if Lottie hired Ex? Or did this man from Lynk hire Ex?"

"I don't know."

She licked her lips, trying to decide how to ask about the other night. There was no easy way, so she'd just have to come out and say it. "But Ex, the man you killed, he was from Avoni." It wasn't a question, but she needed confirmation.

Evander nodded.

Now for the question she feared the answer to.

"How'd he get into the palace?" She kept replaying the conversation she'd heard between Evander and his sister over and over in her mind. While she knew the guards had been called back so Evander could exit the palace without being seen, she didn't understand how Ex knew where and when he could slip past them to get into the compound. And then once he was in, how he got past so many skilled assassins. Like the assassination attempt back in Lynk, something wasn't adding up.

Evander sighed. "I was hoping you wouldn't ask about that." He ran his hands through his hair.

She didn't respond. Instead, she patiently waited for him to explain.

"I'd rather not share anything with you. At least not until I've sorted it all out."

She was about to protest when he held up his hand, so she kept her mouth shut.

"What I can tell you is that someone let the assassin in. It was planned perfectly with my sister pulling the guards so I could sneak out."

"Does that mean you have a traitor?"

He looked at her for a long moment before saying, "No. It means I have someone close to me trying to manipulate the situation. Like I said, I'm not ready to tell you everything quite yet. But I do want to apologize for letting him get that close to you."

It made sense if someone found out about the delegation. She understood someone letting the assassin have a go at her for retribution. What she didn't understand was Evander not wanting to tell her everything. "Why keep it a secret from me?"

"Because I'm still trying to figure it all out."

A vague, noncommittal answer. It hurt her that he didn't

want to be completely open and honest with her. Perhaps they weren't as close as she thought they were.

"Sabine." The way he said her name sent a jolt straight to her heart.

"Sometimes I don't know who or what to believe." While he may not want to be honest with her, she wanted to be honest with him. Tears filled her eyes.

He reached forward and took both her hands in his. "You shouldn't trust anyone completely—not even yourself. That will keep you alive."

Then she didn't want to live. Not like that. A life without trust, love, or understanding was no life at all. "That sounds lonely." Having grown up in a large family, she couldn't imagine living the rest of her life alone, never trusting or depending on anyone.

"But you'll live." He squeezed her hands.

"You can't possibly live without trusting anyone."

"I do."

"What about your friends?" The ones they'd met last night who'd kept watch.

"Not even them."

"What about your family?"

"No." It felt as if his hands shook ever so slightly.

It saddened her that he felt that way. "I trust my mother and father along with my brothers."

"Don't."

"I can't go through life that way. I have to believe that my family loves me and wants what's best for me." She wanted him to understand that trusting someone was part of loving someone.

His eyes darkened. "You're married to Rainer now. That changes how your family sees you." He let go of her. "You need to protect yourself." He rubbed his hands on his pants. "For the first time in my life, I find myself afraid." He glanced away, as if embarrassed to admit something like that.

"What are you afraid of?" She reached out, placing her hand on his knee.

"I don't want you to return to Rainer. I'm afraid for you." He looked back at her, his green eyes intense.

"You have nothing to worry about. Right now, Rainer needs me." Granted, once he had an heir, things could change.

"I hope you're right. I'll never forgive myself if something happens to you."

"I'll be fine," she assured him.

"You may be fine, but I won't."

"He'll never find out about the kidnapping. I promise." She would make Rainer understand that Evander kept her alive from an assassin Lottie had sent after her.

He shook his head. "That's not what I meant." He leaned his elbows on his thighs. "Sabine, I care for you. I don't know how I'm going to live knowing you're sharing another man's bed." His voice came out gruff. "The mere thought makes me sick. I want to ram my dagger straight into his heart."

She didn't know how to respond to that. "Evander…"

"Don't say anything. I know you're married, and I can respect that. But it doesn't mean I have to like it."

His jealousy surprised her. She didn't think him capable of such an emotion. Putting herself in his shoes, she imagined him marrying Lottie and sharing her bed. The thought of him touching Lottie, putting his hands on her, and kissing her, seemed vile. Repulsive. Especially since he'd never be friends with someone like Lottie—they were too different and had nothing in common. Lottie didn't deserve him.

"Sabine?"

She understood what he'd meant by not being fine.

"Are you okay?" he asked.

She shook her head. Suddenly, everything felt different. It was hard to breathe. Sadness filled her. If felt like she'd been tossed into a dark lake, boulders tied to her feet. She sunk, unable to free herself. Unable to change her fate.

And then she remembered the plan she'd been considering. "Evander, do you want to be with me?" Or was he simply attracted to her like she was to Rainer? She thought they shared a connection, but she needed to be absolutely certain.

"What I want is irrelevant."

She understood, all too well. "What if I told you I have an idea? And if it works, we could be together?" She was curious to hear his response, knowing his parents probably wouldn't support the match.

"What is this idea of yours?" he asked, moving to sit beside her on the bench seat.

More than once, she'd thought about telling him what she had in mind. If anything, he could help her come up with a solid plan on how to enact it. And she could trust him—he wouldn't tell anyone. But her gut told her no one could know, not even Evander. In order for this to work, she had to do it all on her own, and no one could see it coming. "I can't tell you."

He took her hand, drawing circles with this finger on her palm. "Avoni has a plan as well."

"What is it?" she asked.

"I can't tell you." He smiled wryly, still drawing circles on her palm. "What if we worked together?"

She shook her head. "I have to do mine alone." It was the only way.

"Please tell me you don't intend to commit treason because if you do, you can be killed."

"I will not break any laws," she said. Quite the opposite.

She would live by the law. "If my plan works, if I pull it off, we could potentially be together." Although she wasn't going to do it for that reason. She was doing it for all the kingdoms.

She looked into his eyes, wondering how her view of him had changed so much over the course of the past couple of weeks.

"Don't look at me like that," he said. "I'm trying to keep myself from tearing your clothes off."

"Then you shouldn't be so close. Your eyes, your smile, and even your smell make me want to devour you."

The corners of his lips rose even more. "One day."

She nodded, knowing nothing ever went according to plan. While she would do her best to end Rainer's reign, being with Evander had to be secondary.

When Sabine awoke the next morning, she found herself tucked on the floor of the boat, her head resting on Evander's folded cloak. Sitting up, she saw him on the rear bench seat, scanning the water around them.

"Is everything all right?" she asked.

He nodded.

She slid onto the front bench. A thin fog hovered above the water. As the boat floated through the fog, it parted, like a curtain being pulled aside for them. The trees began to thin on either side of the canal. Every once in a while, a tendril of fog reached onto the land, between the trees, like an extended arm, pointing to something.

Sabine remained quiet. Something about the fog unsettled her. Evander didn't bother with conversation either. As the day wore on, the fog lightened until it eventually disappeared all together. They hadn't passed a single boat all day.

Her stomach made a growling noise.

"Was that you?" Evander whispered.

"Yes. I'm hungry. And why are we whispering?"

"You should have told me you're hungry. I have food." He reached into one of the bags and withdrew some bread, handing it to her. "It feels wrong to speak loudly when the weather is like this."

She took the bread. "I agree." Even though the fog was gone, thick clouds covered the sky, promising rain. After eating the bread, she shivered. It felt as if it were getting colder as the day wore on.

"We're almost there," Evander said.

The thought of seeing her brother again excited her.

"Just so you know, this meeting is going to be an official one."

"What does that mean?" She'd assumed they'd meet somewhere discreet like before.

"It means we will each be as we are supposed to be."

"What does that even mean?" It felt as if the closer she got to her brother, the farther Evander was getting from her. She hated the space growing between them.

"You will act as the queen of Lynk should, your brother the prince that he is, and the same will go with me. Titles will be used, and guards will be present."

Then this meant everything was about to change.

"There is something for you in the bag," Evander said. "Something my sister assured me would be appropriate for someone of your station."

She opened the bag and found a dress folded neatly at the bottom. "Am I supposed to change in front of you?" she said in a teasing tone.

"Oh Sabine, trust me, the thought of watching you undress has crossed my mind more than once." He twisted on the bench seat, facing away from her.

Sabine quickly changed into the blue dress. It reminded

her of something she'd wear in Bakley rather than Lynk. "It's safe for you to look."

Evander twisted around. "I was hoping for something more along the lines of what you wore in Lynk."

She raised her eyebrows. "It's a little cold to be half naked."

"There are ways to keep you warm." He smirked. "Okay, my turn." He motioned for her to face the other way.

She gracefully put her legs on the other side of the bench, her back now to him. She heard Evander remove his clothing. Unable to help herself, she glanced at the water, hoping to catch his reflection. There wasn't one.

"When we arrive, please don't think I'm being indifferent to you," Evander said. "I want to make it clear nothing is going on between us. We each have our roles to play."

Pretending they weren't friends would be difficult, but she knew it was for the best.

"I'm decent," he said.

"I'm going to remain facing this way," she said over her shoulder. It was time for her to start preparing herself for what was to come. Not even her brother could question her relationship with Evander. She started chewing on her bottom lip, trying to decide how she wanted to act and treat Evander. He was an acquaintance. Someone who'd kept her safe from an assassin. That made them friends. She needed that to come across. But any sort of attraction had to be concealed. Taking a deep breath, she let it out slowly. She was the queen of Lynk. It was time to start acting the part.

They came around a bend in the canal. Straight ahead, roughly a dozen boats blocked the waterway.

"There's nothing to worry about," Evander said. "They're here for us."

All of the boats were black with a red mark on the side. It made sense *Prince* Evander would want the protection as they made their way to meet Sabine's brother. After all, they were officially themselves now.

"Are you ready for this?" he mumbled.

"Yes." Having been raised a royal, she knew how and when to hide her true feelings and emotions. While she wasn't ready for what she was about to face, she knew it was time.

The boats moved apart, making a path for them. As they got closer, she saw two uniformed men or women in each boat. Without a word, the boats surrounded them, escorting them along the canal.

Holding her head high, she kept her focus forward. Her back felt cold, as if Evander were no longer behind her, as if she were all alone in the boat. She gripped the edge, her knuckles turning white.

After they traveled about a mile, the trees lining both sides lessened, replaced by green rolling hills and the occasional house. The farther they went, the more dense the houses became until they entered a vibrant city with buildings two stories tall, lining both sides of the canal. The waterway became crowded with boats. However, as soon as people saw the procession, they immediately steered their boats out of the way, letting them pass with ease.

Peering down the side streets, Sabine saw people crowded on the pathways. One thing she didn't see were any docks like the previous towns. She was just about to ask when they came to an intersection. Their party turned right, and she realized they'd entered a wharf. It was quite long with dozens and dozens of boats. She supposed this allowed the main canal to transport more boats since it didn't have to house docks on either side.

Their party made their way to the end where a special spot had been designated for them marked by a handful of guards keeping watch. Evander expertly slid the boat into a slip, and someone hurried over, trying it up for him. All the boats that had accompanied them also docked, the guards all getting out. One of the female guards approached Sabine and bowed. She then extended her hand, helping Sabine step out of the boat.

Evander joined her. "We're staying at an inn not too far from here. If it's acceptable to you, we'll walk there."

She eyed him, not caring for this overly formal version of Evander. Unable to help herself, she said, "And if walking isn't acceptable, what are the alternatives?"

His cheek twitched as he fought a smile. "I can get a carriage for you." He clasped his hands together behind his back, awaiting her response.

She eyed the sky. "Since it isn't raining, a rarity here in Avoni it seems, we can walk." The gray clouds looked as if they'd dump water at any moment.

"Very well." He gestured for her to accompany him.

The guards formed two lines, a dozen in front of them and a dozen behind. The pathways between the buildings were wider here in this city. There were also some main streets, though not many. Sabine still found it strange that there were no horses in this kingdom.

As they traveled along the walkway, Sabine noted that many of the buildings looked like those of the previous towns. "I thought there would be taller structures given that this is such a large city."

"It's rare for anything to be above two stories in Avoni."

"Why is that?"

"Safety," Evander answered. "If we had tall buildings, an assassin could strike me or you at any moment from above. That's also why the second levels don't have windows facing the main pathways."

It surprised her that she hadn't thought of or noticed this before. The beds being on the floor she'd picked up on right away, but this was something she hadn't considered. "Doesn't it get exhausting?"

"No."

She could never live in a land of assassins.

The guards escorting them stopped before an inn.

"Let's head inside." Evander opened the door for her.

Sabine stepped into a lavish room with gold framed paintings on the walls, plush sofas, and a desk to the side.

A young woman came forward and bowed. "Your Highness, two rooms have been prepared for the both of you. The rest of your party has already arrived."

"Excellent," Evander said. "Let's go and freshen up."

The woman led them up the staircase.

"I'd like to see Otto," Sabine said to Evander.

"Can you please let Prince Otto know we wish to see him in the receiving room?" he said to the woman.

"Of course, Your Highness," she replied as they headed along the hallway. "Your room is here," she said to Sabine, opening a door on the right.

"When you're ready, just come out," Evander said. "A guard will be posted here, and she will show you to the receiving room."

Sabine nodded and closed the door.

A familiar trunk sat in the middle of the room. She rushed over and threw the lid open, revealing a couple of her dresses from Bakley along with a handful of books and a blanket from home. Her brother must have brought these things with him. Smelling the familiar scent of her castle in Bakley, she closed her eyes and imagined she was there. She could almost feel the stone floor beneath her bare feet, hear the cracking fire in the hearth, and smell the warm embrace of her mother.

She opened her eyes, not wanting to get lost in memories of the past. It was time to face the future. Since there was a wash basin in the room, she decided to wash her face and fix her hair before meeting her brother. The dress she wore would suffice. Once she was presentable, she exited her room and found a guard standing there just as Evander said.

The female guard led Sabine downstairs where she spotted her brother sitting on a sofa beside Evander.

"Brother," she said.

He stood and turned to face her. She had to stop herself from running to him. When she did reach him, she pulled him in for a hug, holding on tightly.

"It's good to see you," he said.

She released him. "You look well." He was dressed in a tunic bearing the Bakley royal family's colors and he wore his crown—something he rarely did. Which reinforced they were all playing their parts respectively, and this was a diplomatic meeting.

"Come," Evander said, gesturing to a door on the far wall. "I have a private room prepared where the three of us can speak." He led them into an adjacent room containing a small round table and chairs. "Have a seat." He instructed the guards who'd been in the receiving room to move closer to the stairway, giving them a buffer so hopefully no one would overhear their conversation. He closed the door, his shoulders relaxing ever so slightly.

Sabine reached out, gripping her brother's forearm. "How are things at home?"

"Everyone is well," Otto replied, twisting the ring on his finger, not quite meeting her eyes.

"What's the matter?" she asked, withdrawing her hand.

Otto glanced at Evander before he said, "Father is upset with your behavior."

She hadn't expected that. "Whatever for?"

"Leaving Lynk, acting independently, not consulting your husband. The list is quite long." He scratched his chin.

Shock rolled through her. She assumed her parents would be proud of her. "I've been acting in Bakley's best interest." Anger replaced the shock. "And mine."

"I know," Otto said. "You don't need to convince me."

Sabine leaned back in her chair, staring at her brother. "Has there been any news about the kidnapped children?"

"Funny you should bring that up," Otto mumbled.

"I don't see how it's funny."

Otto glanced at Evander. "The children have been found."

Relief filled her. "Have they been returned to their families?" She wondered who found them and how they managed to get them out of Lynk and back to Bakley.

"No, not yet." He drummed his fingers on the table. "I am on my way to retrieve them."

"And Rainer has just agreed to hand them over?" She had a feeling she was missing something.

"Yes, because he is claiming he didn't take them."

She snorted. "But somehow he has them." She folded her arms.

"Rainer is claiming he found the children." He cleared his throat. "In Avoni." He glanced at Evander again.

Sabine sat there, replaying Otto's words over and over in her mind. She must have misheard him. "What did you say?"

"Rainer is saying that some of his soldiers spotted boats in Skyfall River. They thought something suspicious was going on, so they boarded and found the missing children. The boats were manned by Avoni sailors." Otto turned to Evander. "Care to explain?"

"I have no idea what you're talking about, so there's nothing I can explain," Evander said as he ran a hand through his hair.

"But we saw the children," Sabine said. "They were traveling on land with Lynk soldiers."

Otto sighed. "Once the soldiers found the children, they escorted them to Lynk."

She peered over at Evander, unable to fathom him being responsible for kidnapping children from Bakley. Although, he had kidnapped her.

Evander raised his eyebrows. "You can't possibly think I'd do something like that."

She didn't answer. "What are the children saying?" she asked her brother.

"That they were taken by men from Avoni."

"Based upon what evidence?" Evander demanded, his voice rising in volume.

"That's what they were told." Otto folded his arms. "So it could be a set up." He shrugged.

Sabine noticed her brother had only been stating facts. "What do you believe happened?" she asked him.

"I think Rainer is ten steps ahead of us." He rubbed a hand over his face. "I think Rainer sought Alina out and designed the marriage alliance to benefit him. He wants Bakley and our food. I think taking over the other kingdoms is just an added benefit for him. I think he has it all planned out with various scenarios."

"We believe so as well," Evander said. "My family is working on stopping him."

"I have a plan," Sabine said. "I think I know how to stop Rainer. But I'm not going to have a lot of time to enact it."

"Good. I'm glad you're taking this seriously since Father isn't."

That didn't surprise her. King Franz Ludwig rarely took matters of their kingdom's security seriously. She couldn't tell if he didn't know how to handle it, didn't care, or if he was truly that naive.

Evander stood and started pacing the room. "Where do we go from here?"

"I will escort Sabine to Lynk and meet with King Rainer. Then, I'll bring the children home."

"And where does Avoni fit into this now that Rainer is all but ensuring Bakley will want to retaliate?"

"I am going to demand peace. When I meet with the League, I will ask for the same. Whatever it is that Sabine plans on doing to stop Rainer, I hope it works because I fear for our kingdoms if it doesn't."

Evander went over to the window, resting his hands on the window ledge and staring outside, lost in thought.

Sabine wished she could ask him what he was thinking. But she couldn't. Her brother couldn't suspect anything was going on between them—even a familiar friendship. She cleared her throat. "When do we leave for Lynk?" She needed to start hashing out the details of her plan.

"Tomorrow."

She thought she'd have at least a day or two. "Very well," she replied. She'd just have to figure it out as they traveled.

Voices grew in volume on the other side of the door. Someone shouted. All three of them looked to the door as it burst open.

Chapter Fourteen

Markis stood in the middle of the doorway, his chest heaving. "Queen Sabine." He knelt on the floor, bowing his head, a handful of Avoni guards and two Bakley soldiers standing behind him with weapons drawn.

"Do either of you know him?" Evander demanded with a knife in hand.

"Yes. Everyone, put your weapons away. This is Lieutenant Markis Belle, my personal guard." Sabine went over to Markis. "Stand." He did as she commanded. "It's good to see you."

The guards and soldiers behind him all lowered their weapons and took a step back.

"I've been searching everywhere for you," Markis mumbled. He took a deep breath before shifting his focus to Evander. "You." He lunged for Evander, only Sabine stepped in front of him, blocking him.

"Stop," she said.

"But this man kidnapped you," Markis said, his eyes alight with fury.

"He did not," she said loud enough for everyone to hear. "An assassin was after me. Prince Evander has kept me alive."

Markis's eyes narrowed, as if he didn't believe her. However, he kept his mouth shut and didn't argue.

Sabine held his gaze. "We have a lot to discuss. Let me finish up with Prince Evander and Prince Otto. I will meet you in the receiving room in a few minutes."

"Of course, Your Majesty." Markis bowed and left the room.

An Avoni guard stepped forward. "Your Highness?" He looked at Evander.

"Give Lieutenant Markis clearance," he said, waving his hand.

The man bowed.

Sabine shut the door then turned to face Evander and Otto. When neither said anything, she decided to speak. "You have guards here?" she said to her brother.

"Yes. A dozen came with me."

She nodded. It made sense he'd have his own protection—especially in a foreign kingdom.

"Those two used to work with Markis," he added, as if that explained why Markis hadn't been killed on sight.

"I thought he looked familiar," Evander said as he casually tossed his knife, catching it by the hilt. "I remember him following you around the Lynk palace." He tossed the knife again.

"Is there anything else we need to discuss?" Sabine asked. She wanted to meet with Markis to see the state of things with Rainer.

Evander shrugged. "Not that I can think of."

"I have a few League issues to discuss with you," Otto said. "If you don't mind us meeting privately."

Evander sat in a chair, putting his weapon away. "Not at all."

Sabine excused herself and went into the receiving room where she spotted Markis conversing with the two Bakley soldiers off to the side. She had to refrain from running over and hugging him.

The three men straightened and faced Sabine.

"It is good to see you, Lieutenant Markis," she said by way of greeting. She knew he wanted to speak freely with her. However, she didn't know if there was a place they could talk without being overheard. She motioned toward the middle of the room, and the two of them moved that way, leaving behind the Bakley soldiers.

Sabine didn't feel like sitting on the sofa since she'd been stuck in a boat for so long. Instead, she stood near the window, looking outside. The place was surrounded by Avoni guards. She turned to face Markis. "My brother is escorting me back to Lynk. We leave tomorrow."

Markis nodded. "I will accompany you both." He watched her, his eyes scanning her from head to toe, as if looking for injuries.

"I'm fine," she said, her voice low, hoping that would be enough to satisfy him for now. "How are things back in Lynk?"

"A conversation for another time," he whispered, folding his hands behind his back.

Sabine noticed his hair had grown longer and his face now sported a short beard. It made him look older. His skin also appeared to be tanner than the last time she'd seen him.

The side door opened, and Evander and Otto exited the room, joining them.

"Has your business concluded?" she asked, wondering what her brother wanted to discuss with Evander without her present. She doubted it was League business, but perhaps it was.

"Yes," Otto replied. "Lieutenant Markis, if you'll join me, I'd like to plan our journey to Lynk."

"Of course, Your Highness."

"And you two," Otto said to the Bakley soldiers, "you're with me." The four of them headed upstairs.

Sabine went over and sat on the sofa.

Evander sat opposite her, crossing his legs and stretching his arms out along the back of the sofa. "You're leaving tomorrow." It was a statement and not a question.

"I am. Thank you for showing me your beautiful kingdom and keeping me alive. Is there anything I should relay to my husband, King Rainer, on your behalf?" She clasped her hands together, unable to believe she was leaving so soon. Unable to believe she had to behave so formally around Evander.

"You can tell him Avoni didn't kidnap the kids." He tilted his head back as he stared at the ceiling. "And I didn't keep you alive for his benefit."

"I will relay that."

He eyed her. "And here I thought I was the one who'd be most transformed," he mumbled so only she could hear.

His words sent a dagger straight to her heart. She didn't know what he wanted or expected from her. He was the one who said they needed to play their respective parts, and she was doing what needed to be done.

"How are you handling this so well?" he whispered.

At that, she had to squeeze her hands together. She couldn't even look him in the eyes. If she did, she'd tear up.

"You're leaving tomorrow," he whispered.

"We both knew this was coming." And while she enjoyed being with Evander, she had a job to do and responsibilities. She had to put that first, above her own wants and desires. She finally looked at him.

His bright green eyes were intense with emotion. "You're

a much better person than me. I want to snatch you away for good."

"Evander," she chided him. They couldn't afford for anyone to overhear them. They were on dangerous grounds.

He leaned forward, his elbows on his thighs. "You going back to him...the thought of him touching you...it makes me ill."

His words mirrored how she felt when thinking of him and Lottie together.

"I don't think I can do this." He shook his head.

"Listen to me," she hissed. "We don't have any other options. You can, and you will, do this. Now pull it together. I have a plan." Sabine was barely keeping it together. If Evander started to question her returning, if he wavered, she feared she would as well.

"I want to know what your plan is," he said. "To see if it's even feasible."

She wanted to tell him, but she couldn't. No one could know. "I'm sorry, I can't tell you."

He ran his hands through his hair. "Sabine. My family... we have a plan in place as well."

He'd mentioned that before. There was something about his statement that concerned her. "How do I fit into your family's plan?"

"You're the wife of our enemy," he said plainly. Matter-of-factly.

That had been what she expected. Avoni had a plan, and that plan might very well be the end of her.

"How much time do I have?" She understood they'd want retribution for the delegation members who'd been killed.

"Not much." He rubbed his hands over his face. "My family will act if Rainer makes a move against us or any other kingdom. We won't let it get out of control. And if we act against him, that means we act against you."

She understood. "I assumed when he blew up the ship that was acting against your kingdom." She was surprised they hadn't done something already. But they did have a unit of men in Lynk. Perhaps they didn't want to do anything until they knew what was going on with them first.

"It definitely got our attention. But since I technically kidnapped you, we're even."

"Ah." Things were starting to make sense now. "My plan is going to work," she said, trying to sound reassuring though she didn't feel it.

"Even if it does, you're still his wife."

Since she hadn't consummated her marriage yet, she could get out of being his wife. However, in order to maintain peace between the kingdoms, she needed to be the queen of Lynk. It was the only way to save countless lives.

"If he hurts you, I'll never forgive myself for letting you go back to him."

"You're not letting me, I'm choosing to go."

"I just need to stop picturing you with him." He laced his fingers through his hair.

"Trust me to fix this."

"I am not used to trusting anyone."

She understood that. But if he wanted any sort of relationship with her in the future, he had to learn to trust her.

That night after supper, Sabine asked Markis to escort her out behind the inn where there was a small garden. She wanted to be alone to get her thoughts in order. Standing in the middle of a pathway through the garden, she stared up at the clouds. She hadn't seen the stars or moon in days, and she missed them.

"I'm surprised you want to be out here since it's so cold."

A light mist began falling, but Sabine barely noticed it. "I didn't want to be inside." Enclosed. Where people could eavesdrop. She needed to at least feel like she had some freedom.

"Are you ready to tell me what really happened?" he asked, his voice low.

"No." She had other things on her mind that she needed to deal with.

"If he hurt you in any way, I need to know."

She looked Markis directly in the eyes so he would know she told the truth. "He did not hurt me."

He rubbed a hand over his face.

"How did you find me?" she asked. He'd come separately from Otto, so he hadn't discovered her location that way.

"When Rainer discovered you were missing, he sent a dozen soldiers to find you. Anton said something about knowing where you were, so Rainer had him go look as well. That's when Rainer told me if I didn't return with you, he would skin me alive and send my body to my wife."

That seemed rather extreme. "Why did he think you could find me?"

"He didn't know if you'd been kidnapped, if you'd run away, or what had happened to you. He thought maybe you'd confided in me or if you had run away, I might know where you'd gone. When I told him I didn't know either of those things, he threatened me. So I left and have been searching for you ever since."

Guilt filled her. She hadn't once stopped to think about how her disappearance could have affected Markis. "Did you get my letter that I sent with Anton?"

"I did not."

She nodded, not at all surprised. "I want you to return to Bakley. Go be with your wife. Otto will smooth things over with Rainer when we get there." She folded her arms, not liking the idea of being alone in Lynk. But she couldn't put Markis's life at risk like that—it wasn't fair.

"I can't," Markis said. "King Rainer *ordered* me to return with you."

Duty and honor were important to Markis, and she commended him for it. "Then after we return, I will request you be released. You will no longer be my guard, and you can return home."

"Is that what you truly want?" he asked.

No. "Your place is in Bakley. With your family."

He watched her for a long, silent minute before saying, "You've changed."

"I've grown up." She'd had no choice.

"I can remain with you in Lynk," he insisted. "I don't want to just leave you there unprotected."

While she knew she'd have guards, she understood what he was saying. "How about we wait and see what things look like when we return?"

"I think that's wise." Markis glanced at something behind Sabine.

She twisted, following his line of sight. Evander had just exited the inn and was heading toward them.

"Am I interrupting?" Evander asked, stopping a few feet away.

Just the sound of his voice made her warm inside. "No," Sabine responded. "Did you need something?" She kicked the toe of her shoe into the ground, not sure how to act around this man out here under the cover of darkness. Her assassin-pirate-prince.

"I...ah...just wanted to make sure your accommodations are adequate." He cleared his throat.

Markis cursed. "You've got to be kidding me," he mumbled.

"What's the matter?" she asked. Evander was being polite. That was acceptable, wasn't it?

"I should have seen it before," Markis muttered, shaking his head.

She had no idea what he meant by that.

"If I can tell the two of you have feelings for one another, Rainer will be able to as well." Markis folded his arms.

"There's nothing going on between us," she insisted, looking at Evander for help.

"How could you tell?" Evander asked.

Markis looked from Sabine to Evander and then back again. "It's the way you two can't keep your eyes off each other," he said gently. "I suggest the two of you try not to be in the same room together. At least not when anyone else is around." He looked pointedly at her before leaving them alone in the garden.

Sabine assumed he'd be waiting for her just inside the door.

"He's right," Evander said, sliding his hands in his pockets. "It's becoming nearly impossible to keep my wits around you."

"I didn't realize you had any wits to keep in the first place," she said, teasing him, trying to lighten the mood.

"Must you joke about my feelings for you?" he said, moving closer to her.

"If I don't joke, I'll cry." A true admission.

Evander moved even closer, his toes almost skimming hers. As close as they could be without touching. "You're leaving tomorrow," he whispered.

"That's the plan." It felt as if a hole had appeared in her chest.

"I'm going to miss you."

"And I you."

"Sabine, there are some things I want to tell you." His green eyes appeared unusually dark tonight.

"But let me guess, you can't?"

He nodded.

Unfortunately, she understood. She had things she was keeping from him as well.

"I want you to know—no matter what happens—my feelings for you are real. Regardless of what you hear or what people tell you when you return to Lynk. Understand?"

"Okay." She had a feeling his family's plan was already in motion. If he told her what it was, when she returned to Lynk and discovered what was going on, she wouldn't have the right reaction. Her not knowing was better. But it didn't mean she had to like it.

"I wish I had something to give you, like a token, for you to remember me by. Something for you to hold on to when times get rough." He reached out to take hold of her hand.

Sabine took a step back, away from him. "I have memories of our time together." Her eyes filled with tears. And then because she had to, she said, "We shouldn't be out here alone like this. My accommodations are sufficient. Thank you for checking on me."

He closed his eyes and nodded. "Excellent." He turned and left her alone in the garden.

The stillness of the night surrounded her. Taking a slow breath, she tried to rein in her emotions. After a few minutes, she called out for Markis who immediately appeared from the doorway. She asked him to escort her to her room for the night.

***

Sabine stood in the receiving room, Otto at her side. Markis and the two additional Bakley guards were behind them.

"Queen Sabine, Prince Otto, my guards will accompany you to the Avoni border," Evander said, his focus solely on Sabine. "Thank you for gracing my kingdom with your presence." He bowed then left the room.

And just like that, he was gone. The hole in Sabine's chest expanded. She had to bite her tongue to ensure she didn't tear up or do something stupid. Evander meant nothing to her. "Brother," she turned to Otto. "Shall we be on our way?"

"Yes." He held out his arm for her to take.

She slid her fingers around his proffered arm, and the two of them exited the inn. "Are we taking one of the smaller boats to the ship?" she asked, realizing she didn't know where he'd docked.

"No. We'll travel by carriage the two miles to where the vessel is."

"They don't have horses in Avoni."

He patted her hand. "I know."

Without horses, Sabine had no idea how they'd take a carriage.

Four men rounded the building carrying what appeared to be a wooden bench with a back, similar to a sofa, with two poles sticking out on each side. The four men stopped before Sabine, setting it on the walkway.

Otto took hold of her elbow, escorting her toward the so-called carriage.

"I would rather walk," she hissed. "That doesn't look safe."

"Just get in," Otto muttered. "I don't have the energy to argue with you right now."

With so many Avoni guards around, Sabine didn't want to offend anyone or appear ungrateful—perpetuating the rumors about her upbringing—so she gracefully sat on the wooden sofa.

Markis and the two Bakley soldiers stepped behind the carriage.

Once her and Otto were situated, the four men each took hold of a pole, lifting the sofa-turned-carriage. The Avoni guards surrounded them, then they started running. The motion was jarring and not at all comfortable. Sabine feared she'd bounce right off the bench and would land on the ground. She gripped the seat, trying to remain in place.

"Two miles?" she asked, not sure how she would handle this for that long.

"Give or take." Otto shrugged.

It was difficult to keep her head forward and not look back. But she couldn't—she had to focus on the path in front of her, ignoring the growing hole in her chest and the empty feeling coursing through her body. Evander was no longer part of her life. "Why aren't we taking the canal to the ship?" she asked, trying to distract herself.

"I was told something about this way being faster." Otto shrugged.

The Avoni guards led them to a well-traveled road that skirted around the city. When people saw them, they immediately stepped aside, letting them pass. When they reached the next town, they headed straight to a large port containing hundreds and hundreds of docks filled with boats of varying sizes. Sabine had never seen a port so large before.

They stopped before a massive ship with the flag of Bakley raised and flapping in the wind. The men set the bench down, and Sabine and Otto got off. Markis immediately stepped to her side, taking her arm and escorting her to the gangplank. She stepped on it, carefully walking across with Markis right behind her. A couple dozen Bakley soldiers were onboard, waiting for them, standing at attention. One reached forward, helping Sabine step onto the ship.

This was by far the largest vessel that she had ever been on—at least three times the size of Evander's boat.

"Let's get out of here," Otto said once he boarded. He started barking out commands.

Sabine moved to the front of the ship, wanting to get out of the way as sails were hoisted, soldiers hurried about the deck, and the anchor was raised. The boat moved away from the dock. They traveled out of the port and into Skyfall River.

Otto joined her at the front of the ship.

"Are we sailing north straight to Lynk?" she asked.

"That's the plan."

Which meant they wouldn't be stopping by Bakley first as she'd hoped. She missed her family terribly and wished she could see them.

"Everything all right?" Otto asked.

She nodded. "I just wanted to make sure we're staying in Skyfall River where the water is calmer rather than going around, out into the open ocean." At least this way she wouldn't get seasick.

"We're going this way since it's the fastest route."

The wind blew her hair, so she quickly braided it to get it out of her eyes.

"I have a few things to attend to. There's a room for you below deck." Otto rubbed her back before going to speak with one of the soldiers.

Her chest tightened and her eyes stung, but she refused to cry. Instead of thinking about Evander, she watched the other ships as they passed by. Several were stacked with supplies, probably traveling from port to port selling goods, others had large nets for catching fish.

She was not going to cry.

Evander was just a man whom she happened to have feelings for. But it didn't matter. She was married and had a job to do. Just because she'd left him didn't mean she needed to cry over it. Just because her life wasn't what she wanted it to be didn't mean she had to be sad about it. She was a queen. By all appearances, she had it all. Crying meant she was a spoiled brat. She would not—*could not*—be that person. Her sister would be disappointed in her if she gave in to her emotions like that.

Otto joined her again, this time placing a cape over her shoulders. "Is there anything else you need to tell me?" he asked, his voice low.

"I'm worried about what's going to happen when I return to Lynk," she admitted.

He rested his arms on the railing, looking out at the water. "The Sabine I know would never cower." He peered at her, eyebrows raised. "So whatever happens, you must be strong and not show weakness or an ounce of fright."

She nodded, wishing it were that easy. "Who do you believe kidnapped the children?" she asked.

He shrugged. "It's hard to say. We saw Lynk soldiers traveling with the Bakley children. It makes sense Rainer is responsible for kidnapping them. However, his explanation about having found them and his soldiers escorting them to safety also makes sense."

"Yes, but given everything else—his ships spotted off the coast of Carlon and the rumors about him preparing to invade other kingdoms, what do you think?"

"It doesn't matter what I think. What matters is keeping the peace between all kingdoms. You need to do whatever you can to make sure that happens."

"You're right." She took a deep breath. She would not back down. She was the queen of Lynk and would act like it. For far too long, she'd allowed Rainer to dictate how their relationship went. Well, no more. She lifted her chin.

"There she is." Otto smiled.

Sabine found that she did not care to be below deck for long periods of time. Other than eating and sleeping, she spent most of her time on deck, watching the scenery and enjoying the sun for the first time in what felt like weeks.

A few of the soldiers had shoved some crates together for her to use as a chair. She was sitting there when an eerie feeling came over her, making the hairs on her arms rise. The nearby coastline changed from sandy beaches and ports to tall, rocky cliffs. Squinting, she caught sight of the imposing wall that separated the kingdom of Lynk from Carlon and Nisk to the south of it.

The ship sailed past the wall. Waves near the cliffs crashed against the rocks, revealing just how rough the waters were. It would be a death sentence to sail too close as any boat would be smashed to pieces. Now she understood why the wall hadn't been built along the river—there was no need with the cliffs serving as a natural barrier.

Sabine recalled the first time she saw the wall and how scared she'd been. There was no reason for her to be frightened now. Lynk was her kingdom. Her home.

Looking the other direction, toward Avoni, she spotted the bay she'd sailed in with Evander when they'd stopped at the port to fix his boat. That felt like a lifetime ago. Today, several large ships blocked the mouth of the bay. Each one had the same flag raised. A flag she recognized.

Otto joined her.

"Those ships are from Lynk," she said as she stood, going over to the railing to get a better view.

"I was afraid something like this might happen," he murmured as he joined her.

The sound of a horn blasted through the air, making

Sabine jump. One of the Lynk ships started moving directly toward them.

"Here we go," Otto said. "Are you ready?"

Her heart raced. "Who do you think is on board?"

"Lynk soldiers." He folded his arms, observing the nearing ship. "I need to speak with my men."

These soldiers were probably out looking for her. They might even insist she return with them. "What do you think is going to happen?"

Otto shrugged. "I'm not sure. But remember, you're their queen. Act like it."

He was right. These Lynk soldiers couldn't tell her what to do. They were her subjects. It was time she mustered her strength and acted queenly.

When the Lynk ship neared, Sabine saw that the soldiers onboard had arrows trained toward the Bakley ship. No one owned this river, and those soldiers had no right to behave with such hostility. She glanced up at the mast to her left, confirming that not only did the Bakley flag fly, but also the one indicating a member of the royal family was onboard. Which meant these Lynk soldiers were acting extreme and dare she say, as if they were at war or owned the river.

Markis joined her. "I think it best if you go below deck," he said, a short sword in hand.

"I may be needed here." She watched her brother climb onto the crates. "What are you doing?" she called out to him.

"I'm fairly certain piracy has been outlawed," he replied. Then he shouted at the Lynk ship, "Lower your weapons!"

A man came forward bearing the uniform of a Lynk captain. "It's a little far north for a Bakley ship."

"Lynk does not own these waters," Otto said. "And that's Prince Otto Ludwig of Bakley to you. Now order your crew to lower their weapons."

"What's your business this far north?" the captain demanded.

Sabine rocked back on her heels, shocked at the audacity of this man. It was time for her to intervene. She stepped forward to the railing. "Drawing a weapon on your queen is considered an act of treason. Shall I have you all killed?"

The captain's eyes widened, but he made no move to order his men to stand down.

"I am Queen Sabine Manfred," she continued. "I demand you lower your weapons and address my brother with his proper title. If I have to repeat myself, I'll have all of you killed for insubordination." She lifted her chin in the air and slid her hands over the railing, being sure her ring was visible.

The captain ordered his men to lower their weapons. "We've been searching for you," he said.

Not wanting to acknowledge his comment, she ignored it and said, "I am eager to return home to my husband. If you have no other purpose here than to sail these waters, you will escort my ship north so we don't encounter any further… disturbances." She turned and headed below deck, not giving the captain a chance to respond.

With her arms and legs shaking, she made her way to her cabin which consisted of two rooms. The first one had a desk and acted as an office. The door at the back of it led to her sleeping quarters. Markis had insisted she take this cabin so he could sleep in the office to make sure no one got to her while she slept in the back room.

Sabine forced herself to sit at the desk, pretending to read the maps and letters strewn about.

Shouting came from above. She ignored it and kept staring at the papers before her, as if they held the answers to whatever it was she needed to know.

A few minutes later, someone knocked on her door.

"Enter," she called out.

Markis opened the door, revealing the Lynk captain at his side.

"Your Majesty," Markis said with a bow. "May I introduce Captain Higman."

"Why are you on this ship?" she asked, leaning back in the chair.

"I've been tasked with returning the king's property."

"This is a Bakley ship," she said, her hands gesturing to the walls.

"No. I am referring to you."

She had to stifle her anger. It was time to play her part. A smile slid across her lips. "I thought I was clear before. However, in case you didn't understand your orders, I'll repeat them. I am on my way home to Lynk." She made sure not to break eye contact. "As your queen, I bid your ship escort this one."

He shifted his weight. "I, uh, was going to disembark and take you through the mountains to the palace."

"I don't want to go that way." In reality, she much preferred traveling on land than sea. However, this was a battle she would not back down from. "The ships will head north. You will take us to the port closest to the palace. You're excused."

When the man went to open his mouth, Markis grabbed him, shoving him out of the office. She could hear them speaking in the hallway. Markis returned a moment later.

"Your Majesty, Captain Higman wishes to remain onboard in order to ensure your safety."

She drummed her fingers on the desk. "If his ship has a suitable captain to replace him, then I think that is an excellent idea. However, since we don't have any accommodations for him, he will have to sleep on the deck."

Markis chuckled. "As you wish."

Chapter Fifteen

Sabine found it difficult to enjoy her time on the ship with Captain Higman following her around like a dog. She snorted, realizing he reminded her of Harta. At least she would be reunited with her dog soon.

Standing at the bow of the ship, she watched the lush landscape pass by as the vessel cut around the land, heading for the small port not far away. Sabine imagined Evander doing this very thing only weeks ago when he'd arrived here with his delegation. That had been on her wedding day. The irony wasn't lost on her.

"Are you doing okay?" Otto asked as he came to stand beside her. He gripped the railing, scanning the land before them. "There are a lot of hills. And everything is so…green."

She chuckled. "I'm fine. And yes, it's a vastly different climate than you're used to." She hoped he could stay for a bit before he returned home. Having him nearby felt reassuring. However, it also made her nervous knowing what Rainer was capable of. The last thing she wanted was for her brother to be hurt in some way. Same with Markis. As soon as it was safe, she needed to send Markis home. Hopefully he could accompany Otto and the missing Bakley children.

Speaking of which, she was curious to hear Rainer's explanation of events. She still didn't know what to believe.

Drumming her fingers on the railing, Sabine realized the first thing she needed to address with Rainer was Lottie. She couldn't very well have her sister-in-law plotting to kill her. Rolling her shoulders back, she wondered when Lottie would marry Evander.

"You seem tense," Otto murmured.

"I'm fine."

As the ship neared the dock, Sabine caught sight of dozens and dozens of Lynk soldiers standing at attention. A chill slid over her. "How did they know we were coming?" she asked her brother.

"I'm sure Rainer has watch towers." He put his hand on her lower back. "It's going to be okay."

Given what happened with the Avoni delegation, perhaps the Bakley soldiers accompanying them should remain here on the ship. If Rainer had planted poison and cut holes in the Avoni ship, he could do the same with this one.

"You and Markis will be the only two disembarking. Are we clear?"

"Yes."

"No one from Lynk is allowed to step foot on this ship."

He eyed her but didn't argue. "Okay." He went over and spoke to one of his men.

The ship reached the dock and the soldiers ran around the deck, securing the sails and dropping the anchor. The gangplank was extended.

Captain Higman joined them. "Let's go." He reached for Sabine's arm.

She leaned back, away from him. "That's Your Majesty to you, and you will not lay a hand on me." One of the first things she needed to do was discuss this matter with Rainer. His men needed to speak to her appropriately.

Turning away from Higman, she gazed out at the rows upon rows of soldiers standing at attention. This was not the welcome she expected or hoped for. She spotted Rainer standing slightly in front of his men, his sword strapped to his waist. She shivered. He looked fierce and commanding. She thought she'd have the journey to the palace to figure out how to handle her first meeting with Rainer. However, it appeared she'd be reunited with him in five minutes.

Whatever happened, Rainer had to believe he had the upper hand. He couldn't see her as a challenge or threat.

"Are you ready?" Markis asked, coming to stand at her side.

She looked into his eyes. She was not ready. In fact, she was terrified to step foot off this ship. Rainer could welcome or arrest her. She truly had no idea what his response would be. However, there was only one way to find out. Besides, she had to prevent a war and make sure Lottie paid for her crimes.

"Yes," she said. "I'm ready."

The Royal Throne

LEAGUE OF RULERS, BOOK 3

Vengeance brought her home.
Love might be the reason she burns it down.

Sabine has returned to Lynk to deliver justice for her sister's
murder and stop her husband from waging a war that could

destroy the realm. To succeed, she may have to topple the very crown she swore to protect.

But Lynk's court is deadlier than ever—brimming with treacherous allies, spurned lovers, and rivals eager to see her fall. And in the shadows waits the assassin–pirate–prince, whose touch tempts her to abandon duty for desire. Every stolen moment with him threatens to unravel the kingdom she's sworn to defend.

The final battle for the throne will demand more than Sabine's crown—it will demand her heart, her life, and the truth she's feared all along. Because some destinies aren't given...they're taken.

OTHER BOOKS BY JENNIFER ANNE DAVIS

True Reign:

The Key

Red

War

Reign of Secrets:

Cage of Deceit

Cage of Darkness

Cage of Destiny

Oath of Deception

Oath of Destruction

Knights of the Realm:

Realm of Knights

Shadow Knights

Hidden Knights

Reigning Kingdoms

Sword of Rage

Sword of Desire

League of Rulers

The Queen's Crown

The King's Sword

The Royal Throne

The Order of the Krigers:

Rise

Burning Shadows

Conquering Fate

Single Titles:

Evil Lurks Beneath

The Voice

The Power to See

ABOUT THE AUTHOR

Jennifer Anne Davis graduated from the University of San Diego with a degree in English and a teaching credential. She is currently a full-time writer and mother of three kids. She is happily married to her high school sweetheart and lives in the San Diego area.

Jennifer is the recipient of the San Diego Book Awards Best Published Young Adult Novel (2013), winner of the Kindle Book Awards (2018), a finalist in the USA Best Book Awards (2014), and a finalist in the Next Generation Indie Book Awards (2014).

Visit Jennifer at:
www.JenniferAnneDavis.com

facebook.com/AuthorJenniferAnneDavis

x.com/authorjennifer

instagram.com/authorjennifer

bookbub.com/authors/jennifer-anne-davis

goodreads.com/jenniferannedavis

pinterest.com/authorjennifer

tiktok.com/@authorjenniferannedavis